Double Her
Pleasure

by

Tanya Sands

Double Her Pleasure

The Chasers Series, Book 1

Copyright © 2016 Tanya Sands

Cover design by Hardline Images

Graphic assistance by Jennifer Zapata

Prologue

Miranda Michaels fastened her seatbelt and pulled out of The Haven's parking lot where she worked. It was a no kill animal shelter started on donations long before Randa came along. She started out volunteering while her second husband, James, was still alive, and eventually became a silent donor, enabling it to keep its doors open. Randa's love of animals kept her volunteering until they offered her a job as the manager.

On the drive home she ran through the conversation that she had earlier on the phone with her friend, Lani. After catching up, Lani had questioned her about her love life, and Randa had gone on to complain about her relationship troubles after James passed away. Lani had bluntly told her she needed to get back up in the saddle. Randa just didn't know if she could. Or even how to start to go about doing it. She did know she didn't want Lani to call Josie and the other girls for an intervention. Her only saving grace was Lani lived in Chicago and the rest of the girls lived in San Diego like her. Thank god for small favors.

Her choices in ways to meet men were limited. She wasn't crazy about the bar scene. It was way too tempting to drink, leaving you in no condition to judge. And she'd heard horror stories about disaster dates from online dating. No way was she going through that.

She had gone on some blind dates her friends had set her up on. Sure, the men were nice, but they just didn't have the wow factor she'd been looking for. She'd had years of comfortable companionship, and she was over that. She wanted excitement, that 'oh my god' moment. Not that she expected it. Hell, she couldn't even provide that for herself. She'd had years of self-pleasuring, even if she blushed when she did it, but she'd never had the fireworks.

What she really wanted was to find a man that would accept her for her. She was tired of dealing with losers. Her latest mistake was Philip. She'd thought he was a nicer guy, so when he broke it off with her, it had been yet another blow to her self-esteem. Once again she scolded herself because she should have expected it. Instead, she was blinded by the fact such a gorgeous guy would want to date her at all.

What the hell was wrong with her? Here she was, a mother of two grown boys, widowed from a strained marriage and thinking about sex all the time. Okay, so she wasn't dead, but with all of the 'mommy porn' out to read, it was no wonder she had sex brain going on. It was all wistful reading for her though, since she knew no man would want a woman like her.

It's not like she was bad looking. Hell, standing back and seeing herself through someone else's eyes, she would say she was pretty cute. Society would definitely call her size eighteen full-figured. And she hated society. Having battled a weight problem all her life, Miranda Michaels, Randa as her friends called her, finally came to terms she would never be able to maintain a size smaller than a sixteen. She had married young, to a man who probably had a complex himself. He had moved on to a younger woman while still married to Randa, but he made sure to dig at her by stating no man would want to have sex with her, due to her weight and frigidness.

But she knew there was a man out there for her. Someone who would love and appreciate her for who she *was*, not what *size* she was. She dreamed of being swept off her feet and treated like she knew she deserved to be.

Chapter One

Randa pulled into her driveway, immediately annoyed at the noise coming from the house next door.

There were a couple of moving vans backed up to the house and many trucks parked all over the lawn. Such a shame too. The Hamilton's had taken pride in their beautiful lawn when they owned the house. Now, with their kids grown and gone, the couple had sold the house and moved.

The front door was wide open and country music was blaring from open windows. Male laughter could be heard over the music, and quite a lot of cursing too. After a long day at The Haven, all Randa wanted to do was complete the laps she had committed herself to since the pool was put in her backyard. It was now her routine every night after work. Since San Diego was fairly warm year round, the pool was not only a good investment for property value, but it enabled her to do some toning. So, despite the ruckus happening next door, she would make use of her down time before the stress of bringing on the two new vets began.

Randa unlocked the door and could hear the usual thump, and then nails racing down the hall to come to a halt in front of her. There sat her baby, barely containing herself. The bundle of fur was definitely *not* the size of a baby though. Since the dog thought she was a lapdog, and had indeed been tiny when she first arrived at The Haven, she had been named Baby. In reality, there was no way the Irish Wolf Hound looked like anything but a small horse. Baby sat patiently waiting as Randa stood there. Obediently, the dog watched keenly, waiting for the sign she had been taught. Her tail thumped heavily on the floor, and her wiggling back end belied her stillness. A big smile on her face, it always amused her how such a big animal could appear to tip toe around her, obviously very aware of its size. Randa had a 'proud mama' moment since she was the one who had trained the dog.

Randa's house had been targeted during a string of break-ins in her neighborhood not too long ago. Since her schedule had her out of the house a lot during the day, it made her home a prime target. But after the man came in through a window, Baby had tackled him, and simply sat on top of him, growling for about three hours until Randa arrived home and was able to call the police. Then with the subsequent arrest, closing of the case, and recovery of thousands of dollars of stolen property, they'd awarded Baby with an honorary detective's badge. Randa's neighborhood was now the safest around and probably why the house next door had only been on the market for a couple of weeks before it sold.

"Baby, house all in one piece? I trust no trouble? Why didn't you let the new neighbors know this is a shenanigan free zone, hmm? I guess you left me the hard work. Okay, girl, let's get changed and go for our swim."

With those few words, Baby knew she had done a good job and would be rewarded with a swim. Due to her breed and size, lots of exercise was needed. Thank goodness Randa had a huge fenced in backyard. Of course she had to have the fence built tall enough for Baby. She was able to get out into the yard from the house if she needed to, but the pool was off limits unless family was with her.

Randa undressed and pulled on the one piece swimsuit. She was glad for the fence because, despite the resignation of her size, she wasn't comfortable putting herself on display. She was not the type of woman who wore clothes to flaunt, instead she dressed for comfort with a touch of flattery. She knew with her blond hair, despite the slight graying, certain colors would bring out the green in her eyes and compliment her skin tone. Randa grabbed a towel and headed down the stairs, out the back door to the deck, and then stopped.

From her vantage point, she could see the neighbor's backyard. It was full of men—shirtless men. There had to be a half dozen men milling around. The grill was going and the smell of the meat reminded her she had missed lunch. She watched all the activity as they tossed a football around, a Frisbee sailed through the air, a couple of dogs ran around, and there was even the clang of horseshoes in the pit. She stood staring, mouth agape, as six gorgeous, well-fit, athletic males all turned her way.

***

Chase stood at the grill, the first thing that had been taken out of the moving van. The thing was massive. He had it custom built by his friend, Gerald Sutton, aka Pac. The man could re-purpose anything, as the grill attested to. It was big enough to grill a small horse, and that was before it was butchered. The heat of the day, combined with the grill, was what did it for him. It screamed home to him. The day was winding down after all of the help he and Jack had received. But then again, the group of men had been friends for years and nothing would stop any of them from helping each other out however they could. The grill was more of a necessity to feed the bunch of cavemen that tended to spend at least one full weekend together every other month.

Five years prior, the group had started out with four of them having to attend traffic school to avoid points on their licenses. They had received tickets for a variety of reasons: speeding, running a stop sign, etc. Trace happened to show up the day the others were leaving to talk to the officer in charge of the class. During a break, the original four: Chase, Jack, Pac and Iain, had made conversation about general topics. When careers were mentioned, it was then that Chase and Jack became friends because of their love of animals. Chase, originally from Texas, expressed his love of grilling, but his disdain for the grills on the market. Pac had offered to build him one. The one thing that they all had in common, other than their traffic court issues, was horseshoes. Ironically, all of them had grown up with fathers that had their own pits and would play at every opportunity. Thus began a lasting friendship that continued strong.

Their monthly BBQ's were a way for them to make sure they kept in touch, even though impromptu card games happened, and sometimes a basketball game at a nearby court. Chase loved it because he was able to showcase his grilling talents, even if he had to go to Pac's house to use it. It gave Pac and his son more of a support system since Pac's wife had died years before and they were still recovering. Most of all, it was a way for them to relax and just get their heads out of any stress everyday life piled on them.

Meat tended to, he turned to watch the rest of the group relaxing in one way or another. He raised the bottle of beer to his lips, letting the cold liquid run down the back of his throat. They had been at it since the crack of dawn. Luckily, Sam Jensen was the owner of a trucking company and owned a fleet of trucks, two of which they were able to get for a day to move his and Jack's stuff from storage and their old apartment to the house they had co-purchased. When they were employed by competing vet hospitals, it did nothing to deter their friendship. Work was always left there. The only work conversations allowed were about the animals, not the surroundings. Then, when they had heard The Haven was looking to permanently fill two vet spots, they both jumped on the opportunity and were hired.

Their friendship didn't stop at their shared occupation either. They hung out a lot and tended to date the same type of women. After they had played together in multiple threesomes, they decided that they enjoyed it more than one on one sex. They were very comfortable with each other, and there were plenty of women out there that had fantasies of being with two men at the same time. A lot of their friends shared their love of the bigger women. Not obese, but women who were put down for being full figured. They hated that term, would rather the type be classified as lush. The house they purchased together, with the hopes that somewhere down the road they could possibly find a woman that would be open to a relationship, and hopefully kids, but that wasn't set in stone. They had even adopted a dog together. So the search was on for the one that could be theirs. Shit, she could be the girl next door for all they knew.

Right at that moment, Max went strolling by, not able to run faster than a trot, after a ball one of the guys had thrown for him. If for nothing else, certainly not a guard dog, Max was great entertainment. He grabbed the ball and trotted back to Iain Sinclair, who laughed and threw the ball again. Barreling beside Max was a new animal friend, Jackson. Their friend, Trace Wilde, had just completed training with a dog Jack had recommended for police dog work. He had been surrendered since the owners couldn't afford the medical treatment when Jackson was protecting a child from another dog. The German Shepherd mix had good instincts and made it through the canine training with the police academy at the top of his class. He and Max were best friends, despite them both being males.

Chase had had a case come into his hospital of a Bassett Hound being thrown out of a moving car. A clear case of buyer's remorse. When it was witnessed, and the police got involved, the owner claimed they didn't have the time to take proper care of the animal. He had been furious when the three month old puppy had shown up on his table. Poor little guy was scared, but longing for love. He had instantly fallen in love with the mutt. There were no internal injuries, but he needed to stay due to a broken hind leg and major road rash. Chase had assumed responsibility of all his medical bills. The pup was such a fighter the office had taken to calling him Mighty Max. Since they lived in an apartment at the time, and couldn't have a pet, Chase had arranged with the hospital to be able to keep him there until he and Jack found a place that allowed animals.

A loud, deep bark from the house next door stopped all activity and caused them to direct their attention to the deck off the back of the well maintained house. On the top step was the most beautiful sight Chase had ever seen. No stick figure there. The kind of body he and Jack preferred. How was it possible that he and Jack didn't know this woman lived next to them? If the real estate agent had even brought up the fact, they would have paid more just to be able to live next to her. With a glance at Jack, it was obvious that they both were thrilled. The type of woman they were both attracted to was only yards from them.

Hell, all six of the men were eying the woman like they had recently been sent ashore from an all-male crew on a naval ship. Hungry much? They had all noticed the pool earlier and jokingly said maybe they could cozy up to the owner or owners to get use of the pool. Now? They would definitely be offering free checkups for that horse of a dog standing chest high to the woman. A beautiful dog for a lovely lady. But the trick was to convince her that the dynamic duo of ménage was right for her.

**

Jack had been talking to Trace about the graduation ceremony for Jackson that would be held in a week. Jack was invited, due to Jackson being his "god-dog". In fact, the damn dog was named after him—a joke at first, but Jack was touched. Yes, he'd heard the barking, but hadn't thought anything of it. It wasn't until he turned and saw why all of a sudden the group quieted. She was gorgeous. He couldn't tell from where he stood how old she was, but he could guess she was in her forties. She had on a one piece swimsuit that showed every curve she possessed. She looked like a deer in headlights with all of them practically panting after her. He turned, trying to see what she saw. Sure enough, they all looked like they had recently been released from prison, not having seen a woman in years. She probably felt like she was a buffet of some kind and she was the main course.

She was a bitty thing. Judging by the size of her dog, which was a beauty too, she couldn't be that tall. Jack figured that she would fit nicely in his arms, in their arms. Chase turned and caught Jack's gaze and they shared a knowing look. They knew she was the only person that lived there. He remembered the realtor saying something about Mrs. Michaels being a widow, but she was really well liked in the neighborhood. It was explained her dog stopped a group of burglars that had been plaguing the area. For some reason, they assumed the widow would be some little granny who crocheted. Now, wasn't *this* a pleasant surprise.

Jack walked to the fence that separated their yards and leaned against it. She waved and smiled shyly. He grinned and returned the gesture. She looked like she was ready to bolt and go back inside, but started down the stairs of the deck to head to the pool. The time it took her to walk down the steps, gave him ample time to see that she wasn't slender—*yeah, thank god for that*—but she was in good shape. Her face was red and he knew he was making her a bit self-conscious, but he just couldn't help himself. Her blonde hair looked so soft and fell to her mid-back. And her breasts? He could just about feel the hard tips in his mouth and hear her moans when he licked and nipped them. Before his thoughts could go further, her dog came bounding to the fence and jumped up. As a vet, he knew not to invade in a strange dog's space, so he took a step back.

"Well, hello there. And what might your name be, fella? Do you think you could wrangle an intro with your mom?"

The woman, Mrs. Michaels, called out and dove into the pool a moment later. The dog turned, gave one last dirty look to Jack, and then ran to jump into the water with the woman. Jack swore he saw a huge grin cross the animal's face. And why not? Warm day, big pool of water, and a human to dote on you. Then the name the woman shouted before jumping in the pool registered. Baby. He laughed and walked over to where Chase was standing with a dazed look on his face. The other men went back to talking, but Chase and Jack exchanged a look.

"Hey, buddy, feel like putting a plate together and walking with me next door? I do believe we need to introduce ourselves to the widow," Jack spoke to Chase in a low voice.

Chase smiled at his friend. "You read my mind. And did you see the dog? What a beauty. Yeah, let's get these knuckleheads fed and see if they can get to moving stuff around. Maybe even read what's written on the boxes and put them in the right rooms?"

The others heard the last comment and started arguing and throwing out a lot of bitching about not appreciating free labor, but it was all in good fun. They would all help each other move across country if it came to it. They pulled the meat off the grill and all went into the kitchen to begin dishing up plates. Chase got out a plate and put together a variety of the meats and sides— store bought, but hey it was an offering, right? When Jack grabbed a beer and a hard cider, Chase snatched up bottled water, just in case she didn't drink alcohol, and the plate of food. Then they walked out the front door, yelling to the others to keep an eye on Max.

Since they knew she was in the pool, it made more sense to go through the gate for the back yard. Chase unlatched the gate and they both walked through to the pool area. Jack rounded the corner first and Chase almost ran into him and spilled the food. Luckily, he swerved to avoid the fiasco and came face to face, or snout to groin, with their neighbor's 'baby'. They had full intentions of announcing themselves, but the wet dog snarling at them kind of halted any progress they might have had of doing so. They looked at each other and then the dog. Their vet knowledge and appreciation of all things animal had them admiring the dog.

Chase, the unofficial dog whisperer, began talking to him—quick glance, nope a her—trying to get her to at least go from snarls to warning growls. Jack, despite his knowledge of animals and their need to establish their territories and to make sure intruders knew of those boundaries, stood still and allowed her to smell his legs, picking up the scent of Max. The hairs on the dog's back were ridged, defining her irritation of encroachers.

"You are such a pretty girl. Oh yeah, I can see those lovely teeth of yours. And protecting your mama? That's a great job. No bad men gonna get her with you looking out, huh? Okay, so I'm Chase, and... nope, eyes on me, pretty lady." The dog had looked at Jack and was starting to snarl again, but then turned back to Chase. "Good girl. Yeah, I'm Chase. And I'll have you know I adore dogs. Got one of my own, yeah? Course, he doesn't look nearly as pretty as you. I'll tell you a secret, but you can't let him know I told you. Okay? Max can't even come close to being a watchdog like you. Maybe you can give him lessons?"

Jack watched as the dog slowly began to loosen up, never taking her eyes off of them. The woman was stepping out of the shallow end of the pool and had just wrapped a towel around her body—what a shame that was—when she saw them talking to her dog.

"Baby! Come away from there. Come!" She called out. Her voice was only raised slightly, but it was firm.

The dog gave them one last look of disdain and then loped to her owner's side.

Chase and Jack waited where they were as the woman came over to where they were standing. She looked at them. Well, more like checked them out as if she was starving, and they were her next meal. Jack liked it, a lot. He was sure Chase did too. And since she was just their type and they both had an ulterior motive for coming to introduce themselves, they let her look as much as she wanted, and then grinned at her to let her know they approved of her looking. Her eyes came up, noticing their smiles and she blushed and called her dog.

"Baby, come here." She looked up, way up, at them because they towered over her quite a bit. "Hi, I'm Miranda Michaels. Welcome to the neighborhood. This is Baby, she's a good girl, but has become very protective toward me." She had Baby sit then waved them over to introduce them. "Baby, these are our new neighbors. Be nice to them or no more swimming for a while."

The dog looked at her as though she understood every word. Her head lowered slightly as though embarrassed and then came up again. It was almost as if she was seeing how far the pouting look would get her. Chase and Jack looked at each other in wonder, then at the dog. Never had they come across a dog so well trained and so in tune to their owner's emotions and words. This Miranda was a wonder with animals. To the two men, it was as though Ms. Fate had stepped in and handed the woman to them on a silver platter, a woman they were both immediately attracted to. Plus she liked and was good with dogs. It was too perfect to be a coincidence.

Since Jack had just bottles in his hands, he went down on his haunches and placed the bottles on the ground. He held his hands out for Baby to come inspect. With one last look at her momma, she crept forward and sniffed his hands. Tentatively, her tail began to move until she had practically jumped into his arms. He laughed and held her away from him to stop the massive amount of doggie kisses she was raining down on his face.

He stood and relieved Chase of his burden and allowed his friend to introduce himself too. The canine was less hesitant, figuring since they came together, and one was okay, then the other was too. Chase had less notice than Jack did before he had that pink tongue all over his face. Since she did her duty as hostess, Baby got off him and ran back to Miranda. They both liked the doting mama look on her face when Baby came back to her and sat by her side, barely containing her joy.

***

Randa watched as the men fawned over her dog and couldn't help the silent, wistful sigh from crossing her mind. What she wouldn't give for two gorgeous men to act like that with her. She would do the crawl and wiggle her ass thing for them. Her face turned red at her thoughts. She raised her eyes to theirs and saw that they both wore huge grins on their faces, as if they knew exactly what she was thinking.

21

They were both still shirtless, skin poured over hard muscles and bones. She could see they were both very well defined, though the blond seemed to have more of the chest hair and happy trail situation going on than the darker haired man. But that didn't mean that one was any less attractive in any way, shape, or form. She closed her eyes and a scene from a book she recently read immediately came to mind.

She could almost picture Jack leaning back against her car, hands wrapped around her and cupping her breast, while Chase dealt with her nuisance of a skirt. She could feel the breeze created as cars drove by, but their actions blocked from view. She could feel Jack's breath as he spoke into her ear what they wanted to do to her. It was as if the three of them were substituted for the characters in her book. Now *that* was a fantasy so many women dreamed of—to have two men making sure her pleasure was achieved before their own.

"Hi there, I'm Chase and this is Jack. It's so nice to meet you and Baby. Although, I must say she isn't much of the size of one." Chase offered his hand.

His words snapped her out of her fantasy world. Her face flamed again, and she just knew that they could tell what she had been thinking. When their skin touched, she inhaled. It was almost like he walked across a carpet and shocked her. But his friend had other ideas. He walked up and, juggling the plate in his hands, pulled her into a hug.

***

Shoving what he held to Chase, Jack shook Miranda's hand then pulled her into his arms. He was trying to be nonchalant about it, but could feel her tense up, so knew he'd better say something. He leaned back and looked down into her lovely face, smiling. He'd felt her body quiver, just slightly, when he enfolded her in his arms. As he pulled his arms back, he allowed his fingers to just graze the underside of her breasts. When she jumped, he kept his expression purposely blank.

"Sorry. I grew up in a family of huggers and this is just part of the hand shaking ritual for us. I hope you don't think me too forward." He had a very welcoming smile on his face, trying to coax the same from her.

Miranda Michaels was a beautiful woman, but Jack could tell with the way she wrapped her arms around her waist and held herself back from them that she was not aware of that fact. She would quickly learn that when the two friends set their minds on something, they tended to get what they wanted. And they wanted her.

"We decided to come and welcome you to our madness. See, we tend to have our friends over quite bit. Keeps all of us out of trouble, and sometimes out of jail. So, consider this an apology for what will probably be a loud night." Chase held the plate out for her to take.

"We weren't sure if you drank alcohol, so we brought a bottled water too. We were hoping since it's Friday night and you're home, and you probably hadn't had a chance to eat, it would help you out."

***

Miranda didn't want to be rude, so she took the plate from him. Looking at the drinks Chase held, she chose a bottle of beer. When eating food from a grill, beer should be the only beverage permitted. The food on the plate looked delicious but there was no way was she eating in front of these two men. With her luck, she'd spill something on her and look like a slob. She looked up at them and smiled her thanks.

"Well, that was really nice of you and greatly appreciated. I don't cook as much as I used to since my boys are grown and gone. It's just no fun to cook for one." Miranda cringed and thought to herself how pathetic that sounded. "You didn't have to do this, though. I understand if you have friends come over; no big deal." Yeah, she thought, like she ever had wild times in her house. The most wild she'd ever had was when she burnt the popcorn and Baby got upset by the noise of the smoke alarm.

"Well, any time you want to come over, you are more than welcome," Chase invited then went on to explain. "Most of the time when they come over it's just to watch a game or play poker. Maybe your pretty face would distract them enough to allow us to take their cash, so yeah, come on over anytime." He laughed.

Miranda blushed and looked down. Wow, she hadn't blush so much in years.

***

Chase really liked the look she was giving them from under her lashes. It was almost as if she wanted to say more, but lost her nerve. *Well*, he thought, *maybe she would be open to a quiet dinner with them.* Once she was comfortable with both of them, they'd definitely want to take her out to dinner. There was a new place they'd wanted to try called Flavour; maybe they could take her there.

"I have an idea. This should not count as dinner. Why not come over some night this week and we'll cook you dinner? Then we can also introduce Baby here to our other roomie. He's very short, although don't tell him because he doesn't know it, and he's about her age. Our Mighty Max will definitely get along with her." Jack threw out the offer without talking to him because he knew they both wanted her in their house. "Then we can all get to know each other, become friends, and then you won't think we're trying to not get the cops called on us when the guys are over. Come on, what do you say?"

Chase liked how Jack jumped right into getting the woman in their house. Hell, if it was up to either of them, she'd be in their bed right now, but he doubted she'd be up to that just yet. He smiled at Miranda, nodding his head when Jack invited her for dinner. Then he thought about the new jobs they would be starting in a couple of days. They weren't even sure what their schedules would be like. But they'd cross that bridge when they came to it. They wanted to get her to agree to date them and get to know them first. Chase just got a feeling in his gut that there was something about her that he didn't want to lose out on.

***

Miranda was a bit flustered. And she definitely was not used to being asked to dinner by a man, let alone two. But it was probably just for the reason Jack mentioned. There was that unwritten rule that if you're planning a party, you should invite neighbors to avoid any complaints about noise. She was sure that was the case here. She didn't want them to think she was a desperate, overweight, lonely woman that needed to be fawned over to ensure they weren't turned in to the police. Besides, looking at them, there was no way they didn't already have girlfriends, or at the least, women they dated on a regular basis. No way were either of them hitting on her.

"That is really kind. Let me think about it and I'll let you know. I've got some training to do this week at work, and I'm not sure what my schedule will be like," she replied with a smile.

Chase pulled his phone out and looked at her, then reached out to take the plate and beer from her.

"Would you be okay programming your number in my phone? I'll send you a quick text to yours, that way you can call or text me to let us know. Now, we don't want to keep you from the rest of your swim, or the beginning of your weekend. Besides, who knows what those animals are doing next door. We'll talk later in the week. Okay?"

Miranda typed her number into Chase's phone while he set her food and beer on a nearby patio table, gave it back, and then she was enfolded in two very strong arms. This time it was Chase and he smelled good. He smelled like hot male mixed with smoky barbeque, and a touch of an everyday deodorant that worked well with his natural scent. Then before she could even truly enjoy the arms, she was spun and wrapped in Jack's arms and he smelled just as good. Both of them smelled like outdoors and grilling. Miranda could spend hours just sniffing them. And there it was again, that telltale blush that would clue them in on where her mind went.

***

Jack liked how she looked in his friend's arms and was glad he had another chance to hold her before they left. When he let her go and her face was red, he looked at Chase, but he was too busy looking at the woman's ass. Jack couldn't blame him, though. He'd be doing the same if he had the opportunity. After a quick pet for Baby from both of them, and lots more doggie kisses, they left and went back to their house. Now to get through the ribbing the guys would give them when they got back. But then again, they all had the same taste in women, and the rest of the group knew that Chase and Jack shared everything. Their love of animals, their love of grilling, and of course, their love of lush women. Their friendship was the ultimate in sharing.

They walked back into the house, Max and Jackson acting as though they'd been gone hours instead of the fifteen minutes or so. Apparently, the guys were more interested in what happened next door than helping put boxes in the proper rooms. At least they cleaned up after they finished eating, but all that said to Jack and Chase was that they were expecting them to give details on the lonely widow next door.

They were sitting in the living room and each had switched to bottled water, knowing they had hit their limit. Trace was sitting in front of the fireplace and Jackson took a seat right next to him. They would make a good team once graduation was over. Pac sat with his legs spread out in front of him, looking relaxed as hell, but they knew he was antsy. He had said he was done listening to the rest of the guys talk about getting laid, and not getting any himself. Iain sat there checking out his phone. He was expecting a call any minute on a delivery at his shop. He got the okay on a dream project. He was expecting a '67 GTO convertible to come so that work could begin the following Monday. He was given carte blanche. The only thing the owner wanted was for it to be painted canary yellow. When he was told, Iain cringed then talked the guy into red with the classic black top and a black interior. Iain was thrilled the owner agreed.

But the coolest cucumber of them all, the one the others were watching his hands closely, was Sam. It was his two trucks that were rented. As the rest of the group watched, he knotted and unknotted the piece of rope he always had on him. He said it relaxed him, and honestly it was a bit mesmerizing to watch him show off his Shibari knowledge. The intricate knot work was a thing of beauty, even for someone not in the BDSM lifestyle. And Sam was the first to ask.

"When's the first date?" He smirked in their direction. He knew the dynamic duo worked fast. "You will let me know when you want to learn the ropes, so to speak, yeah? That body of hers was made for Shibari, guys."

They all tensed as Chase clenched his fist. He had taken a couple of steps toward Sam, but Pac calmly stood up and stepped into his path. Jack backed up Pac by standing behind him, but he understood Chase's reaction. Sam was only doing exactly what any of them would do—bust their balls. This got him thinking. They *just* met her. Why would it matter that Sam wanted to dominate her?

"Chase, come on, man, you know he didn't mean anything by it." Trace slowly came up to Chase's side and spoke softly to him. "You know it's what we all do when we see something we like. And, buddy, when you and Jack stood talking to her, you looked good together."

Jack saw the look on Chase's face as he looked at Sam and knew his friend felt like shit. In the back of his mind, he knew his friend was yanking his chain, but it bothered him for a reason he couldn't quite figure it out yet. He felt the need to protect the woman. He had never felt like this before, never would have thought he would have reacted as he just did.

Jack listened to Trace and knew Sam was aware he'd overstepped and came forward to apologize. Sometimes, Sam's power of observation didn't quite connect with his mouth. Just like married couples, the group didn't like to walk away angry. There had only been one instance where anger crowded them, and it was over a woman, Sam's ex-wife to be exact. But then again, Sheila had played him like a fiddle, so that one time shouldn't really count. She hadn't been worth the possibility of losing a friend. If he hadn't seen her trying to get with Pac, he would have lost the friendship of a truly great guy, who had turned her down anyway.

Jack watched Chase's face. It was almost like he'd had an 'ah-ha' moment. But what could he have been thinking? He wondered if it were anything like what was in his head. It would take some getting to know her, but Jack couldn't let go of his initial reaction to the woman. Would it lead to anything long lasting, or just having fun? Who knows until they all got together and got to know each other.

"Damn it, Sam. I'm sorry. No reason for you to apologize. I overreacted." Chase ran his fingers through his thick hair and sat down.

"Nah, man, we're good. This was bound to happen. My Jedi mind powers weren't totally connected tonight," he joked.

"Good. Glad we're okay. And fuck your Jedi shit. It's the Dom thing and you know it. Just don't think you can fucking read my mind or dominate me." Chase got a distant look on his face. "There's just something about her."

Chapter Two

Randa spent the weekend catching up on her favorite shows, reading a couple of books, and taking Baby to Harry Griffin Park, a place for dogs to play. By Monday, she was back on track to start the new doctors' training. She had all of their paperwork ready for them to fill out.

She had tried to turn down the small salary that she was paid for the work she did at Haven, but Josie said that it was good for her to have the steady paycheck, even if she didn't need it. And as usual, Josie was right about the pay issue. Better to have the steady income. Randa knew that the veterinary hospital couldn't afford to pay someone to do the work she did there, and she would never ask for that anyhow, but the board didn't want her to ever feel like they were taking advantage of her giving nature so they had compromised with a small paycheck and free care for Baby.

The phone on her desk rang and it was Cheryl, the morning volunteer, telling her that there were two men waiting to see her. A quick glance at the clock showed it was just after eight o'clock. It seemed the new vets were on-timers. Good. The one thing that irked her the most was having a job and being late. Cheryl sounded strange, but Miranda didn't question it. She instructed her to let them know she'd be right there. Off the corner of her desk, she grabbed the two clipboards and pens and walked out to the front. As she rounded the corner,

31

there were indeed two men waiting. They were both talking to an older lady in the process of adopting a small, wiry haired dog that was so craggy looking, but Randa knew she would love him anyway. She'd spent a lot of time with that dog, and had fallen in love with him herself. The older lady was blushing and giggling like a teenager, so they must have been flirting. As they stood and turned, they were all shocked to the point where Cheryl had to say Randa's name twice.

"Randa, this is... Um, Randa? You okay? Do I need to get Dr. Stuart?"

"What? No, Cheryl, I'm fine. Are these the gentlemen you were talking about?" Randa asked. There was no way she could have prepared herself for the surprise of seeing the two men in front of her.

Cheryl giggled. Really? Giggled? "Oh, yes. Doctors Fargo and Benning, this is Miranda Michaels, our administrator. She will get you set up with your entry paperwork, desks, and anything else you might need."

She turned away and answered the phone that had been ringing, but didn't take her eyes off of them. They smiled at her and then turned to Randa, who was staring at them in confusion. They were her new doctors? Her oh-so-hot neighbors would be working with her? This *so* put a new twist on things that she wasn't expecting. Here she stood with men she had fantasized about all weekend. How was she going to work with them? Damn, she would be in a state of perpetual arousal.

"Um, hi there. If you'll just follow me, we can get started." Randa tentatively smiled and began to walk to the small room they used for staff meetings. As she walked in front of them, she worried about them watching her ass. But then again, why worry? They probably weren't interested.

Randa walked in the room and waited for them to come in before she closed the door. She set the paperwork down and sat across from where they had taken a seat. How was she supposed to look at them and work with them when all she wanted to do was have them take their shirts off so she could lick them? *Wait, what? Where did that thought come from?* Randa could feel her face turn red. She was a grown woman, she could do this, even though she was tempted to push everything to the floor, lay on the table and tell them to fuck her. God, she seriously needed to go home and take care of this.

They took a seat across the small conference table from her and she wished a hole would open up in the floor and suck her into it. This was not going to be easy for her. Just looking at them had her breathing a little erratic and she could feel that her face was flush with both arousal and embarrassment of her arousal. She needed to get over this and do her job. She squared her shoulder and went back into work mode.

"In front of you is all of the paperwork you will need to fill out for payroll, your health benefits and 401k." Randa didn't recognize her own voice and she wished she didn't feel so hot all over, "Why don't I just let you two take care of the paperwork and then I can show you around, unless you have any questions now?" She waited for a moment and then turned to leave the room. She had to get out of there before she said or did something she regretted.

Chase stopped her with just her name.

"Miranda?"

Stopped in her tracks, she didn't even hear Chase as he had stood and come up behind her. His hands were on her upper arms, holding her in place. Just the touch of his hands on her made her body run hot. She was a bit surprised that his hands were a little rough. True, he may not operate as much as a people surgeon but his hands were still important. She closed her eyes, the heat from his touch making it impossible to think rationally. Doing so prevented her from noticing that Jack now stood in front of her, effectively sandwiching her between them. With a finger under her chin, Jack tilted her head up.

"Sweetheart, open your eyes and look at me," Jack entreated her.

Randa shook her head and couldn't stop the blush that spread over her again. The vibe she was getting from them wasn't of a 'friend' sort. They had seen her in that damn frumpy swimsuit, so why would they be doing this? Over the weekend she had done a lot of thinking. Was it possible that one of them was really interested in her? Maybe it was just her being hopeful that they weren't doing the 'keep the neighbor happy to avoid complaints' routine. A small glimmer of hope began in the pit of her stomach. Tamping it down, she kept her eyes closed.

"Miranda? We won't bite and we're really friendly. I bet if we were dogs, you'd take us home with you," Chase said teasingly in her ear.

A shiver ran down her spine and she opened her eyes to see Jack's handsome face smiling down at her. She couldn't even speak as she felt like she would drown in his soft chocolate eyes. The combination of Chase's smooth voice and Jack's eyes were enough to make her mouth go dry and she felt like a shock ran through her, but she straightened herself up and attempted to act like they did nothing for her. What a big lie that was. All they had to do was tell her to strip and she would quickly. No questions asked.

"You know you don't have to keep up the act." Randa tried to act like their closeness wasn't affecting her. "And my name is Randa. I prefer to be called Randa."

"Miranda," Jack stressed the use of her given name, "there is no act. We really would like you to come over to our house for dinner this week. You don't want to make us feel unwelcome in a new neighborhood, do you? Come on, you know where we work, you know where we live. What can it hurt to share a meal with us?"

"You're not serious, are you, trying to get me to feel guilty? Come on, guys. You are grown men. Obviously, you can have any woman you want. Why would you want me to come over? I don't mind the neighborly dinner but you don't need to pretend you're interested in me. Okay?" She didn't mean to sound snappy, but all she could think was that they possibly felt sorry for her—or something worse.

***

Chase spun her around so she was facing him. As Jack molded himself to her back, Chase moved in and held her close to him by her hips. He liked the feel of her soft sides in his hands. He liked it so much he could feel himself harden as the blood shot straight to his groin. He stepped closer until not a thing separated them from her. Jack's hands smoothed up and down her arms as Chase's caressed her outer hips. She was so turned on that Chase could feel her nipples peak against him. But he figured it wouldn't be a good idea to let her know he was aware.

"Why would we need a wing man, Miranda? We hadn't planned on inviting anyone else to dinner. It would just be the three of us. We wouldn't have just anyone coming into our home and meeting Max. We don't want him to get attached, you know?" Jack tried to be flippant about it, but it was true. Max was like a kid and wouldn't understand if someone they were only going to casually date were paraded around, then not come by anymore. Besides, as old fashioned as it sounded, their house was their castle.

***

Randa's senses were overloaded and she was hot all over. She felt her heart racing fast, like a sprinter at the finish line. She needed to get out of the room, or at the very least out from between their bodies. She could have sworn she felt hardness nestled against both her ass and her belly, but her brain wasn't making the connection.

"Excuse me, we are at work and there is a lot to do to get you both on rotation. So, can you let me go so you can fill out your entry paperwork and we can get on with our day?"

Randa had two grown boys and knew that when she got into "mom" mode, she was intimidating, despite her size. She realized she wasn't being held tightly, but Chase's hands were still loosely holding her hips. When she looked pointedly at his hands, he grinned and released her. She heard a low chuckle from behind her as Jack's hands left her too. She felt a sense of loss when they let her go, but it was for the best. She ducked away from them and quickly walked out of the room, closing the door behind her. She walked around the corner from the conference room and leaned against the wall, dragging in deep breaths to try and steady her heartbeat.

***

In the closed off room, Chase smiled at Jack. They knew what they wanted, and they were going to get it. But they also realized, there at their place of employment, they would have to play it cool. Sexual harassment laws were very strict, and they certainly did not want to jeopardize their incomes or make it uncomfortable to work with them. Too much had been sacrificed and they had worked too hard to get where they were now. The Haven hospital was the premier facility. They knew for a fact a lot of other vets had vied for the positions they eventually were hired for.

Each man was silent as they began to pour over all of the paperwork. They each had their own vision of how the dinner would go, but both ended the same way. Three sets of legs entwined, two sets of hands caressing a lovely rounded body fit for a goddess. Not to mention a certain female to treat like a queen. A good time had by all. But now that they knew they would see more of their lovely neighbor, the thought of something more came to mind. What that was, neither of them was too sure.

The day went by with lots of introductions, most of which would not be remembered by at least one. Chase was envious of Jack's photographic memory. His friend would have no problem knowing who was who and who did what tomorrow. Chase would be lucky if he remembered where all the rooms were. Oh well, Chase would remember in time. Besides, he figured he could pull a 'newbie' card for a while before anyone got seriously angry. He certainly wasn't above using his smile to be forgiven any slips.

With the first day under their belts, they made their way to their cars and agreed to meet up at home. Chase would be heading straight home to get Max out to do his business, and Jack had to stop and pick up a few things for the house. Now that they were moved in, they needed to get the place looking good for company. Hopefully, they would still be able to get Miranda to come over and they wanted to be prepared just in case. Just the thought of her in their house definitely brightened their moods.

Outside, the sun was working its way down to the horizon, but it would be a while before it actually happened. They both slipped their aviators on and walked out into the still bright sun, the crunching of gravel under their shoes as they made their way to their vehicles. Neither believed classic cars should be locked away. They should be enjoyed while they could. They had different backgrounds to steer them to the vehicle they loved most. For Chase, it was a sentimental one, reminding him of family. For Jack, it was a way to recapture his teen years.

Chase was originally from Texas and loved the truck he inherited from his grandfather. It was a 1941 Chevy half ton, fully restored and painted cherry red. His granddad loved the truck and knew Chase would be the only grandchild to appreciate it. Chase loved the low rumble it made when he first turned the key in the ignition. He had to admit he even loved the looks he got when he drove around. He drove off in the direction of their new home, eager to start the afterhours chase, and feeling like a cowboy riding into the sunset.

***

Jack's taste in cars was very different than Chase's. Where his friend was a 'good 'ole boy', Jack was more into sports cars. Chase came from a family with a moneyed background. Jack's family was lucky if they got to go to the local county fair every year. There were no extras for anything. Jack had to work for any spending money he had. When he was fourteen, he convinced his dad to buy a car from the junkyard—with money Jack had saved—for him to fix up. His after school and weekend jobs paid for the entire project. It needed a lot of work, but between his dad helping, and him taking classes in school dealing with mechanics, he was able to make his Porsche 944 into a thing of beauty. Because he had put all the work into restoring it, he kept up on the maintenance religiously, and since he had the mechanical knowledge, he'd never needed to take it to a garage. He treated that red car like a child. He'd often been asked why he chose the color, and he always explained that his sister had a bottle of fingernail polish he'd seen once called Fuck Me Red. He'd love the color so much he'd stolen the bottle from her to match the color.

They both loved their cars, therefore when they were looking for a house, they both insisted a big two-car garage was a definite necessity.

Groceries stored in the backseat, Jack headed home. As he pulled into the driveway, he noticed Miranda's car was not there. He parked in the garage, beeped twice, and cut the engine. Clicker in hand, he closed the garage door just in time for the side door to open and Max to come running in to welcome him home. The stocky, muscled body always provided a laugh when he came running, and he could just about knock either of his owners over. He forgot how strong he was as he ran to Jack, jumped as high as he could, and ended up knocking Jack back into his car. With bags hanging from his hands, Jack was still able to hold the thick little guy back from scratching the paint.

Chase came out to help with the groceries, and between them, all bags were in the house in one trip. Since he shopped, Chase would put away. It was an unspoken agreement put in place when they first started living together. Bottle of water in hand, Jack leaned back against the counter and Max lounged at his feet, tail thumping on the floor. Jack, lost in his thoughts, didn't realize Max wasn't able to keep his butt still. He was just so excited to see them he felt someone needed to be petting him and paying attention to him, like right then.

"So, she's not home yet. You think she'll shy away?" Jack asked. "I picked up some flowers to give her to sort of apologize for today. Maybe she'll overlook the fact we were practically drooling after her all day. I know I tried to dial it back, but damn, man, she's got me in knots."

Chase sighed and looked over. "I don't know, man. She was pretty 'deer in the headlights' this morning. Did you notice all day she couldn't look either of us in the eye? But I agree, the flowers might get us out of the stalker category. Good thinking."

"Look at us. Hell, man, every time she came into any room we were in, the temperature went up like twenty degrees. Yeah, and that blush? Dude, I was so tempted to kiss her every time she did. You realize we will have to play it cool at work? She's the admin/HR— would be a total disaster to have her claiming sexual harassment."

"I know, right?" Chase replied. "Those slacks she was wearing today cupped her just right. God, man, the image of the fabric pressed against her peach shaped ass had me fuckin' hard all day."

Jack laughed and agreed with a nod of his head. "She's got those curves that make you just want to sink into them." Then he got serious. "But I don't think she knows how attractive she is. She kept fidgeting with the hem of her blouse, pulling down and away from her abdomen like she was trying to hide her stomach. We've come across women like that before. Remember Julie? She kept insisting she was a cow. Floored me when she used that exact word." He shook his head in disgust.

***

Chase finished putting the groceries away and pulled out a vase to put the flowers in, figuring they could give them to her tonight as soon as she got home, but they would have to keep an eye or ear out for her arrival.

"Why do women do that to themselves?" Chase asked.

He couldn't help the pissed off look that came over his face. He had always been very vocal about his views on what made a woman attractive. He was pissed that society dictated to the female sex that they had to be thin with no curves. His experience with thinner women was not good. Were they attractive? Sure. Chase used to be attracted to all types of women, but he'd had so many bad experiences where the slender women he'd been involved with seemed to put way too much emphasis on their outward appearance instead of what was on the inside. Hell, all women are attractive and sexy, but since he and Jack met and started doing the whole threesome scene, curvy ladies were the only type they went after. It was just their preference. They liked a little more to hold onto and the softness of just a little extra.

They were so busy, each in their own thoughts, they hadn't heard Miranda come home. They did, however, hear her and Baby in the back yard. She had a large enough yard to fit the pool and enable the dog to run to stretch her legs and get her daily exercise. Dogs that size needed that, otherwise they could become too curious and destructive. Max decided he needed, right at that moment, to go out and introduce himself. And being the ever thoughtful owners they were, they stopped what they were doing and opened the sliding glass door to the backyard to let him do just that.

Max ran outside, barking his joy. The sight of his bottled up energy could always bring a smile to their faces. Not two seconds later a huge head popped over the fence. They could almost see the grin on the other dog's face. Either she thought Max was a play toy or a prospective suitor. *That* would be a funny thing to see. Max's muscular, but round body was trying its best to jump to Baby's level. He must have gotten high enough for Miranda to see, because she was giggling. Maybe their little guy would earn them some points and get into her good graces. He took that as a good sign and walked to the fence separating the yards, Jack right next to his side. They saw that she was again in a swimsuit, towel wrapped around her, but she hadn't gone in yet.

"Hi, Miranda. I'd ask how your day at work was, but we all know, yeah?" Chase said friendly enough. He really wanted to see if she'd allow them and Max to come over, but figured he'd better not push his luck.

***

Jack waited until he could judge how she would react to Chase before saying anything. That cute blush crossed her face again and he held back a smile. She didn't disappoint him with her reply. He had the vase with the flowers in his hands where she couldn't see them. He knew she'd had a weird day and hoped that the flowers would at least show they were sorry about making her uncomfortable at work.

"You know exactly what kind of day I had. Why didn't you tell me you were the new docs coming in? I hate walking in and looking like a fool." She fumed at them, looking from one to the other.

"Now, sweetheart, when we were here the other night, occupations weren't even discussed, were they? You could just as easily have told us where *you* worked," Jack tried to soothe her.

"Hey! You came into my yard. You should have been the ones to say something. Oh, I don't know, like maybe: Hey we're vets starting a new job on Monday," she said sarcastically. "You know what? Forget it. I need to get my swim in before it's too dark. I don't have lights set up out here yet."

***

Randa was a bit peeved. And because it distracted her, she didn't even think twice about dropping her towel on a chair and diving into the water. Baby, hearing the splash, ran to the end and did a great belly flop. She doggy paddled to her mistress and they both started to swim the length of the pool.

She caught Chase and Jack out of the corner of her eye as they watched eagerly, their arms resting along the top of the fence. Her arms sliced through the water, legs kicking behind her. Not once did she slow down. The feel of the cool water as her arms sliced through calmed her, slightly. She noticed they stood there watching the whole time and she could catch glimpses of Max running back and forth along the fence, in hopes that his new girlfriend would come back to him.

After ten laps, end to end, Randa went to the shallow end and ascended the stairs, Baby right beside her. She walked to the chair and grabbed her towel to begin to dry off when she heard a barking howl and looked up. Baby shook the excess water off and was back at the fence soaking up the attention from the men. They hadn't moved and were cooing to Baby, telling her what a good girl she was and how pretty her eyes were. Baby's tail end was wiggling in pleasure from the affection. Randa knew if they talked to her like that, her reaction would be the same. She'd be flushed and not able to stand still. Hell, she almost wished she had a tail so she could wag it excitedly.

In unison, Chase and Jack looked over at her. She had bent to dry her legs, so they were watching her in profile. The look on their faces showed an interest in her, a bit of attraction maybe. Was it possible? Not trusting herself to even believe that they might actually be interested in her, she was well on her way to thinking that they were just being friendly because they were co-workers. She wrapped the towel around her, wishing her hips weren't so wide or her belly so jiggly. But then again, she wasn't trying to impress them. It wasn't like she had a chance with either of them anyhow. Inwardly, she cringed at the 'woe is me' thoughts. They had her confused, though, especially with how they acted this morning. She had been pressed between them and was so turned on she could have sworn they noticed how hard her nipples had gotten, but they never said a word, just let her go. She had thought she'd felt hardness pressing against her front and back, but she was so focused on her embarrassment that she couldn't swear on a bible if she actually did.

Randa thought about how the rest of the day went. Every chance she had gotten, she had tried to have one of them in front of her. God, they were like stone sculptures. Even through the clothes, she knew their bodies were hard and they took very good care of themselves. She kept wondering how they were so fit and in shape. And their voices... Every time they said her name, it was like someone had taken a live wire and touched it to her body. Her legs had gone weak, and moisture had pooled in a spot that hadn't had any attention in a long while.

Their attentions could certainly grow on her though. She'd seen them flirting harmlessly with older pet owners, thinking it very sweet. She also witnessed them being friendly with the other female employees, nothing suggestive, just friendly and it bolstered her confidence a bit.

So the quiet little voice in the back of her head was getting louder, trying to convince her that maybe, just maybe, they were interested in *her*.

***

Chase couldn't keep his eyes off her as she walked closer to them. When she had been drying off, his mouth had gone dry. The swimsuit was not doing what she had wanted. He figured she was hoping it would hide what she thought might be flaws. Oh no, it was doing the exact opposite. He could see her nipples pushing out, pointing into little peaks, begging for attention. Sure, it could be from being out of the water, but he liked to think it might have also had to do with them. She stepped to the side of Baby and looked first at him, then into Jack's eyes. He smiled slowly as he saw her pupils were dilated, almost entirely black. Just the reaction any observant man wanted to see from the woman he was trying to figure if she was into him or not.

Chase stared at her hungrily. Her mouth was a lovely shade of pink. He could almost picture her nipples looking the same. She was watching as Jack ran his hand down Baby's neck. Chase had a good idea what she was thinking, and could feel himself harden painfully as her lips parted slightly. He could almost feel them wrapped around his erection as Jack slipped into her from behind.

He must have made a sound, because Randa was looking at him like she was starving and Jack was smirking at him. She might be upset with them, but that didn't seem to stop her libido from approving of what she saw and making her want them.

"Uh, yeah, we were wondering if you had thought anymore of our offer to come over for dinner? We really are good cooks." Jack sounded like a schoolboy, and he was anything but. Chase knew this was a first for him. Normally the women they pursued were just as eager. This situation was new for them, being tasked with convincing this goddess that she was indeed more than worthy.

"I won't hold you to it. Really, I don't hold a grudge." Randa sounded resigned, as if she were giving them the out she thought they were looking for.

"Now, you wouldn't be thinking that our work should come home with us? We aren't backing out. We'd like to share a meal with you and get to know you better. Is that so hard to believe? You said yourself you don't cook much, so let us cook and you can just bring your lovely self over. Plus, you can bring Baby. She'll keep Max company. See? Look at your girl there. She's dying to be introduced to our Mighty Max," Chase teased her.

Randa looked at Baby and laughed. The dog was indeed, looking at their pooch as he ran back and forth along the fence, showing off for her. Max looked like a wind-up toy that Baby would have tons of fun with. It certainly would be funny to watch Max woo her.

"So, that's how you think you're going to get me? Because my dog is up for a playmate, you think I'll agree to dinner?" She laughed.

Two voices agreed and then laughed. The fact that she was joking with them was promising, leading

48

them to believe they were beginning to wear her down. Neither of them felt any shame in using Max to get the woman into their home. Any sense of shame they might otherwise have felt went right out the window with the thought that she would be exactly the perfect match for them. They were both picturing her soft curves pressed between them.

***

Randa was trying to figure out their angle. Was it still a matter of staying on a neighbor's good side? Or could it be that they were attracted to her? They seemed to be going out of their way to be friendly with her. They *had* pressed up against her at work, very provocatively. They were even using their dog to, what she hoped, put the moves on her. So, if all of it was for real, how should she handle it? Were they both looking to date her? Would she be expected to choose between them? Could she actually get involved with two men at the same time? None of her friends had ever talked about it happening to them.

One part of her brain was essentially telling her to shut up and go with the flow, the other holding firm that they were just being neighborly. That glimmer of hope sure was getting brighter.

***

Jack bent down and picked up the vase of flowers. Damn it, he felt like a total ass, giving them to her over the fence, but he still wanted her to have them and hopefully they might be that much more persuasive to get her to agree to have dinner with them. He handed them over the fence.

"This is to say we're sorry if we made your day uncomfortable. We'd really like you to come over and have dinner with us. Please?"

He didn't know her well, but he was an observant guy. He could see the internal warring and indecision. And there was a bit of disbelief mixed in too. Jack wanted nothing more than to vocalize that she had nothing to doubt. He wanted hours for them to convince her that she was exactly what they desired.

***

"Oh all right, I'll come over. But I insist on bringing dessert and a treat for Max. Okay?" Randa spoke with a little bit of a tremor in her voice. There would be at least one friend who would find out about, what most would call an atypical date. Kitty. She would get the dessert from the best pastry chef she knew. It was inevitable that someone would find out, and as a pre-emptive strike kind of way, and a way to get the reassurance that this could certainly happen, Kitty was the best bet.

Katarina Campanetti, or Kitty to those who knew her well, was a dear friend of Randa's and was slowly gaining popularity around town. She had proven herself when she was chosen to provide the cake to be served at the opening of a newly built office building. But Randa knew about the woman when she was still baking out of her little house. Kitty made the most delectable sweets. Anything from cakes, pies, and cupcakes, to cookies, and even chocolates. In fact, La Dulce, Kitty's bakery, was part hers. Although she had a stake in the business as a silent owner, she would never try to cash in on it. She would rather do the baking than worry about the business end of it. She was glad she could help a friend when she needed it.

"Dessert? Yeah, that would be great," Chase said softly.

"So, since this is the only week we know for sure we'll all be on the same schedule, how about you pick the night?" Jack murmured.

"Well, would you be open to a BBQ? Here? I have the pool and you both are welcome to use it anytime. The gate is never locked, and it's great to unwind in after a rough day." She stammered through the words that almost failed to be formed in her head. She could almost swear they were thinking about her for dessert. The heat coming from over the fence was enough to make her need to jump right back in the pool.

"Sweetheart, we are grilling fiends. You saw the group of guys here this past weekend. We do it as often as we can. Less mess when grilling is involved. But Chase here is too picky about where he does his grilling. Since Pac made him the grill," he pointed over his shoulder at the monstrosity, "he swore he'd never grill on anything else. So, we can still do the swim after, but are you okay coming here to eat?"

It seemed like they didn't want her in her safety zone, wanted to throw her off a little. Maybe so she couldn't throw them out of her house when dinner was over. Not that she would, but maybe they were worried about it.

"Oh, okay. I guess that would be all right. But what about Baby? Do you still want me to bring her over? She loves other dogs and since she's normally way bigger than others, she's learned to be mindful of her size."

"Of course, bring her over. She's a big girl and will love the extra yard space with no pool. Max can court her to his heart's content," Chase laughed. "So when would be a good night?"

Randa hoped that her nervousness didn't show. For that matter her mind was awash in uncertainty. Could that tiny voice trying to convince her of their interest be right? Though her mind still challenged the thought they wanted *her*, she was curious about them. How they had met? Had they always lived together? Clearly, they weren't gay, but maybe bisexual? Wow, maybe not *that* question—no reason to offend if they weren't. It was an unusual situation, though.

"How about tomorrow night? Would that be okay? I don't want to bother you tonight since we're all home already. Besides, that would give me the chance to get dessert and treats for the dogs to occupy them."

They all agreed the next night would be good all around. With Baby still pouting over not being able to properly greet her new friends, Randa said goodnight. She only had to call Baby once, and the dog reluctantly dropped her front feet down from the fence and turned to trot to her mistress. Randa had to admit she was looking forward to their dinner date. Not even thinking about the consequences, she unwrapped the towel from her body and began to rub her hair to aide in the drying process. That was until she felt the suit begin to ride.

***

Jack and Chase stood at the fence, watching as she went inside. They weren't worried about her safety. That huge dog would deter anything or anyone from hurting Miranda. Oh no, they were clearly enjoying watching her hips sway. Some of the material was beginning to ride between her ass cheeks, and from the way she was subtly walking, they knew she was dying to correct it. As one, they turned to look at each other and grinned.

Jack stayed at the fence long after Chase went inside. He was still thinking back to the dessert issue. He was tempted to tell Randa to wear pudding smoothed all over her body. To him, *that* would be dessert. The image so vivid in his mind, his cock strained against his zipper, looking for a new home. Giving one last look to the top of her deck, hoping she would reappear, he turned to go inside, adjusting his suddenly too tight jeans.

Chapter Three

The next day was hell for Randa. Luckily, she didn't have to escort the two new docs around, but every time she saw them, she blushed and couldn't meet their eyes. She had worn a casual and flowing skirt today, but only after she had debated over it the night before. She was satisfied that this particular skirt hid some of her most noticeable flaws; her thicker thighs and her self-perceived too wide hips. At work, she had on her heels to match, but tonight she would wear flip flops, as she hated footwear at home. She needed that comfort of foot freedom.

Both of the guys had each been assigned a volunteer guide for the remainder of the week. So, unless they had a question on something only she would be able to answer, they had no need to seek her out. Plus, she made herself look so busy they really wouldn't have a chance to, even if they wanted. Not that she could work too much since she was constantly thinking about them. And when she wasn't thinking about them, she saw them or heard them and there went her concentration. She knew it was inevitable, but right now she couldn't deal with them in her space.

Since she was pretty much able to make her own schedule, Randa had arranged to leave early. True, she didn't think of it as a date, but if they ended up in the pool she certainly was going to be smooth and look her best. Plus, she had to stop at Kitty's bakery.

Earlier, when she had called and told Kitty about the dinner tonight, and how she was to bring over dessert, Kitty oohed and ahhed over what Randa should bring. Her friend finally decided it would be a surprise and told Randa to pick it up at three p.m.

At two-fifteen, Randa shut her computer down. She went looking for Josie and told her she was leaving for the day. It took another fifteen minutes to actually be able to leave the building because Josie was in detective mode and trying to get Randa to spill as to why she was leaving.

Josephine Stuart—no one dared call her anything but Josie—was one of Randa's closest friends. When Randa first began volunteering at The Haven, Josie had been a bit standoffish. When Randa's then boyfriend had come to the shelter demanding to see her, he had become increasingly belligerent with the staff, forcing Josie to step in and tell him off. Josie hadn't liked how the man had treated Randa. Belittling her and trying to come across as funny when he called Randa his 'chubby puppy'. The look on Josie's face had instantly made the others smile and pity the guy since her ability to cut a man down was legendary. Randa and Josie had immediately bonded after that moment.

With the promise of a later explanation, she escaped out the employee entrance to her car. She could feel Josie's gaze follow her out of Haven, and if she didn't know better, the woman probably watched as she got in her car.

Ten minutes later, she was walking into heaven on earth. The smell of the shop alone should be

56

outlawed and Randa could have sworn she gained five pounds from just the aromas. Kitty came rushing around the counter to grab her into a tight hug. The girl behind the counter had a bit of a panicked look on her face when Kitty told her to watch the front. She must have been really new.

"Come on back, I've got your man winner waiting. We haven't seen each other in a couple of weeks and I need to know how you met the man you're having dinner with."

"Well..." Randa wasn't sure how to break it to her that it wasn't just one man, but two. "You remember the empty house next door? It didn't stay empty long. The new owners moved in last weekend. They invited me over for dinner to get to know them."

"Oh, so it's not a man, but a couple? Well, shit, girl, I thought you had a hot date." Kitty pouted and looked like she would change the dessert.

"Uh... well, not exactly. It is a couple, a couple of guys. And before you ask, no they are definitely *not* gay. At least, I don't think they are. They bought the house together, but don't seem the type to swing that way. Actually, that was going to be one of the things I ask them tonight. They just seem so masculine and straight, I'm not sure I want to make them angry asking if they are."

Randa went on to explain they were the new doctors at Haven. She even confessed they were extremely good looking and she was attracted to both, how they had acted their first day by sandwiching her between them, and how when she was swimming it felt like they were undressing her with their eyes and wanted to lay her out for them to feast on. But, fat lot of good that would do for her; no way would they be interested in a thick woman like her. She knew it could have been just her imagination, but a part of her remained hopeful. Could it be that she was just deprived and hadn't realized it until they came along?

"You did *not* just call yourself fat, did you? You know how much I hate that word. And you could have any man you want if you stopped thinking of yourself like that. You are beautiful, smart, and have a great sense of humor. You're so kind you'd take in Jack the Ripper if he showed at your door homeless," Kitty ranted.

Randa hung her head. She so wanted to believe Kitty, but she could count on one hand how many times a man had ever approached her. Kitty was a full figured woman too, but she carried herself taller than Randa did. With her Sicilian upbringing, food was an important part of Kitty's life. But like Randa, she was in no way unfit. She came to use the pool whenever she could. Plus, she didn't own a car, so she rode her bicycle everywhere. Thank goodness she lived close to all of their friends. Someone was always around to shuttle her to the store to get her groceries.

"No, Kitty, I didn't call myself fat. From your constant corrections, I know better," Randa teased. "I know I am a lush goddess of beauty and sexuality."

The last statement they both said at the same time then laughed. Kitty had made it her mission to help any plus size woman see that curves were a good thing. She hated that there were people out there telling heavier women their size wasn't considered fashionable or sexually attractive, and they were unhealthy. Besides, Marilyn Monroe, who was a sex kitten in her day, was a full figured woman. Hips seemed to go out of style in the sixties—maybe early seventies. But not all men went along with fashion. Kitty had politely corrected a girl in her culinary classes that men who found her attractive were not chubby chasers. That there was a difference between being fat and being full figured. Sure women could be fat just like men could, but it was in a sense of not being fit, not being healthy. Besides, if the woman and her significant other were happy, what right did anyone outside that relationship have to criticize?

"So, you've literally got a double date tonight? Well, sweet thing, my chocolate cream pie will be just the thing to take. That way, if things get naughty, you can use the pie to paint their bodies with and then lick off," Kitty cooed to her. "Please give me details the next time we talk. And you had better at least kiss them and have fun. You so deserve it."

"Thank you," Randa replied as she checked her watch again. "But it may just be a neighborly dinner, so don't be disappointed if nothing happens."

Kitty gave her look of doubt for her last comment, but she took pity on her for once, and let her leave without more of a lecture on how beautiful she was and not overweight. Kitty had her best interest at heart and she appreciated it. She wanted to kiss her for being such a great friend, but she just wanted to get out of there. She was anxious to get home and she still needed to make a quick stop to pick up the dog treats.

Randa gave her friend a hug and kissed her on the cheek, then rushed to her car, made two quick stops and drove home. She immediately began to fill her tub with very warm water, including her favorite white tea and ginger scented bath oil. She didn't want to wear perfume tonight, but still wanted to smell nice and she knew the oil wouldn't be overpowering. Thank goodness she had recently had laser hair removal performed and didn't have to shave any longer. Her hair pinned up, she got in and sighed. Despite the warmth of the weather outside, the hot bath relaxed her. Work was not stressful, there were no bills to worry over, and the boys were doing very well for themselves. Nope, all of her stress was self-inflicted.

She thought of the two men with whom she would be having dinner. She truly thought that they had invited her to keep the peace of the neighborhood, or to break the news that she had no worries about being uncomfortable at work. They probably just wanted to be friends with the owner of the closest pool. Well, if that was what they wanted, she was okay with it. It wasn't like she wanted a relationship. That would be weird, wouldn't it? How could something like that actually work? Maybe they would make her choose between them. She wasn't sure she could decide between the two. There was just something about them that complimented each other. She closed her eyes and soaked. The thought of two men pleasuring her at the same time was definitely a turn on. She had never pictured herself in a situation like that, until recently. Hell, the men that had been in her life already had been shining examples that some men were only looking for superficial.

On the edge of her hearing was an alarm. Confused, she sat up in the now lukewarm water. The clock on the side showed four-thirty. *That* got her attention. She was due to go next door for dinner in an hour. Thankfully she had set the alarm. Randa stood and stepped out of the water. She grabbed the fluffy towel that sat in arm's reach and wrapped the soft fabric around her body. After tucking it beneath her arm and securing it, she padded into her room to figure out what to wear. No shorts or slacks. It was definitely a dress or skirt situation. The skirt she wore to work that day was actually the perfect look, but since she hadn't hung it up when she undressed, it was now a puddle of wrinkles. Luckily, she had a similar skirt from the same designer.

Leaving her hair pinned up, she slipped the skirt on. Now for the shirt. Again, it was a very warm day, so she decided on a camisole with a built in bra. The color contrasted the skirt nicely. She looked at herself in the mirror and could almost see what Kitty was talking about. Her skin was a healthy cream color, and she had her honey hair up, but tendrils had escaped to give her a just loved look. Her blue eyes shone with excitement that the rest of her body shared.

No makeup was needed since it was just a casual dinner, and since she had soaked in the bath oil for quite some time, the scent mixed with her own, made Randa smile. She loved that subtle scent, loved how it made her feel very sexy. Not that she was shooting for sexy, but a woman always wanted that feeling. It was definitely a woman thing.

Baby came through the doorway and cocked her large head to one side. It was almost as if she were judging how Randa looked. Her tail began to thump on the plush carpet in approval. Randa didn't know what she would do without someone to talk to, even if that someone couldn't talk back. It made her think she was a little less crazy. Of course, her boys might not agree with her.

"Well, are you ready to meet your new friend, Baby? I'm going to apologize now for the leash, but I don't need you trying to find the Henderson's kitty. The last time you ended up coming to work with me to get stitches when he didn't like how you played. Besides, Max is waiting for you."

At the mention of the other dog, Baby's attention was grabbed and she woofed lowly and begin to whine softly. She started walking away toward the stairs where she stopped and looked at her mistress as if to say, 'well let's go'. Randa laughed softly and followed down the stairs. She had made a trip to a good butcher shop and picked up a couple of really nice bones to keep the dogs occupied. Then her last stop was to her favorite wine store to pick up a bottle to give to Chase and Jack. She had picked a nice red wine so they could enjoy it with whatever they would eat that night, or for the friends to open another time.

Leash clipped to her collar—knowing that Baby would not pull, even around Max—Randa grabbed the wine, which she slipped under her arm, and then the special pie. Kitty had said it could sit out for a couple hours, especially if they had wanted to use it for something other than eating. Randa, blushing bright red, had adamantly denied any accusations of such a conquest. She stood at the door, about to ring the bell, when the door opened, startling her. The wine came out from under her arm, but was saved by a strong set of hands.

Relief washed over her face, as she looked up. Beautiful green eyes and the longest lashes she had ever seen looked back at her in amusement. Chase had similar coloring to her, but she would call his hair color wheat versus her honey. He had a little bit of a shadow so she knew he hadn't shaved when he got home. But that was okay. With his hair styled as a controlled mess, it was sexy as all hell.

They stood like that for no more than a minute or so, but to Randa it seemed like a lot longer. Having dropped the leash along with the wine, Baby had already torn through the house looking for Max, and by the sounds of the excited whines, they had found each other. That left the two of them. She was just staring into his eyes, not saying a word. She guessed it was too late for her to grab her dog and go back home. She stood there like a deer in headlights, not even sure what to say.

"Are you going to stand there staring, or are you coming in, hon?" Chase teased her.

Randa was mortified and wanted to turn around and go home. But between her dog's blissful sounds and Chase coming out to practically push her inside, she couldn't. She stepped into the house and, knowing the layout, headed toward the kitchen. When Joe and Jennifer Hamilton lived there, she was there a lot since their oldest son and hers were good friends. There were a lot of BBQs and shared holiday dinners.

Chase followed right behind her, making her worry he was watching the sway of her hips. She placed the pie on the counter and turned, catching a smile on his face. Then she remembered the bones were still next door.

"Oh, I forgot Max's surprise. Give me one moment and I'll be right back."

She dashed out before he could say a word, passing Jack as she headed out the front door.

***

Jack watched her go and then looked to Chase to explain.

"She forgot something at home. She'll be right back," Chase promised.

They walked to the deck and watched the dogs take turns chasing each other. They were pleasantly surprised at how well Baby was trained to be mindful of her size. She could easily hurt them or Max—hell, Miranda, too—but she was the epitome of a gentle giant.

The doorbell sounded and Jack answered it this time. Instead of greeting her like he should have, he allowed his gaze to travel down her body. The skirt she wore looked almost identical to the one she had worn to work, though a different color. And that top? He liked how it cupped her breasts. With no bra straps in sight, he was tempted to pull the material down and bare her nipples for a lick. She stepped into the house and immediately took her flip flops off. When she looked at him, she blushed as he raised his eyebrow in question.

"I'm sorry, I don't wear shoes unless I'm going out. I hope you don't mind?" she asked tentatively, stepping back to her shoes, but stopped when his hand reached out for hers.

"Oh no, babe, go ahead and make yourself comfortable."

With his hand on her waist, he guided her back into the kitchen where Chase was taking the marinated meat out of the fridge. Jack picked her up and sat her on one of the bar stools and asked what she'd like to drink. He watched as her gaze quickly flitted over their beer bottles, but landed on a four pack of wine coolers that they hadn't made room in the refrigerator for yet.

"Would you like a wine cooler or hard cider? We keep stuff like that on hand. Depends on our moods as to what we drink."

"Oh yes, a hard cider would be great," she replied with a smile.

"So you brought a chocolate pie?" he asked.

"Yes, my friend owns her own bakery, and when I told her I was coming over for dinner, she made it special for us," Randa said shyly.

"You told your friend you had a threesome planned?" Jack teased her.

"Threesome? Umm, no. I told her I was having dinner with new neighbors who happened to work with me and were two men," she answered a little softly.

Chase stopped what he was doing and calmly walked to the sink to wash his hands. He walked toward her, drying them on a hand towel. Chase spun the chair Miranda was in until she was facing him. She couldn't look at him, just stared at her fingers fidgeting in her lap. With just one finger, he lifted her head until her eyes met his.

"Miranda, Jack was only teasing. We would never expect anything unless you freely joined in. We're not like that, at all," Chase spoke softly to her.

Jack stood behind the chair and rubbed her arms from behind her, then leaned down until his mouth was at her ear. It was true he had been teasing her, but his main intention was to see how she would react to the term out loud. She couldn't be totally shocked, right? It had been insinuated at work the other day, but they hadn't come right out and told her that they would be pursuing her.

"But make no mistake, sweet thing, we would love for you to join in. In fact, we don't play without a female. Let's put that right out of your mind. We are not gay, *very* far from it. Not bisexual either, but we are very comfortable with ourselves which makes us comfortable with each other," Jack whispered.

Chapter Four

Miranda shivered, not knowing what to say. Startled a little, the idea that they *were* interested in her was beginning to take form, for real. She knew she was only just okay to look at. That was something her ex and her second husband had always told her. Of course, her looks were bunched in with her weight. "You'd be so fucking hot if you lost the weight," is what her ex had said to her. And even a recent ex-boyfriend had come close to saying something so very similar to that. "Sure, you're cute, but with those extra pounds, your looks are distracting."

"Why are you telling me this? You really don't have to be nice to me because we work together, or because we're neighbors. I don't mind your friends coming over, as long as the noise isn't too loud. And what you do in your own time is your business, not any of mine," she spoke quickly, feeling her cheeks turning red.

"Miranda, look at me." Chase waited until she did. "Jack told you because we are interested in you. We're both attracted to you and we'd like to get to know you to see if there's anything there. Is there any chance you're attracted to us?"

"You're, uh, both attracted to me? But why? You two are gorgeous and could have anyone you wanted. Why me?" She covered her mouth, wanting to take the words back. *Why couldn't her brain to mouth filter ever work when it needed to?*

Chase lifted her off the stool to sit on the counter. Since she was on the corner of the counter, Jack stood between her legs and Chase moved to her side and slightly behind her. The look on Jack's face was pure hunger. Her breathing stopped and she drew her bottom lip between her teeth. His gaze flitted over her face before settling on her lips. With a groan of torment, Jack leaned forward and captured her lips. He sipped at her mouth, gently moving his lips over hers. She was non-responsive at first, in shock with his lips against hers. Tentatively she began to respond. As she tilted her head to accommodate Jack's kiss, Chase leaned forward and began to nuzzle her neck and earlobe, his hands coming around her to rest below her breasts. Simultaneously, both men backed off slowly. The power of the kiss made her shy and not sure who to look at.

Jack spoke to her softly, "Now, does that prove we're both attracted to you? We could continue if you like, but you might need to eat to keep your strength up to manage both of us." His grin was devilish, but there was hope in his eyes for more.

It showed her they weren't afraid of touching her, but she was still stuck on why. Did they think she was an easy target because she was a lonely widow and easily accessible considering she live next door? She was not up for being used. She just couldn't let herself believe they were being genuine. "But why would you want someone who has a body like me?" she asked, confused. There it was again. She even sounded pathetic to herself. She wanted to crawl in a hole and never come out.

Chase looked upset. "What do you mean someone who has a body like yours? Could you mean a lush figure with curves in all the right places? Do you mean a woman with a body made for loving?"

"Miranda, there are a lot of men who prefer women with real bodies, not sticks that poke us when we're in bed with them. Chase and I are like that. In fact, most of our friends are like that." Jack's smile was soft this time. "Chase isn't upset with you, babe, he just hates that society, or anyone else for that matter, feel they can dictate to him who he should find attractive. He's not one for following the rules, much." Jack laughed softly.

Randa was so stunned that these two men could both want her that she never even noticed that Jack's hands were under her skirt, caressing her thighs. Or that Chase had raised her camisole and was running his hand up and down her back. Once she realized it, she blushed again and batted at their hands. Once their hands left her body, she immediately felt empty. Not able to explain it to herself, she focused on the other question that was running rampant in her mind.

"I guess I can accept you are attracted to my body shape, but how can you both be thinking to pursue me? I'm flattered, but not sure about the dynamics?" she asked, curious. How could two men hope to have any kind of a healthy relationship by being attracted to and sharing the same woman?

If she were honest with herself, she *could* picture herself dating these two men at the same time. Heck, what woman hadn't dreamt of two gorgeous, hard bodied guys pleasing her at the same time? But how could that be fair? What if things got intimate and one of them got jealous? She'd have to break it off with both, making it awkward living next door and working with them.

They watched her closely and she just knew they could see the wheels turning in her head. They must have had this happen before. She had so many questions and concerns, but there they stood, calm as can be, as though that particular conversation was an everyday occurrence. Damn, she wished she could be nonchalant about it too.

"Well, that's another thing, sweetie. Sure, we've pursued women on our own and have enjoyed it, but the last few years we've had more satisfying relationships as a threesome." Chase explained, leaving Jack to finish the rest.

"Absolutely. We noticed our tastes were similar a while back and we've been involved in threesomes for quite a few years now," Jack said.

She was shocked over that last bit of news, so she just stared at them, not knowing what to say. Two men at the same time? Was that—well, it *was* possible, but how did a true relationship build from a situation like that? How did they figure out who went where and who went first?

"Okay, I think you're right. I'm going to need food. But maybe not for keeping up with you, as you stated earlier. I need to wrap my brain around things and I need to know what you want from me out of this dinner. So, let's get dinner going. You can introduce me to Max, since by the looks of them outside, Baby is in love with him already. Then we can talk. Is that okay?" She tried to act as though such a situation happened to her all the time.

Chase and Jack looked at each other, smiled brightly, and then looked at Miranda. "Sounds like a plan."

Steaks, salad, and other sides were brought outside to the deck. Between Chase and Jack, the cooler was stuffed with drinks to minimize the trips inside.

Settled in a chair, and told to not move, Randa took the size appropriate bones out of the packages for the dogs and called them over. Baby knew exactly what to do, Max watching her, followed suit. Both animals waited patiently. Randa placed both bones on her knees, well within reach of the dogs, and pretended to ignore them. It was a test she liked to do to make sure Baby kept her manners. After a minute or two, she called Max forward. His entire body was one big wiggle, but he was very gentle about taking the bone he was offered. Baby did the same, taking the bone daintily in her mouth and wandering off to chew on it. Max lay right next to her, not allowing her to get away from him.

***

Jack and Chase looked at each other, then at Max. He had been taught basic commands, but manners? Nope, *that* they never showed him. Probably because they still pictured him as a puppy. So for him to pick up on that so quickly, was a surprise.

"How did you do that, Miranda?" Jack came over and sat with her. "That was amazing."

She blushed and tried to brush it off. "It's nothing. My dad was a dog trainer for the military and we always had dogs growing up. Seemed he'd get one trained and he or she would go off to its handler, then another would come to live with us. I loved it and hated it. I was never allowed to have a dog of my own. Dad was afraid that it would interrupt the dog training."

Chase was giving the meat time to cook, so he came over, took a seat on her other side, and drank some of his beer. Watching her with Max reminded him of Jackson. Prior to his training for the police department, he had been a sweet dog, but a little unruly. If she could take the wild Max and teach him manners in two minutes, what could she do with other animals? Especially service animals?

They started talking about various topics. But when the topic of age came up, Randa looked a little concerned to learn Jack and Chase were younger than her. Not young like her boys, but still younger than she was. They both could care less about the difference. It was just a number to them. With many discussions, both he and Jack found it was just a matter of preference. They had found that older women were more mature, were more focused on what they wanted. Oh yeah, and they were certainly better in bed. Since they discussed different aspects of women, and had dated a few older women, they agreed the older women were the ones they would pursue.

Getting Randa to talk about her past relationships was harder than Chase thought it would be. But when they finally got Randa to open up about her two marriages, they were both upset for her. The thought that she'd endured verbally and emotionally abusive relationships throughout most of her life made his heart ache for her and made his stomach sour. They told her both of her husbands deserved nothing less than to be strung up and beaten. How could any man cheat on a woman as beautiful and loving as Randa? She truly deserved better. Despite the strangeness of their arrangement, neither of them would or could deal with infidelity. Randa would never have to worry about it with them.

With dinner done, the three of them continued to chat, while the sun began to set. The dogs were still very busy with their bones and not interested in being disturbed.

Chase peered at Randa and as corny as it sounded, in the dying sunlight, she looked so beautiful. He continued to study her, watching as the blush crept up from her chest to her hairline. Feeling like she might be getting uncomfortable with him and Jack staring at her, he stood. Jack followed suit and they each held out a hand. She slowly placed her hands in theirs and allowed them to pull her up to stand between them. When they tried to lead her inside, she hesitated only for a second then allowed them to pull her into the house.

"Would you like a glass of wine?" Chase asked. "Jack is going to get a fire started. We thought we'd have some of that pie in the living room, in front of the fire."

***

"That sounds really nice. Can I use your restroom?" Randa responded timidly. She needed to get the jitters out of her, although she didn't think they'd voluntarily leave.

"Sure. You know where it is, right?" Jack teased her.

She did. Randa quickly made her way to the bathroom, locked the door, and stood there while running the water. She stared at herself in the mirror while she contemplated their offer. Was she seriously considering entering into a relationship with two men at the same time? She couldn't keep two other men happy—separately—and one even called her frigid. She'd had a few dates comment on her size and say men wanted someone they could feel protective over and with her being full figured, it didn't instill that feeling. What if they were all right? She was almost fifty years old. Did she want to start over with not just one man but two? That doubled the pressure to possibly disappoint.

Randa left the bathroom and headed toward the fireplace. To her knowledge, the fireplace had never been used by the Hamiltons. With kids, they didn't have a lot of opportunities for a romantic setting, and this part of California didn't really have a need for the warmth. Then she thought about the set up. Were they going to make a move on her? Would she have both men kissing her in front of the fire? God, just the thought made her knees weak and she felt her body tingle for the first time in a long time, at least with real men present and not in just her fantasies. Sure she had been attracted to other men, but it seemed it was one sided and that hadn't exactly gotten her juices flowing. If two men, especially two men such as Chase and Jack, wanted her as much as she wanted them, she'd turn into Niagara Falls.

She stopped in the open doorway of the living room and watch as Jack lit the fire. A bottle of wine and three glasses were on the table close by. Chase was carrying a plate and two spoons toward her. With the look of a predator on his face, he looked like he would tackle her right where she was and eat her up. Just the look alone made her nipples pebble and she could feel heat travel down her body. Chase smiled knowingly at her, but his gaze was on her breasts, watching their reaction to his stare. She stood there, not able to move.

He had her so mesmerized with that raw desire in his eyes, she hadn't heard Jack get up and walk toward her. They were both wearing casual clothes, but their shoes had been removed, making his steps almost silent on the plush carpet. Chase set the plate down and joined Jack. They each took one of her hands and brought her to the blanket and pillows they had strewn on the floor. Chase sat first and gently pulled her down to sit next to him. Jack joined them on her other side. With the wine poured, Chase pressed the glass stem into her hands, and began to talk.

"Miranda, Jack and I really like you. You're funny, smart, generous, and sinfully sexy. We come as a package deal, though. If you're not interested in both of us then this won't work. That's not how we work." He smiled at her to soften the bluntness of his words.

Jack nodded his head and continued where Chase left off. "We think the three of us could really have a good thing together. So, do you think this is something you can handle? Us—together—at the same time? We'd like to show you how good the three of us can be together."

It was the second time that week they told her they were interested in her. Randa wanted to answer right away, but couldn't as her throat was too dry. She was so tempted to kiss one as she ground against the other, but she wasn't sure if it was because it had been so long or because of the attraction she knew was there, for both of them. She took a sip of the wine and moved to sit on the step in front of the fireplace. They watched her with a look of disappointment, until she began to talk.

"I am attracted to you, both of you, but I've never done anything like this before, and if it doesn't work out, I will probably never do it again. I want us all to go into this with our eyes wide open, although that is more for me than you since you've done this before." She took another sip of wine to fortify herself. "Most of the men I've been with I trusted with not only my body but my heart. I'm not sure my heart could take being trampled on like that again. The first called me frigid and the rest insinuated it. For all I know, I could be. I just want you to know what you're getting into. If this doesn't work out, I'd rather have a clean break, and an agreement that work will not suffer."

For the longest moment, neither said a word. They looked at each other, and then back at her. Randa could see Chase clenching his fist, his face turning red and Jack was gritting his teeth in what looked like anger. Were they angry at her? What had she done besides just being honest with them? But then Chase came to his knees in front of her, took the glass of wine out of her hand and set it on the table.

***

Chase wanted to beat the shit out of the cowards who told her she was frigid. All you had to do was look at the woman to know she was anything but. He had a feeling, though, she wouldn't believe his words, that actions would definitely speak louder than anything he could say to her. His anger quickly morphed into a driven desire to make her feel what she deserved to feel. Beautiful, appreciated, *cherished*. He looked at Jack and saw the same thoughts running through his mind. It was like their minds were connected. They both smiled and nodded at each other, knowing what they were going to do.

Chase gently pulled her back down to the floor with them. Jack came up behind Miranda, his hands sliding down her arms until he reached her fingers, then back up to her neck. He tilted her head to one side and held her so Chase could lean forward to lick from her nape to her earlobe. Chase then slid the straps of her camisole down her arms until only her breasts were holding the top up. With a quick tug, it pooled around her waist, baring her sumptuous breasts. He continued to kiss and nip her skin along her shoulders, as Jack reached around and cupped her breasts, fingers narrowing in on her nipples. He may not have a physical kind of job, but his hands were just rough enough to cause her to gasp and her head to fall back to rest on Jack's chest.

Chase lifted himself away from her, only to be rewarded by a whimper. Quickly, he pulled his shirt up and over his head, tossing it somewhere behind him. Her hands immediately went to his chest. Soft and warm, her touch sent shivers through his body. She pulled gently on the hair that was sparingly scattered about his pectoral muscles before sliding her hands behind his head to draw it down to hers.

***

Randa had never been so forward before, but they made her feel so confident. Already they were a good influence on her, enticing her to behave like she normally wouldn't. And she had to admit to herself that she really liked it.

"Please, I need..." She was not even sure how to voice how much she needed both of them at that moment.

"Soon, baby. Let us play a little. Okay? We promise we'll all go over that edge."

She was impatient. But his words and subsequent actions settled her a bit. But they also excited her. Jack's hands quickly pulled the front of her camisole up and over her head and slid it down her arms, effectively trapping them behind her back so she couldn't move. She tried to pull her arms free with no luck. Then he leaned down, licked her earlobe, and said, "This is the proof that you affect us."

He pressed her hands to the front of his pants, showing how much the sight of her with his friend had affected him. Quickly, her camisole joined Chase's shirt and then her hand was pressed to the front of his pants to show the same.

Chase started to caress her legs under her loose skirt, moving gradually toward the apex of her thighs. His movements were a slow, deliberate journey. She was a little embarrassed at how wet she was and that he would know soon enough. He wouldn't have to remove her panties to test her readiness, they were soaked and he seemed pleased that they were the cause.

Chase lightly rubbed her through the material before he slipped past the barrier with two fingers and caressed her, allowing his thumb to stroke her nub. He pulled his hand away and brought it up to show her the moisture on his fingertips. He placed his mouth to her ear and said words that made her shake, "This is proof you are not frigid."

Mortified, she tried to grab Chase's hand, but Jack stopped her. The two of them laid her on her back before the fire.

***

As Chase started pulling her skirt and panties off her hips, her scent washed over him, making him want to run his tongue and lips all over her. Instead, he watched as Jack kept her mind occupied by leaning over and kissing her. He imagined Miranda's mouth must taste like the wine they had just enjoyed and couldn't wait to taste her for himself as Jack sipped and licked at her lips, coaxing them to open.

Chase stroked her calves languidly as he continued to observe Jack's lips tasting and caressing hers, feeling the softness. Jack's hand went to a breast, tugging on a nipple gently, then pinching it. When she gasped, his tongue slipped past her lips and began to play with hers. Her hands came up to run her fingers through his hair, but Jack lifted up and pressed her hands to her own nipples. He covered her hands with his and together their hands moved over her breasts.

"Feel what I feel, Miranda. This is all hot, eager woman," Jack told her. "No way is this a frigid woman. The man, or men, who claimed you were, had no clue how to please a woman. My guess is you probably have never had a true orgasm," Jack whispered as he looked down at their hands. Four hands cupped, tweaked and pinched her breasts. Her chest lifted up and she moaned, closing her eyes. "Oh no. Open those beautiful eyes. You need to see how you much you affect us and how much we affect you."

Chase, having removed her skirt and panties, started to massage her left foot. As she relaxed, he worked further up her leg. When he reached the juncture of her thighs, she stiffened again in anticipation.

***

She almost begged him to take her right then, right there. She needed them to soothe the ache raging in her body. He disappointed her by starting on the other leg to begin the same routine of massaging, but this time licking, kissing, and nipping as he worked his way up.

Randa had never had one man pay so much attention to her, let alone two. If that was how they made love together, she could only guess that alone they were just as attentive. She arched her back as Jack licked her nipples between their fingers. He guided her fingers to pinch them lightly, causing her to moan, but when Chase reached her core and was lightly tonguing her, the moan seemed to go on forever. How could a woman not be turned on by two men whose objective was to give the most pleasure? But why wouldn't they let her return the gesture?

"Please, Jack, Chase, I want to touch too. Please, won't you let me?" she moaned out as she moved restlessly.

"The way you're responding is pleasure enough, sweetheart," Jack replied in a whisper.

They switched positions so that Jack was now between her thighs and Chase was tonguing her nipples, first one then the other. Jack positioned her legs so that her heels were practically imbedded in his back, but she didn't care at this point that she was spread bare for them to see. Every time Chase's tongue swiped, so did Jack's. Every time Jack sucked on that little bundle of nerves right above her moist heat, Chase would suck hard on one nipple then the other.

The two sensations were going to send her over the edge soon, but she didn't want to go alone. She bowed her back and tossed her head on the blanket. She could feel it coming, but she was trying to fight it off. She had always been a generous lover. A big woman had to make sure her man was satisfied or he'd look elsewhere, right?

***

Chase wanted to know why she was fighting them. He knew they were pleasing her. Her low, breathy moans and the sexy movements of her body were proof. He figured it was just that she wanted them to fly with her.

Her skin had a fine sheen of perspiration. The flush of her skin and the sensuous sounds she was making was driving him closer to a climax.

"Baby, please, let us take you over. This is for you and you alone," Chase whispered to her.

"But I want you to come with me," she pleaded.

Chase waited as Jack came up on the other side of her. Obviously the pleasure was there, but he could see the wheels turning too when her arms immediately covered the scars and stretch marks that they had noticed. One looked like an appendectomy, and one horrific scar spanning her abdomen was probably a hysterectomy. But they weren't going to make love to a scar; they were attracted to the woman inside.

Chase pried her arms away from her stomach and kissed each scar. "Miranda, we want to do this. We want to show you how beautiful you are. Believe me, we'll join in. Neither of us are saints," Chase murmured with a soft chuckle. "We just want you to see what we see and feel what we feel. Okay?"

"He's right, sweetheart," Jack whispered. "I can't wait to sink into you as you use that pretty mouth on Chase. Can't wait to hear more of your moans. Can't wait to see your face when you explode all over me, or all over my friend here."

***

He was giving Randa visuals of what was to come with both of them. She was pretty damned sure that separately she would see stars, but together? There would definitely be planets involved, and comets too. But she was still torn. In the past, sex was a lot of work for her. It was almost like her partners chose her out of a sense of obligation and not true attraction, which made her do most of the work and they seemed to get the majority, if not all, of the pleasure.

"You're thinking too much. You need to feel right now, not think," Jack said.

After she took her time looking deeply into one set of eyes and then the other, she decided they were right. Up until now, *they* were the ones who had pursued her. *They* initiated everything. How could she not believe their actions? So, she was going to throw caution to the wind and let someone else do the work.

"You convinced me. I welcome any ministrations you boys would like to bring to the table." Randa tried to sound cocky, but wasn't convinced she didn't come off as more than uncertain.

Chapter Five

They weren't going to allow her to change her mind. Jack stayed near her head, because he truly loved her breasts. He could spend all day showing this woman how much she turned him on, but he doubted she knew how much just her breasts made his cock throb. He loved to watch them as they perked up and begged for his mouth and tongue. And just when she wasn't expecting it, his teeth would gently nip, just to send a jolt through her, making her back arch. So, that is where he would be playing and showing her pleasure. He leaned down and took her mouth, roughly. He had been thinking about this for the last two nights, her mouth, her breasts… Hell, everything about her. She had invaded his dreams and made him wake up in a sweat and covered in his own release. He hadn't done that since he was fifteen.

With his lips and tongue dueling with hers, his hands were far from slacking off. Each had cupped the bottom of each breast. Jack had never felt skin so soft. It was as though she had rose petals for skin. And right now she had just the slightest of blushes spreading across her body. Her hands came up and tangled in his hair, holding him steady as she moaned against his lips.

***

Chase had sat back at first, just watching his friend and Miranda. She was so responsive. There was no other reaction for him to have but to be aroused. But sitting back became too much for him, he needed to be a part of her pleasure. Head lowered to her abdomen, he licked and kissed his way to the juncture of her thighs. Her personal perfume would have brought him to his knees if he were standing. The further south he went, the more the bottom half of her body tensed. He was amazed that she was able to keep track of what half was feeling what. Her pubic area was not fully shaved, but she did have what looked like a bunny's tail right above her clitoris.

His fingers combed through that patch of hair. His breath caressed her as he leaned down and allowed his tongue to come out and lick her. He could taste her wetness and when he set his mouth completely on her, he hummed his approval of her taste. Her folds called out to him and he couldn't help but to push her thighs further apart. He lay on his stomach, arms under them around her thighs to hold her as he claimed her heat for his own. His fully seated mouth caused her to buck her hips to get closer.

***

They were barely started and Randa couldn't think straight already. In the past, her lovers weren't as attentive. It was almost as if they were only interested in the end result. A lot of times, she wasn't even brought to climax, but left hanging, and they hadn't even known or cared. She was so close to coming that she wasn't sure how much longer she could hold on. Chase's mouth was so hot and soft and his tongue was doing magical things to her. And Jack at her breasts...his hands should be registered as most likely to make a woman wet with just a flick of the finger. But since they said this was more for her than for them, she would hold out as long as she could. It would be a challenge since it had been so long since she had received such pleasure. Actually, she hadn't *ever* felt like this nor had such an intense burn of desire. Her whole body was on fire. She had felt desire and attraction before, but never like this. It was as if their bodies were made for her and hers for them. They played her body like expert musicians with an instrument. Not even with her husbands had anything like this happened.

***

Jack moved his head from her lips down to her jaw and then her ear. "Absolutely beautiful," he whispered to her. The words spoken, he could feel her breathing speed up and her body tense, but Jack still felt her holding back. Why was she fighting it? He worked his way down her neck to her nape. From there, he licked until he reached her breasts. Both hands cupped a breast, pushing them together so he could lick a trail from one nipple to the other. Using quick flicks of his tongue, they hardened to the point that Miranda released his head to grip the blanket and push up. She must not have known to do so would only bring her closer to not only his mouth, but to Chase's. Jack turned his head and continued what he was doing, but also watched his friend.

***

Chase opened his eyes when almost all of Miranda's body rose for his and Jack's convenience. The only eyes that looked back at him were Jack's. He saw his friend smile around the nipple he was laving. He caught the nod Jack gave him and he went back to the sweet heat before him. With one hand, he spread her folds. He could see her essence, shiny and wet and waiting for him. Right at the top, her little bundle of nerves sat, plump and engorged with blood. He could tell that she was close, but he knew a woman's body well enough to know that she was holding back.

His tongue came out and ran along her folds, his taste buds going nuts for her. The tip pressed on her button, then flicked it quickly, making her moan loudly. His second hand joined the fun by thrusting two fingers inside. He curled them up to hit her g-spot and she moaned long and loud. Her inner muscles were gripping his fingers and he felt her body shake. The two friends' gazes met again and they decided enough was enough. It was time to make her lose control. They each ramped up their attentions and got down to business.

***

Randa thought she would be strong enough to hold off, but the two of them seemed to be determined to break down her defenses. Despite her body needing to let her climax flow from her, she had held out. She had wanted them to join her, but now she wasn't sure she would be able to stop it from cresting again. They were reading her body as if it was a well loved novel and saw the signs. She could feel the slight roughness of Jack's tongue and the scrap of his teeth across her very responsive nipples. Currents of electricity seemed to travel straight to her womb with every pull of his mouth or the slight nip of his teeth. And Chase seemed to know this and had quickened the movement of his fingers thrusting in and out of her very ready body, thumb resting on the engorged button, alternating between stroking and pressing down. She could feel the climax fast approaching.

Her eyes were closed, but a burst of white light hit behind her eyelids and she cried out. Neither slowed their movements, but seemed to draw the climax out and push her towards another. Never had she experienced a climax that intense. With two husbands and a handful of lovers, not a single one had made her scream like she just did. And they had done it without coming themselves. *That* was definitely not something the men in her past would have done. She always had to pleasure herself after they came and passed out next to her.

She watched with desire as Chase stood, unbuttoned then unzipped his cargo shorts. He pushed them below his waist and kicked them in the general direction of his shirt. His cock rose proudly from the trimmed hair at his groin, veins running along its length, the head engorged with blood. He sat next to her and began kissing her gently. He maneuvered himself so his back was to the fireplace, then pulled her into a sitting position between his legs, facing Jack. With his arms under hers, he cupped her still sensitive breasts, tweaking her nipples while they waited for Jack to undress.

"Can you feel my cock up against your ass, Miranda?" he whispered in her ear. "Do you think you're still not sexy enough? Watch Jack, baby, see what he's got for you too. He's been talking about watching you suck me. Would you like that? Have to say the thought has crossed my mind countless times since we saw you coming down the stairs of your deck to swim last weekend. Then the other night we both wanted to jump in your pool with you and peel that suit off of you and take you right there in the water."

Randa closed her eyes and listened to Chase talk. The picture he painted for her had her gasping and wanting to beg them to just do it, take her. His hands on her breasts made them feel fuller and his hard length against her ass made her fight temptation to lift up and take him into her. She forced her eyes open in hopes of relieving some of the sexual tension. Instead, seeing Jack lose one piece of clothing after another, ramped that tension to a whole new level. She squeezed Chase's legs, digging her nails in as Jack stripped, revealing hard muscle and a body that would make a nun—released of her chastity vows—salivate.

Randa may not have extensive history with the male body, but she did know enough to realize that Jack and Chase were larger than she had ever been with. It thrilled and scared her at the same time. She licked her lips nervously, which Jack saw and grinned at her. She felt her face flush because she had a feeling he was thinking of her mouth on Chase. Hell, she was thinking of the same thing. Behind her, Chase chuckled and dropped a hand to her groin.

Her head leaned back until it rested on Chase's shoulder. She was still stimulated from her climax moments before, and now Chase's whispered words and their masculine bodies made her more than ready for whatever they wanted to do to her.

***

Jack stood a few feet away from them, but could hear everything Chase was saying. His shirt already lay on the floor and his hands were now at the waistband of his jeans. One other thing they had in common was the fact that neither liked to wear underwear, so when the material left his hips, his erection jumped free. Since they had been in the threesome situation before, they were both comfortable with each other's nude bodies. Not gay or bisexual, but each secure with themselves. So, Jack knew for a fact he was bigger than Chase, not that there was anything lacking in Chase's length or girth.

Jack grabbed one of the chairs in the room and brought it closer to where Chase and Randa sat. The chair was close enough to the fire to be in its glow, but not enough to be too hot. Chase got up and sat in the chair. His knees spread wide, he beckoned her with one finger. When she went to him, Jack could sense the stiffness in her body, as if she were unsure of herself. But she seemed to settle once she stood between Chase's legs. Jack *almost* didn't see the evidence of her arousal, the trickle slowly moving down her leg. Standing behind her he could hear her softly pant when Chase placed his hands on her hips and pulled her forward.

***

    Randa felt Jack press to her back. His thick cock pressed along the crease of her ass. Her legs almost gave out as she felt him distinctly from the middle of that seam to just above the dip in her lower back. To see how large he was and to feel it were very different. *Oh my god*, she thought, *he is huge*. And she thought Chase was big? As the thought crossed her mind, the man in question sat back with a slight nod at Jack. She felt his hands on her shoulders, gently pushing her to her knees and she knew exactly what Chase wanted. She smiled to herself because she wanted it too. He had such a sexy, lopsided grin on his face as he looked at her from under lashes so thick most women would kill or maim for them.

    Confidence took residence in her at that moment. This part of sex was something her past lovers had always praised her for. She knelt down between his legs and leaned forward. She used just the tip of her tongue to touch him. Slowly, she ran it from base to tip, where she circled it, tasting the moisture that had wept out for her. She felt a thrill when a groan came from Chase. Jack had pressed his body to hers as she bent over his friend. His hand alternated between squeezing her breasts, to running the seam of her ass to her pussy. With two fingers, he thrust into her as she took as much of Chase into her mouth as she could. Finally, with her jaw opened wide and having conquered her gag reflex, the tip of his cock hit the back of her throat, making them both groan.

***

Chase looked down at the woman. Never had a sight been more erotic. His best friend pressed tightly against her back, finger fucking her, and her mouth wrapped around all of his cock. Sure, he'd had women give him blowjobs, but for some reason this one outshined the rest. With a nod almost in thanks, he watched as Jack used a free hand to reach up and pull her hair off to the side helping Chase see better.

"Take her, Jack. Now, from where you are, take her as she sucks my cock," Chase ground out.

Chase pushed a lock of her hair aside again and watched her head move up and down on his cock. He could see the shine her hot, moist mouth gave him when she would lift her head, but nothing could compare to the feel of her lips engulfing him again.

***

Jack was right there with Chase. He moved her body so that she was leaning over the arm of the chair that

93

Chase was sitting in. Condom at the ready, he slipped it on then looked at her. The position was perfect for Jack to slip right in. So he did, slowly so that she could adjust little by little to him. He leaned over her back to nip her earlobe and to get her reaction.

"You're so wet for us, baby. You're pussy's not having any problem pulling me in. And you look so goddamn hot taking his cock in your mouth and mine in your pussy at the same time. You're so tight, baby. Do you know how much harder you make me? Either you've never had cock this big, or you haven't had sex in a long time, or both. So think about that as I fuck you, as you suck Chase's cock. Then later, I'd love to hear the answer."

Jack had begun to pump his hips loving her sheath grip his cock and the feel of her ass against his lower belly. He picked a rhythm that when he pushed forward she would be filled by both him and Chase. Leaving one hand on her waist, the other slid down to squeeze an ass cheek. After a few minutes of enjoying the feel of her tight pussy, he pulled out long enough to run two fingers through the wetness of her channel, coating them, then pushed his way back into her and brought his fingers to her puckered ass.

***

Randa had never, ever let anyone put anything in her ass. She just wasn't sure if it was, as her BDSM loving friend said, a hard no. When Jack thrust his cock in her, at the same time one finger went in her ass. She tensed

94

at first, uncertain how she felt. Past lovers had never been interested in exploring this area of sex, telling her it was dirty and unattractive. Initially, she told herself it was too taboo, but quickly changed her mind. She lost her breath when he added the second finger and began to move.

The feeling was unlike anything she'd ever felt. To have her mouth wrapped around Chase and then her ass and pussy filled, it was mind boggling the fullness she felt. The rough texture of Jack's fingers was sending pleasant zings throughout her body. Every inch of her was super sensitive to his touch and his strokes. Right then and there she decided she liked it. A lot. She liked it so much that she could feel her climax starting to roll through her. Oh no, she didn't want to come until they did. Not this time.

***

Jack and Chase were now aware of the signs her body put off when she was about to climax. They couldn't believe she was fighting it again. Their eyes met and they grinned. She didn't know them well enough to know they would wrench it from her, then and only then seek their own release. They needed to see that look of ecstasy on her face. Sure, they could come just by fucking her, but they wanted to enjoy the whole package.

Chase wrapped his hand around her long hair and started to pump his hips up and then back down. Miranda's hand formed a tight circle at the base of his cock, but he grabbed both of her hands so that there would be more leverage for Jack. He knew his buddy would be pounding very soon and would appreciate the help. With a grin, he could feel himself start to thicken, so he slowed down slightly so that Jack could catch up. They had it down to a science to be able get to that edge at the same time, and they were taking Miranda with them.

Chase could feel Jack pick up his pace of thrust and withdraw. If he closed his eyes he could almost see her ass shake as Jack pounded into her hard. Plus, it made her mouth work faster on his cock. She was now making mewling sounds that were starting to get louder. The vibrations enhancing the already awesome feeling. He could see that Jack's fingers had stopped moving in her ass, but began moving his hips in a staccato rhythm. From their many experiences, Chase knew that Jack was close.

"Can you feel how close Jack is to coming? Is his cock thickening in your pussy? I can feel the pounding he's giving you. Right now, you can't know how badly I want to be in your ass instead of Jack's fingers."

***

The sound of Chase's voice was pulling her toward that edge, but when he mentioned fucking her ass, Randa was thrown head first into the ravine. She cried out with her mouth full of Chase's cock, making her screams muffled. She had full intentions of swallowing, so she had wrapped her lips tightly around the head of Chase's cock, flicking her tongue rapidly. That, in turn, triggered climaxes for the men. Jack shouted as he thrust one last time, trying to get as deep inside her as he could. From his words, she knew Chase had watched them both. He was waiting until the last possible moment, before either of them were done climaxing, before he growled out his release into her mouth. She swallowed and hummed around him as she savored the taste.

Chapter Six

Jack cradled Miranda and walked to the blanket, laying her down next to him. Jack positioned her so that Chase could curl up behind her, draping an arm over her waist. Jack lay on his side facing her, hands sifting through her hair as he adoringly studied her face. Randa's eyes were wide and had a panicked look, but it was fleeting. As if someone snapped their fingers, she calmed and looked right into his eyes, smiling tremulously.

Jack ran his hand down her arm and then down her hip trying to reassure her with his touch. He could think of nothing better than to lay with his best friend and the woman who they'd just had sex with, and he wanted her to feel the same. Just the feel of his hand on her skin soothed him, made him feel like he was home. This time was so different from any other, it made him think. But he didn't want to actually put to words yet, even mental words, the direction his thoughts were heading.

A little frightened by the direction his mind was going, Jack grabbed pillows off the couch for them all to prop up on. After they repositioned themselves, he grabbed the chocolate pie they hadn't even touched, and dipped a spoon into the treat. He held it to her mouth and waited for her to take the sweetness. He offered the second spoon to Chase, who scooped another bite of the sweet and placed the spoon at her lips. She laughed softly and took his offering too. Then both men handed her their spoons and allowed her to feed them bites. They did this until the piece of pie had been finished. Despite the delectable flavor of the chocolate, all Jack could think of was giving the woman between them much more pleasure.

***

Randa was stunned. For over twenty some odd years she had the cruel echo of words spoken to her out of spite rolling around in her head. Because of those words, she had limited herself to the type of men she either approached or entertained the thought of dating. Neither of these men fit into the type she tried for. No, they were out of her league, at least in her eyes. Now, here she was with not only one, but two men, both of whom reciprocated the attraction she felt for them. Despite her new found confidence—and what woman *wouldn't* be confident after what she just experienced— old doubts came creeping back in. *Could* this work? The three of them?

Baby and Max had been howling, trying to get their attention. They all looked at each other and got up to dress. With Baby being the size she was, it would be awkward for the men to be nude with her around. She was glad they had left their shirts off though; it allowed her to ogle their bare chests. Jack padded barefoot to the door and let the dogs in. Baby immediately ran to Randa, whining and sniffing her to make sure she was okay. Max just wanted someone to pay attention to him.

Randa sat in the chair Chase had used, feet together, hands on her knees, staring straight ahead, a signal Baby recognized. Max, done with his owners, ran in like a goof and tried to jump onto Randa, but she held her hand out in a typical 'talk to the hand' gesture, stopping him in his tracks. Max swiveled his head between Baby and Miranda, whining. But when he caught on, he also sat, waiting for a sign of approval and love. After another minute, she patted her shin and they both scooted closer, but didn't jump on her. Max seemed to be taking clues from Baby.

Jack and Chase looked like they were in disbelief as their wild Bassett sat there patiently waiting for attention to be doled out to him. Finally, she placed a palm up on her knee, telling Baby to gently scoot forward. Her tail wagging, she laid her head on Miranda's leg. Max looked at them, cocked his head, and did the same.

Chase grabbed a dog biscuit for each and handed them to Miranda over her shoulder, a reward for their polite behavior. Each dog properly rewarded, they took their treats and went to enjoy them.

Both men stared at her, making her feel a little uncomfortable. "What? Do I not have my shirt on right?" she asked nervously.

"Personally, you have too much on, but I'm still shocked at how you get Max to act so polite. I mean, Baby I can understand, you've had her a while and know her, but Max? You've been around him all of five minutes before he ran off after Baby. How did you get him to do that without being a crazy mess?" Jack mused.

"My dad, remember? His job with the government and then for some private companies. I guess I picked up some of his tricks," Randa replied. She shrugged, thinking it was no big deal.

"Do you think you could do that with other dogs? You know a step above basic obedience? See, most of our friends have dogs. We've all been wanting to have a big BBQ and have everyone bring their dogs, but we've had issues," Jack explained. "It would be great to have a true family party with the dogs and all."

"Well yeah, I guess I could try and help out. Would the friends you're referring to be the ones that were here last weekend to help you move in?"

"Yeah, they are. We're not a really wild bunch, but it can get a little loud from time to time. That's why when we have our monthly poker game, we each take turns. Since there are two of us, we get our turns more often." Jack shrugged. "I know the guys would appreciate any help they can get with their dogs. Maybe we could invite them over and have you come talk to them?"

Blushing, she spoke hesitantly, "Yeah that would be okay. Would I be the only female here?"

She watched Chase and Jack looked at each other and then at her with big grins lighting their faces up. The dogs were curled up together napping, since they apparently had run themselves ragged outside. She looked at them expectantly, wondering what they were thinking. As they walked toward her, their hands went to their waistbands. They each stopped on either side of the chair that she sat in. Chase was first to speak.

"Would it be a problem to be the only female here if they all come over? What do you think will happen, Miranda?"

"Um, would you please call me Randa? Miranda is what my ex would call me when he put me down and I hated the connotations he gave it," she answered breathlessly.

Jack chuckled, "Randa it is. But you're avoiding the question. Would you be nervous in a room full of men? Or would it excite you to know that they all wanted to be with you? Being showered with attention by all of us?"

The question made her breathing speed up. Randa may not be knowledgeable about too many things, but what Jack just described was a gangbang, right? One woman, several men? She wasn't sure if she was brave enough for that, but knew these two men sure got her going. Would they ask their friends if they wanted to be with her?

"No! Uh, I mean, I don't think that would be okay. Besides, no way would they all want to be with me. You guys like heavy women. Those guys I saw last weekend? No way would they date anyone like me."

Chase's featured morphed into anger at her words. "Are you going to sit there and start in with that 'not me' shit? I thought we had resolved that issue just a bit ago in that same chair. I believe some reinforcement is needed, Jack."

Jack nodded, leaned down, and picked her up. She made a protesting noise, saying she was too heavy, and tried to get him to put her down, but he wasn't having it.

Randa knew the layout of the house and that there were three bedrooms on the second level. She held her body still, a bit embarrassed that Jack was carrying her, fear that her size might throw him off balance. Up the stairs, they passed two of rooms that were furnished differently from each other. They walked into the third and Jack set her on her feet, turning her around to face the room. She stood in front of the biggest bed she had ever seen, clearly big enough for at least four or five people. She stared in amazement wondering how on earth they find sheets to fit a bed that large.

Chase had followed them and closed the door. Randa peered at Jack while he took his pants off and she saw that he was hard. Again. Chase took his shorts off and pressed against her ass. His hands on her hips, slowly, tortuously, Chase pushed the rest of her clothes down her legs until she stood before them naked. Jack leaned down and took her lips, hard and hot, forcing her lips to open and surrender to his. Breaking the kiss, he sat on the end of the bed and pulled her closer so her breasts were at eye level. He gave them each a quick kiss before he swung himself around so that he was lying on his back, head at the end.

Chase, still standing behind her, gently pushed her forward so that her hands were flat on the mattress on each side of Jack's head, her breasts dangling above his mouth. All Jack had to do was reach up and guide them, which he did. When Jack flicked her nipple, the look on Chase's face was such a turn on. The groan that seemed to be torn from him brought an answering one from her. Chase inserted two fingers inside her depth and slowly began to pump. She was so wet, she could feel the moisture running down her leg, embarrassing her, but Chase quickly put that to rest.

"Do you see? You see how your body reacts to ours? Look up, baby. Do you see that hard cock? You will have that cock deep inside you very soon. And mine," Chase ground his hips into her ass. "My cock will be in your ass. You'll have two hard cocks in you at the same time. Do you think you'd be excited if our friends walked in right now to watch? What if, while we fuck your ass and your pussy, another fucks your mouth? The other three would watch and take over when we've come inside you."

Randa knew she couldn't be with so many men at one time, but could not stop herself from moaning and moving her ass while Chase finger fucked her, getting her ready for Jack. Because of their size she had originally thought to steer clear of anal sex, but she had to trust her instincts. That was the only thing she had right now because she was so hot, she couldn't think straight. And those instincts were telling her they would not hurt her, at least not intentionally.

She heard Chase open a foil package and slip the condom on. Then, with eyes closed, she could just about picture exactly what Chase had described and at the moment he thrust into her, hard, Jack took a nipple into his mouth and bit down just enough to hurt slightly, then sucked on it hard. Already sensitized, she came, her sex pulsing around Chase, causing him to groan. Randa answered Chase's sound with a keening wail and she began to push back against him to get him to take her harder. She looked down Jack's body and saw his cock bobbing for attention, making her need his cock in her mouth.

Chase pulled out, leaving her feeling empty and Randa cried out a protest. Jack spun his body around and let his legs hang off the side of the bed, his upper body laid back on the mattress, making his cock point straight up toward her. Chase pushed her forward again, her mouth naturally sinking down on Jack. There was no chance she would be able to take all of him in her mouth, but she lowered her head as far as she could. Jack, lifted up on his elbows, watched intently.

Chase began to thrust into her again, the angle just right for hitting her G-spot over and over. With every forward thrust, he pushed her mouth further onto Jack. Amazingly, she was able to take him all the way into her mouth, causing Jack to groan this time from deep in his throat. Randa peeked up at him. He was watching as her head raised then lowered over him again.

"That's it, baby, take it. Just like that. You got that cock all the way in. Now suck it, baby. Suck that hard cock," Jack said softly, encouraging her.

Randa couldn't believe how she was acting. They were proving to her once again she was a desirable woman, no matter her size. But they were the last in a long line of friends that had been working on that for years. If the passion of these two men couldn't convince her, she wasn't sure what would. Both men pulled away from her at the same time. She cried out, the loss of their touch and their bodies disappointing her, and shook her head.

Jack scooted back until his head lay on a pillow, motioning her to come to him. Randa turned and looked at Chase. With no expression on his handsome face, he just nodded. She crawled up and beside Jack. His expression as he looked down at her was just as blank as Chase's. His hand lazed its way along her arm until Chase joined them. Jack slipped a condom on then leaned down and kissed her. Chase lifted her and positioned her over Jack's cock, allowing gravity to guide her down. She watched as Chase opened the draw of the bedside table and pulled out a bottle.

Randa moaned loudly as her body lowered over Jack's. He felt so good, so thick and hard. He tugged her down until her mouth touched his. As he kissed her, he began to thrust up into her with slow strokes, letting her feel every inch. She felt something cool trickle down the crack of her ass and tried to rise up. Jack held her still, his mouth to her ear.

"Relax, Randa. Let him get you ready. We both want to be in you," he whispered to her.

The words served to heat her up again. As Chase was moving the liquid to her puckered hole she gasped, but then held her breath until first one then two fingers entered her ass. Jack continued to thrust slowly below her, keeping her mind off of Chase and his exploring fingers. She was ready for that rough ride, but she was unsure as to how to tell them.

She decided to just spit it out. "Please, Chase, now. Take my ass now as Jack fucks my pussy. Please..."

He needed no further encouragement. Lube poured on his cock, he pressed the head at her rosebud entrance. Jack stilled his slow thrusting and grabbed her hips to stop her too.

"Relax, baby. I don't want you to hurt you. Pleasure, baby, that's all this is about. Now just bear down for me." Chase pleaded with her.

With an inaudible pop, Chase pushed through the tight ring and slowly began to push further inside her until finally, he was fully seated. The time it took from initial entry until he was as deep as he could go seemed to be hours. A fine sheen of sweat began to cover her body and she could feel Jack's arms shaking from his control. The burning was a bit disconcerting at first, but it seemed to dissipate quite quickly. Randa let out the breath she was holding in. Slowly as Jack would thrust in, Chase would withdraw. Randa never thought she could feel so sensitized, so full. Positioned as she was, her clit was getting worked over so much she thought she would go off. The constant barrage of sensation finally bringing her to a peak, she looked into Jack's eyes and pleaded with her own she needed to come, to please make her come.

The look was all that Jack and Chase needed to see. They began to move in sync. Both thrust in, then withdrew in tandem. Randa groaned and urged them on, telling them she was so close. Simultaneously, she could feel each cock thicken even more than they already were and then they were all falling over the edge. Chase's hands gripped her hips tightly, and Jack had her head pressed into his neck. Chase withdrew one last time and lay next to Jack on the bed, trying to catch his breath.

In the back of Randa's mind she was concerned about laying on them, no matter their obviously strong bodies. She rose up enough off of Jack and nudged them to move so she could lay between them. They stayed like that for quite a while until they finally heard Baby in the hall crying, and Max was right there almost as if to comfort her. Jack barely got out of the way before both dogs had run into the room and jumped on the bed. Since they were whimpering around Randa, it was a good conclusion that Baby thought her momma was getting hurt by the big bad men. She laughed as she reassured her.

"I hate to say this, but I really do need to get home. I have to get to bed...well, back to bed," she laughed. "To sleep. Tomorrow, I'm up early. And I believe one of you has surgery first thing?"

"Yeah, that's me. I have Mrs. Kennedy's poodle coming in for neutering. Poor little guy is losing his nuggets." Jack cringed as he said it and Chase covered his own groin. "Do you want to ride in together? No sense in taking two cars, huh?"

"Uh, well, I really think we should take the two cars," she stammered. "I, um, might have some errands to do after work and don't want to hold you up. Okay?"

When the topic of sharing a ride was brought up, all that ran through Randa's mind was what people at work would say. Would they think something sexual was going on, with both of them? She wasn't ashamed of it, and there was no policy stating that employees could not date, but a small part of her mind couldn't bear it if someone thought poorly of her for dating two men at the same time. Or them for dating a woman like her. Randa didn't want to have rumors go around before there was really anything to spread them about.

***

Jack knew a story when he heard it and he was puzzled that it bothered him. He figured she needed the security of taking her own car for whatever reason. He wanted to confront her, but knew it could push her away. What was happening between the three of them was new and he didn't want to scare her off. Besides, he and Chase needed to talk too.

"No, that's okay. Just thought I'd offer, being neighbors and all," he responded, trying to sound nonchalant.

Jack lay there looking between them both with a slight smile on his face. He was always the type to do the pleasing, making sure he and their partner were taken care of before he went onto himself. Chase was more of a 'let the chips fall where they may' kind of guy. Jack assumed after Randa left they would be having a chat. "Randa, go give Chase a good night kiss and I'll walk you home. I think you wore the poor guy out," Jack teased.

Chase held his arms out and waited for her to come and lean down. He pulled her onto the bed until she lay on top of him. Rolling her over, he kissed her until she began to moan and breath hard, then he rolled again so he was on his back and she lay on top of him. She looked like she was about to lower her head and kiss him again, so he chuckled and smacked her ass light enough to not hurt but hard enough to snap her out of her stupor.

Jack watched her blush then began picking up her clothes. She got up, taking her clothes from Jack. She got dressed with both men watching intently. Who would have thought watching a woman dress could be as arousing as undressing? Jack was still not dressed, so the slightly impatient look from her made him grin sheepishly, pull his pants on, and grab up his shirt from the floor. He pulled it on and slid his feet into a pair of slip-on sandals. After Randa gave Max a kiss goodnight, Jack picked up Baby's leash, clipped it to her collar, and they walked out into the dark night. Neither said a word until they got to her door. She unlocked it, opened it enough for Baby to get through, then stood there staring down at her feet.

Jack didn't want her to feel awkward in any way. He figured it might have something to do with the car issue, so he placed a finger under her chin and raised her head until she had no choice but to look at him. She looked worried. He crowded her against the door jam, leaned down, and took her lips in the sweetest, hottest kiss he could muster, all the while fighting temptation to get her horizontal again.

"Hey, don't worry about it. I'm not upset. I truly didn't mean anything other than a carpool offer, baby, nothing more. So you stop worrying, okay?"

She released a breath and smiled at him, nodding her head.

"Good. Now, get to bed, rest up, and we'll talk soon. Okay? You must be dead on your feet," he teased her.

She blushed, which made him laugh softly and kiss her again.

He waited on the top step outside her door as she closed then locked the door. Only then did Jack head back to his and Chase's house.

***

Randa watched Jack through her blinds as he walked home and turned off their outside light. She figured they were both going to talk about what happened tonight. Maybe they were going to decide she wasn't worth seeing again. Could they have only been interested because she was handy or because it had been a while? Maybe she was just over thinking things?

Randa and Baby made their rounds on the lower level of the house, making sure everything was locked up and the alarm was set. She turned off the lights and they walked upstairs to her room. She changed into her boy shorts and tank, and climbed into her king size bed. So, here she was, coming down from the best dinner date she'd ever had—with two gorgeous men—to come home and sleep alone. Sure, it was her own doing, but they hadn't asked her to stay either. Baby, tuned in to her momma's emotions, curled as close as she could and placed her head on Randa's pillow. Randa fell asleep feeling hot breath in her hair, dreaming it was her men.

***

Jack got back next door, locked up, and turned out all the lights. He went upstairs with the full intention of he and Chase talking about what happened. He walked to the room they had just had sex in, the bedside light giving off a soft glow. Under the covers of the huge bed, Chase lay asleep, Max curled against his chest. The dog cracked one eye open and then decided it took too much out of him, so he closed it again and went back to sleep.

Jack shook his head, turned the light off, and walked to his room. Flipping on the light on the bedside table, he sat, dropping his head into his hands. Why did this not feel like the end of a normal three-way date? Usually they both had no problem taking care of a woman two or three times in one night and moving on. This was different, at least for him it was. *Shit*, he thought, *not good*. Stripped out of his pants, he crawled between the sheets, crossed his arms behind his head and looked around. His room was done in shades of green and blue, his two favorite colors. The brand new bedroom set was comfortable enough, but a small niggling thought had him wanting to share the custom built bed with Chase and Miranda. To sleep in a bed with his best friend and the woman they were...what? Dating? Yeah, for now, dating would have to do.

The numbers on his bedside clock read a little after midnight. No more time left to think about what ifs.

He had surgery at eight a.m., but needed to be to work by at least seven-thirty to prep. He clicked the light off and closed his eyes. The last thing he saw behind his eyelids as he slipped into unconsciousness was the satisfied smile Randa had given them right after their second round of sex.

Chapter Seven

With the last suture in, Jack left the rest to the tech to handle. Poor little guy was now a eunuch. But since King had impregnated several females in his neighborhood, something had to be done. King's legacy would carry on in all of his pups the owners of the females were trying to find homes for. Mrs. Kennedy even said that since she wasn't paying full price, he could have the pick of any King combo'd puppy in her neighborhood. He'd chuckled and said he'd have to think about it.

He rounded the corner and walked toward the locker room to change out of his scrubs. God, he needed caffeine. He didn't care the variety, just as long as it was cold. Once changed, he headed to the employee lounge where there was a soda vending machine. Lost in thought, he didn't hear the gasp behind him until the soda came down. He twisted the cap and turned. In the doorway was Randa, looking elegant in dress pants and heels. The blouse she was wearing was so thin and with the coolness in the building, he could see the pebbling of her nipples. Nipples that he had savored many times last night, to both of their enjoyment. When he raised his eyes to her, they were wide and she was panting softly. She knew exactly what he was thinking and her nipples got harder and more noticeable.

"Good morning, Randa. Did you sleep well?" he teased her.

"I did, yes. Thank you. A-and you? How was your night?" she asked breathlessly.

He walked to the doorway, stuck his head out, and looked up and down the hall. Seeing no one nearby, he pushed her against the wall of the break room and quickly took her lips. His knee came up between her legs to press against the apex of her thighs. His lips devoured hers, tongue running along the soft seam until she slightly parted them and then his tongue dove inside. Just as her hands had come up and tangled in his hair, he pulled away. He backed up trying to catch his breath, and he was pleased to note she was having the same problem.

"My night was the best I've had ever. Great food, wonderful company, and memories to last a lifetime," he spoke softly so only she could hear him. He turned back to grab his soda and walked out.

***

Randa stood there in shock. She had felt a little unsure of how they would act once they returned to work. *That* was certainly not how she pictured it would go. No way was there going to be a case of grabby hands when she was on the clock. So why hadn't she protested the kiss?

She may not needed the job, but she wouldn't lose her co-workers' respect either. Sure, she was now breathless and wet, thank you very much, but also uncomfortable. And she forgot why she was in the break room.

Luckily, when Chase made it in, Randa had enough to keep her busy for the rest of the day. Not that she was avoiding anyone, but after the episode with Jack, she wasn't sure she could make it the rest of the day without melting into a puddle. And then there was Josie. They were such good friends that one look and the other woman would know something was up, which was sure to send Randa into a spin. She just couldn't handle it right now.

The possibility of a Josie interrogation was bad, but the thought of what Kitty would say made her blush. Her friend had been texting her all day to find out how her pie went over and she would blush when she remembered the activities before and after it was consumed. It was almost as if Randa had convinced herself that Kitty would somehow know.

At the end of the day, Randa was sitting in the lunch room sipping on a cup of water. She had managed to avoid being alone with Josie all day, but her luck ran out when Josie came in and stood there with arms crossed over her chest. Randa, lost in her thoughts, didn't notice until the other woman loudly cleared her throat and smiled when she looked up. The look on Josie's face said a lot. Concern, and a little amusement, showed in her expression. Randa looked away hoping to hide her thoughts for just a bit longer.

"How long have you been standing there?" she asked.

"Oh, I would say long enough to hear the three sighs and to see you twirl your hair. Who's got you twirling, sweetie? You seeing a new guy? Oh hey, how are the boys doing?" Josie was one of a handful of women that could say she knew Randa well. And if all the girls got together? It was like they were all attuned to each other's emotions.

"Oh no, the boys are fine. Bradley is doing well with JAG in DC, and Colton…Yeah, he's had full capacity seating every single night since the grand opening. Oh, by the way, he did say that any night you want to bring a date, let him know and he'll make sure he takes care of your meal."

Colton was Randa's youngest. He graduated top of his class in culinary school and, despite his professor's advice against it, decided to use his trust fund to open his own restaurant. He chose to call it Flavour and from the nightly attendance the last six months, he felt confident he'd be in the black very soon. Randa was so proud of him.

Randa purposely did not reply to the guy comment.

"I can recognize avoidance when I hear it and you're avoiding. You *are* seeing someone! Holy shit, woman! Where did you meet him? How old is he? What's he look like? Does he have a job?"

Face on fire with embarrassment, Randa tried to shush her as she got up and rushed to the doorway. She pulled Josie in and closed the door quickly. Eyes closed, she leaned back against the door and took a deep breath before releasing it.

"Damn it, sometimes I hate that you can read me so well. And since I know *you* so well, I am going to tell you, because I know that if I don't, you will hound me and probably not let me leave until I do. So, yes, I am seeing, uh yeah, you could say a new guy. We've only met for dinner once, so there's not much to tell yet. He's a new neighbor, single, and has a great job. And he's very attractive and very fit."

Randa stopped talking and Josie looked at her suspiciously. She should tell Josie. Randa knew that her friend wouldn't push and wouldn't judge, but it was just too new to say anything. She also knew once Josie set her mind to something, she got it.

"I expect to be told when the next date happens, because this came way too much out of the blue," Josie teased.

Randa didn't like keeping things from her friends. The fact of a possible boyfriend, or two, was a big deal. Josie could be as tenacious as a bulldog, but Randa knew she would be patient. For a bit. There were plenty of men over the years that had come to The Haven to either work, volunteer, or even adopt an animal, but Randa had always felt her social life should never mingle with where she worked. Or as Josie would say, "Don't shit where you eat."

Computer shut down and lights turned off, Miranda left her office and headed out to her car. Before she could get out of the building, she heard her name and turned. Chase was walking toward her. Immediately, visions of what happened with Jack that morning flooded her head, and there was no way she could deal with that happening with Chase too. She slowly walked backward while shaking her head. He had to know this was not the place?

"Randa? Can I walk you to your car?"

Randa tried to ignore Chase, but he was still walking toward her. She didn't know what to say so she continued to walk, shaking her head. She hadn't intended to, but had caught a bit of the reaming that Chase had given Jack. It surprised her as she would have thought since they were friends he wouldn't make a big deal of it. She was confused and needed time to think. Work was definitely not the place to discuss what happened. As she approached the exit, she gasped in surprise as Jack opened the door that led to the parking lot. Effectively, she was trapped between them. Her body stiffened, but she pushed past Jack and quickened her step leading away from both men.

Randa didn't give them a chance to catch up or to talk to her. She didn't even know who drove what, but she headed right to her own car. No way was she getting into anything in the parking lot. With her luck, she'd have herself talked into being on her knees with a cock in her mouth, not caring who came along. Not that she thought either of them would do that.

***

Jack knew he'd fucked up that morning. He'd practically attacked her, not even caring that someone could have walked into the break room. He could have really made trouble for both of them if they had been seen. His only excuse? He couldn't get her out of his mind and needed to feel her again. After Chase threatened to beat the shit out of him—*yeah, like that could happen*—he avoided both of them the rest of the day. No hard feat either, since there had been a lot of transferred animals come in that day.

***

Chase felt like a piece of shit at the frightened look on Randa's face. He watch as Randa got in her car, without even a look at either of them, and drove off. Chase threw another glare at Jack and walked to his truck. They had to make this right if they wanted to continue to see her. That was *if* she decided to give them—Jack—a second chance. Once back at her house, Chase figured she would probably close herself off from them. They couldn't let that happen. But they might be able to throw her off guard if they waited for her while she was swimming. That was the only predictable part of her day. They knew from talking to her last night that she relied on that pool as a way to relax after work, get her exercise, and allow Baby to get rid of energy that was held in while her momma was working.

They got home within moments of each other and both noticed that Randa was home too. They knew that she would be changing into her swimsuit at that moment. Just that quickly, Chase hardened enough that his cock could push through his zipper without major effort. Inside their own house, they changed into more comfortable clothes. Chase went out back and fired up the grill to get it hot. Normally, they wouldn't grill during the week, but he knew it would be a quick meal, and knew Randa would smell the meat as she swam.

Max ran out to join him and immediately made a beeline for the fence, hoping that Baby would come say hello. Jack came out with a couple of beers and joined Max at the fence. They were each watching their girls in the pool. Randa's arms sliced through the glassy water fluidly, with the large dog paddling her way easily beside her. A very corny description came to mind: poetry in motion.

***

Randa was fully aware of her audience. Every time she came up for air, she could see Jack leaning on the fence, and she could hear Max yelping because he couldn't see. Normally, she would be done with her laps by now, but she was still upset with Jack. She was only slightly upset with Chase, only because he helped Jack box her in back at work. So, to help wear that anger down to just irritation, she had decided to add five more laps to her normal ten. She was tempted to add more, but her arms were tiring and she was beginning to get irritated with herself now. She never thought herself a coward, but her avoiding them was clearly made her one.

Every time she lifted her head out of the water the mouthwatering scent of the grilled hamburgers would make her stomach growl. Chase walked through the gate to her backyard and sat on the bottom step of her deck, waiting. She eventually approached him, towel wrapped around her. She was starving, but she was also still upset. Upset won. She stopped right in front of Chase. When he reached out and pulled her between his legs, she didn't fight him, but neither was she pliant.

Randa stood stiffly while he just sat there patiently waiting. His hands were soothing her lower back, just rubbing in circles, pulling the tension out of her. She closed her eyes in pleasure and made a small sound. He pulled her closer still, until his head was pressed into her belly, just holding her.

"He was wrong, babe. He knows that, knew it when he did it. I do have to get his back, though, and say I understand why he did it. You are so fucking amazing. You get into a man's head and it's hard to not want another taste. Come eat with us. Let's talk and work this out. Please?"

She dropped her head until her cheek rested on the top of his head. Her arms came up, curled around his head, and she threaded her fingers through his hair. They stayed like that for a few more minutes then she pulled back and nodded. Fingers interlocked, they walked next door, Chase holding Baby's collar so she could come and play with Max. Once in their backyard, Chase broke away and went back to the grill.

Jack came to her with a wine cooler. Twisting the top off, he handed it to her and she took it thankfully. As she was about to raise the bottle to her mouth, Jack wrapped his arms around her waist and pulled her close to him.

"Randa, I'm sorry for this morning. I shouldn't have acted like I did. I need to be honest here. When you said last night that you wanted to take separate cars, I guess I was upset. It kind of felt like you were ashamed of what we did. Ashamed of us. I'm hoping that's not the case. I would have no problem telling people the three of us had a great time last night."

Hesitantly, she replied, "No, I wasn't ashamed of what we did. Nor of either one of you. But you have to understand, that is where we work. I can't have my personal life affecting The Haven. Not after all of the hard work that was put into getting the place up and running. And that work wasn't done by just me. If it were all just on me, I would shout it to the world, but there are others involved. You know?"

They both heard Chase calling out that everything was ready. Interlacing their fingers, Jack led them back to the table to sit. A handsome man on each side of her, what more could a lady ask for? They ate the burgers and salad amidst very general talk. When Baby ran barking to the gate near the front of the yard, they thought nothing of it. And then didn't even bat an eye when Max ran off with Baby loping behind. It wasn't until Randa heard a voice that she felt the blood drain from her face. Chase and Jack looked at her in concern and asked if she was okay. Then they all saw a tall man walking into Randa's backyard.

Randa jumped up and ran toward the fence, angry that he was there.

"What the hell are you doing in my yard, Philip? Didn't you say all you needed to say the last time you were here?"

The man looked at her and sneered. "Well, I was curious if the pool had done any good. When my company put it in, you had said you'd be using it for exercise."

Immediately, Randa felt the color drain from her face from his comment, but quickly burned with rage. And Philip? He looked like he wanted to say more about the pool, when he suddenly got dollar signs in his eyes seeing someone had moved in next door where there was no pool.

"Hey there! I'm Philip Conrad. I'm a sales rep with Jarecki Pools. Good to see someone moved in here. It's a great neighborhood and this yard has potential for a great pool. I don't see any kids, but a pool isn't just for them, ya know? You guys look like a great couple. Would you be okay with me stopping by in the next few days to sit down with some numbers and options?"

Randa was incensed at Philip comments. Like the only reason two good looking guys would want her around was because they were gay. Well, that and her pool. Randa was mortified, not only for herself, but for the two men flanking her.

"I think you should take yourself out of my backyard before I call the police and have you arrested for trespassing," she fumed.

"Aw, darlin', you know you won't do that. You must be missing me and came to see your friends because you have no company. We can go out for drinks if you like," he drawled. "I'd be happy to keep you company, and am pretty certain you aren't seeing anyone. You did say you were hoping the pool allowed

125

you to lose weight, remember? You had promised to let me buy your first bikini when you could fit into one?"

Randa's eyes pooled with tears and she felt like she would get sick. She knew for certain she could not face Chase and Jack right now. She grabbed hold of Baby's collar and as fast as she could went into her backyard and started up the steps to her deck. What she didn't see was Chase and Jack had followed. She only got half way up the steps before she heard Philip again.

"So how long have you two been together? Randa and I used to date. Yeah, when she told me she wanted to lose weight I got her a sweet deal on this pool. I see by the swimsuit she's wearing that she at least uses it, but we all know it won't help if she won't stop eating, right?"

Just as she got to the top, she heard a growl from below her. She turned to see Chase had pinned Philip to the side of her house with his forearm across his neck, holding him in place. She couldn't hear, at first, what Jack was saying so she started back down the steps. The closer she got, the more she liked what he was saying and decided to sit a few steps above to listen in. Call it morbid curiosity, but she needed to hear what they said to him.

"You are a worthless piece of shit. How dare you talk about her like that? I can't believe she dated a fucking asshole like you, ever."

"What the hell do you care? You just met her. I've known her a lot longer than you have and she's been fat the whole time. Besides, you guys are gay and she was probably looking for girlfriends, if you get my drift," he taunted.

Just like that, Chase drew back his fist and hit the man. Philip went down without another word, landing on his ass, and stared up dazed. Randa screamed and came down the stairs until she was in front of Chase, wanting to stop him from any more violence. Jack had knelt down and was grinning in the asshole's face, clearly enjoying the other man's discomfort and surprise.

"You need to leave while you can still walk. Don't ever come back here again. No, we don't want a pool. We're pretty sure our *girlfriend* will let us use hers. Oh yeah, and for the record, we're not gay, not in the slightest, not even bisexual. If you'd like to press charges, I'll give you the name of my cop friend who can certainly help you do so, but keep in mind you were trespassing and Randa will be able to countercharge you."

Confusion spread over Philip's face for a moment. When the realization of what Jack had insinuated came over him, his features turned to disgust. He stood on shaky legs and backed away from the trio, but made one last parting remark.

"Well, Miranda, will wonders never cease? You must have the only two chubby chasers in the San Diego area, huh? Or maybe they're in a dry spell and you're convenient."

With that, he turned and practically ran to his car, gunned the engine, and sped off. Randa felt like she was going to throw up. She couldn't even look at Chase and Jack. She was so afraid to see the truth on their faces. She wouldn't be able to handle it if they confirmed what Philip said.

Chase had his hands on her arms, and Jack had come closer, boxing her in again. Randa refused to look at them, didn't want to see their pity. She didn't even hear Chase had been calling her name. Finally, it took Jack wrapping his hand around her hair and pulling, gently at first then a little harder, making her protest, to get her to look at them.

"We. Are. Not. Chubby. Chasers. You. Are. Not. Chubby. You. Are. A. Lush. Fucking. Sexy. Woman. If given the chance to repeat last night, we would...willingly. Do you understand? If you don't, then let us know and we'll gladly show you right here where anyone can see."

Eyes locked with Chase's, she still wasn't sure what to believe. She needed time to think, time away from them crowding her in. She needed...god, she didn't know what she needed. She felt hands and lips on her, trying to convince her she was worth their attentions, but there was that one small part of her brain that sat back and pointed and laughed at her as if to say that she was nuts for thinking this could work out.

"I can't do this right now. I'm really sorry. I had a great time last night, but I need to think. Okay? I need time to figure this out. Please?" There was a tremor in her voice. She couldn't help it, and didn't want them to feel bad, but she had to protect *herself*.

***

Chase and Jack didn't stop her from pulling away and practically running up the stairs into the house. Baby looked down longingly at them, but followed her. They walked back to their house and started cleaning up from dinner. Then they both went into their rooms, both in their own thoughts.

Jack was in the chair that he had owned since college. It's wasn't necessarily comfortable, but for some reason he thought better in it. He and Chase had plenty of experience playing with women on the threesome level, but was there ever a connection? Never. The episode in the break room that morning with her? Never had he had the need to do anything like that with any other woman. Never had he slept with the image of a woman being the last thing he saw and the memory of their time spent together the first thing he pictured the next morning. Never had he and Chase wanted a repeat of time spent with a woman. Until now. But to a confirmed bachelor, what the hell did that mean?

***

Chase was in his room doing pretty much the same, thinking. But for him it was on his bed. He sat there nude, except for the towel he wrapped around his waist after his shower. All he could think about were the words that piece of garbage had the nerve to say to his woman. *Wait, what?* What the hell was he thinking, his woman? He and Jack had been doing the threesome bit for years and they had never met a woman they had wanted to date, as in on a regular basis. All of the others had been the means to an end. But Randa? She was different. Sure, they had only known her for less than a

129

week, but time wasn't a big deal. All of their friends had asked them what they would do if they met a woman they both felt serious about. Good fucking question. And Chase believed that time had come.

***

Randa was in her very large whirlpool tub, jets turning the hot water to soothe away her stress. Shoot, she had to admit the extra laps she gave herself out of spite definitely made her sore. But that was what the tub was for. To get rid of those aches and stress.

She and Philip had broken it off more than three months ago. It had been an eye opener of a breakup, and at the time she took responsibility since she couldn't get the weight off and be the size six that Philip was looking for. Hell, she'd been shocked when he showed any interest in her at all. Now though? She wondered if it was all about the commission he probably got on her pool being installed. And she was beginning to suspect that the 'deal' he got her probably wasn't a deal. She could have tried to rationalize the whys with Philip, but her eyelids began to droop. That was her last thought on the subject before she drifted off.

Chapter Eight

The following weeks seemed to drag by, for all of them. Jack and Chase were now working their new schedules and fitting in really well at The Haven. The vets would have staggering shifts, but they'd all be off by seven o'clock. Since Chase and Jack lived ten minutes from work, they could be called if there was any kind of medical emergency. Randa kept to herself. She went in before the men did and left before they did. She hadn't used her pool since the night of Philip's visit, instead choosing to walk Baby to stretch her legs. When the weekend hit, she decided that it had been too long since she had seen Colt, so she called him to see if he'd have dinner with her—at his restaurant, of course. He agreed and told her he'd even pick her up and pay. Well hell, it was his place, he should pick up the tab for his mom.

***

The guys had not seen hide nor hair of Randa. They had full intentions to knock on her door and find out if she was okay, and for all of them to sit and talk things over. They were out front washing and waxing their respective cars when a beautiful Lexus pulled up in her driveway. The guy got out and didn't even have time to walk up to the house. Randa came running out of the house to greet the mystery man. She was wearing a dress that made both Chase and Jack want to rip it off and do wicked things to her body. And those heels? Jack decided right then and there that he wanted her to be wearing them the next time they were together, whenever that might be. They stopped and blatantly stared as she ran to the guy and threw her arms around him, hugging him tight. They got in the car—she opened her own door, so no gentleman there—and left.

Chase threw down the rag he'd been using and walked away. Jack was upset too, so he went to find his buddy. On the patio, Chase had two opened beers. Silently, he handed one to Jack as he sat down. What the hell did they just see?

"Are we that easily replaced? Did you see the guy? He looked young enough to be her son," Chase said sarcastically, "and she said she had to figure things out? Maybe she's not up for two guys in her life. Maybe she only wants one guy at a time? Maybe she's just not into us? She hasn't said any more than 'hello' and 'have a nice day' to us in over a week. Man, I have to confess something. She's it. You know what I mean? How the fuck this happened so quickly I can't even begin to explain. In fact, the only thing I know for sure is she is like no one I've ever met. That is before you and I started our threesome gig, and after. There has never been a woman that fascinated me more."

Jack listened to his friend's confession and was floored. Everything Chase said was dead on for both of them. What the fuck were they going to do? She was out on a date with a much younger man, so it seemed like maybe she was moving on.

"Chase, we've got to step back and think about this rationally. Has she ever led us to believe that she's the type to sleep with two guys then go on a date with another soon after? I'd like to believe she couldn't do that, wouldn't do that to us. She's a special lady. We shouldn't jump to any conclusions, okay?" Jack placated his friend. "And I feel exactly the same way. I hate what she went through because of us. I've got to wonder how many times she's had to deal with guys that have either voiced the same thoughts or just blew her off for her supposed weight. God, man, she doesn't even know she's so fuckin' gorgeous and has a body that could get a guy hard even if he were in a room full of nuns."

***

It had been a couple of months since Randa had seen Colton, but it wasn't for lack of desire. It was Colton's new restaurant. The responsibility took up most of his time. She had told him the months leading up to his decision to open his own place, that he was a great chef. He always teased her, saying as his mom, she had to say that. After the meal she just ate, she teased him she was right. The menu at The Flavour wasn't of a particular culture. Italian, Greek, even a little Szechuan. There were also dishes that were considered diner food, but ramped up to be served in a classy restaurant. Colton told her even if it wasn't on the menu, to pick something and he'd make it for her, or have his head chef do it, since they had gone through culinary school together.

She had chosen a dish that, growing up, had always been a favorite of her English grandmother's. Simple, but good nonetheless. Bangers and mash, basically mashed potatoes and either grilled or baked sausage. Her grandmother made it every time she visited as a child. Just the mention of the dish brought back a lot of good memories. Colton knew she would pick it, knew his mama's favorites, and so earlier in the day had made the sausage himself. When it was brought out, it was perfect. She truly enjoyed every bite, as Colton had enjoyed sweet potato cottage pie. They talked about how well the restaurant was doing and apparently, it was the new 'in' spot to be seen at.

As they sat sipping rich, sweet coffee and enjoying her favorite dessert of strawberry cheesecake, Colton got quiet. "Mom, what's going on with the guys that moved in next door?"

"What do you mean, sweetheart?" She tried to calm herself and slow her breathing. Just the mention of them and she wanted to go to them.

"Well, remember that guy Philip, the guy who sold you the pool? He was in here the other night and had the nerve to ask for a break on his meal. When I told him I'd give him a break like he did you for the pool, he got real nasty." Colton seemed reluctant to go on, but she needed to know what was being said about her.

"I'm probably not his favorite person right now, sweetie. In his eyes, I cost him a possible pool sale commission." She tried to make it seem as if it were no big deal.

"Mom? He said some really nasty stuff about you and those guys. He says you slept with both of them. At the same time."

Randa closed her eyes and felt sick to her stomach. Her boys knew she had dated after their father died, but hadn't cared as long as she didn't get hurt. And now, to have them know details? So not good. But just as she knew they wouldn't go into details about their own sex life, she figured they wouldn't want her details either.

"Colton, would you feel comfortable talking about your private life with me?" As he shook his head no, she went on. "Well, I am not comfortable talking about mine. All I will say is that I'm an adult and I'm not going to get hurt."

Colton looked at her with wide eyes, blushed a deep red, and finally grinned. She had pretty much confirmed what that douche Philip had said and Colton caught on. She knew how protective he and his brother were of her.

"Let me just stress to you that ultimately, anything that deals with my personal life I have to be able to handle. And this particular hurdle? Yeah, I'm still in a good place, despite the small blip. Okay, sweetie?"

"Yeah. But, Mom, I can't be held responsible for anything I say or do to anyone who hurts you. And you know Bradley would tell you the same."

On their way out, Colton spoke with the hostess, who was very pretty and watched him like he was her last meal. Randa tried to contain her smile when he chucked her gently under her chin and smiled at her. When he saw his mother watching, he laughed. "What?"

"She likes you."

"I know, Mom. We're dating," he said, chuckling.

"So why not introduce me?" she asked curiously.

"We're not at that stage yet, Mom. When we are, I will definitely introduce her—or whomever I am seriously dating—to you. Right now, we're just having fun. Okay?"

She squinted her eyes at him then had the last word by saying, "Well, I certainly hope you're wearing condoms. Unless you plan on making me a grandmother...?" Slowly one eyebrow rose as if daring him to answer. All he could do was stare at her in shock.

The drive back to her house was a pleasant one. They talked about how Bradley was doing in DC. No, he wasn't seeing anyone. Yeah, he'd put down a bid on a condo in a great neighborhood. She was kind of hurt when Colton mentioned the condo. But then realized that he was very busy with his military career and it was probably just an oversight. She couldn't expect her *grown* sons to tell her every detail of their lives, as proven by Colton's current girl. As long as they talk to her when it *really* matters is all that was important.

Back at her house, Colton came around and opened her door. She got out, grabbed her take home containers, and they walked her into the house. Barely through the door, Baby came barreling into the hallway and jumped on him. It still amazed her that the dog and her boys always acted like siblings. He roughhoused a little with her until it was time to leave.

136

***

Chase, flipping through channels and not finding anything good on TV, sighed when the doorbell rang. Standing before him was a young man barely in his twenties, holding out his hand. This was the *kid* that had picked up Randa earlier. Immediately on edge, Chase pointedly ignored the hand at first.

"Hey there, I'm Colton. I remember this house being on the market, and since you're here, thought I'd come over and introduce myself."

"Yeah, my friend and I bought the house and just moved in recently. I'm Chase," he said cautiously, not sure what Colton's intentions were.

Why should he make things easy for this *youngster?* He wanted to tell this *Colton* to get off his doorstep and get the fuck out of there. But at least *he* was an adult. He'd hear the guy out.

"Yeah, that's what I heard, all right. Well, like I said, I just wanted to introduce myself. I come over a lot to see Mo...uh, Miranda. She has me spend the night on occasion, since our visits can be a bit long. Helps me out to not drive around too late at night. You know how it is, right? Working hard all day and then out late at night. It's the leaving early sometimes that gets me. Hate early mornings," Colton said with a small smirk on his face that Chase wanted to wipe the fuck off. "Well, I've got to get back to work. It was great meeting you."

The little speech made Chase sick to his stomach. He couldn't say a word. He was afraid if he did he'd threaten to do bodily harm to the man standing in front of him. Watching Colton walk back to Randa's house, climb into the Lexus, and leave, took everything in Chase not to stop the younger man and tell him that there was no way Randa could be with *him* and then knock his teeth in. Instead, he slammed the door, leaning back against it breathing heavy to rid himself of the rage coursing through his entire body.

***

Randa was aware Baby knew exactly what was going on when she saw her change into her swimsuit. Her tail started wagging and she had trouble sitting still, knowing it was going to be play time.

Towel wrapped around her neck, they headed out to the deck and down the stairs. She could smell Chase and Jack's grill, but they were not outside. Relieved, she put her water and towel down on a poolside chair, then walked to the pool's edge and dove in. Since it had been quite a while since she swam, she punished herself with a grueling fifteen laps. She needed it, not just to give her the exercise, but to help her sleep. Since she had told the guys she needed time, she hadn't slept well. Oh shit, who was she kidding? She hadn't gotten more than five hours each night. She kept waking in the middle of the night from dreaming of hearing Philip call her fat and Chase and Jack would nod their heads, not looking at her as though they were embarrassed they had slept with her.

The last lap finished, she walked up the steps of the shallow end and wrapped the towel around her shoulders. Baby was whining at the fence and had stood up on her hind legs to look over the top. Max was outside and apparently they were looking to play. Randa looked over and saw Chase sitting in a lounge chair, beer tilted back as he drank deep. On the table beside him were three more bottles, but she couldn't tell if they were empty or ready for him to consume.

As he finished the beer he was drinking, he lifted it up in a silent salute to her, mockingly. The smile on his face was strained. She looked at him, confused, not sure why he was looking at her as he was. After a tentative smile at him, she called to Baby. They both climbed back up the steps to the house and disappeared inside.

***

Chase had enough to drink. He was hard as a rock from seeing her in her swimsuit, and in a way, pissed off about it. She hadn't looked like she was missing them. In fact, she had looked radiant when that young pup dropped her off. He'd been honest with himself and even told Jack how he felt. He was in love with Randa Michaels, damn it! Or at least that's what he thought it was. He had never been in love before, but he was pretty sure that's what he was feeling now. So now what the fuck was he supposed to do? No one had told him that when he fell in love there would be angst. A new job, new house he shared with his best friend, and the woman he'd waited all his life for. So why did he feel like shit?

What a clusterfuck his life was. As he grew up he'd never seen his parents or grandparents have moments like this. None of them had told him that love could produce emotions like this. He'd heard the expression 'nothing worth having comes easy'. Man was that the case. He'd never thought the woman he and Jack ended up with, permanently, would be served up to them on a platter, but also didn't expect the obstacles to hit this soon in the game.

**

Jack was in the living room trying to read up on some veterinarian journals to keep current on treatments and surgeries, but all he could think about was the other night. He could still smell her arousal as if his face was pressed right up to her flesh. And those beautiful nipples of hers were so responsive. His cock punched the zipper of his jeans. With a groan, he set the journal down, palmed himself through the material and laid his head back on the seat. He knew he cared about Randa, knew she was a special lady and wanted to continue to see where this thing between the three of them went.

What the hell were they going to do now? If it were only a matter of dating, he thought they could handle it. But when the heart was involved? But then again, it was a moot point as they weren't even talking to said woman. Or rather, she wasn't talking to them. Or was it that she was also seeing a third man, a much younger man? Chase had told Jack about the Lothario having the balls to strut from her house to theirs and introduce himself, saying they might see him occasionally. The kid had mentioned late night visits, sometimes overnight, frequent visits. He was trying hard to not jump to conclusions but the shit thrown in his face had him reeling. Was Randa really involved with that kid? Chase said he was a cocky, young bastard that drove a Lexus. They wondered if a sugar mama bought it for him.

"Damn, buddy, you feel the need to rub one out, take that shit to your room," Chase growled.

Jack ignored Chase's comment. "I can't get her out of my mind. What does she see in that young kid? Shit, I like to think I can last as long as a younger guy can. Hell, I never come unless our lady does. We are both great at making sure she has plenty before we blow, ya know?"

"Yeah, man, I know where you're coming from. But do we stand back and watch this punk take our lady, or do we fight for her?" Chase held up a hand. "No, I don't mean beat the shit out of him. I mean we do the old fashioned thing. We romance her. But how do we do that when the only time we really get to see her is at work? We need to get her friends involved. Do we still have the box from the chocolate pie Randa brought over?"

Chase explained his idea, but it would take a couple of days to put together. They sat and went over the details, to fine tune, to get names. And so began Operation Wear Her Down.

***

Jack was in charge of tracking Kitty down. They found out by asking around at work, the owner of the bakery, Kitty Campanetti, was a good friend of Randa's. He was pretty confident she could help them out. He dialed the shop's number on the way home. He figured if anyone knew Randa's likes and such when it came to desserts, it would be her friend. If she was at all shocked at the whole ménage factor she hid it very well. Within a half hour of talking with Kitty, a plan had come together. She would give the first bit of ammo for their plan, and then she would get in touch with the others to see if they could help.

Chapter Nine

Friday morning rolled around and Randa woke in an insipid mood. How could it be so beautiful out, and she felt like rolling over and just going back to sleep? Within an hour, she had showered, let Baby run around in the backyard, and was dressed and in her car on her way to work. She walked through the side door near where she parked and followed the hall down to her office. She had seen Jack's sports car and Chase's truck already parked when she pulled in. *Damn it.* She had planned on another day of early in/early out to end the week. She loved the fact she could make her own hours. Since she helped out, and they felt obliged to pay her, she could come and go as she pleased.

She flipped the switch for the lights in her office and gasped. On her desk were two roses in a vase, a beautiful yellow one and a purple one, a purple so dark it was almost black. She knew instantly who they were from. The roses sat next to a flat box with a window. When she looked inside, she saw an oatmeal raisin cookie with icing letters. Only one person would know this kind of cookie was comfort food for her. But it wasn't just the type of cookie, it was the lettering written on it that made her so emotional. 'When angels ask what we loved most about life, we'll say you.'

Her eyes welled with tears. No one had ever said anything so sweet to her. But she still wasn't sure what they wanted from her. How could they want her? She was fat, just like Philip said, just like every man who had come into her life had shown her at one time or another. Sure, they may have showered her with attention, but in the end they went their own way. Something better always came along for them. Always.

A sob escaped her and she decided she couldn't deal with this today. She needed to get out, she couldn't face anyone for fear they would ask her what was going on and if she was okay when she wasn't. The rawness of her emotions rendered her incapable of thinking clearly. She needed to go somewhere to think and she knew just the place.

She called Cheryl at the front desk and told her she wasn't feeling well and would be going home for the day. She also promised she would be back in on Monday. She grabbed up the vase and cookie, not wanting to be rude and allow either to be wasted. The roses would look lovely in her kitchen window and the cookie a good snack for where she suddenly planned on going. With the light turned off again, she walked back down the hall toward the exit and to her car. She'd almost made it outside when she heard her name.

***

Chase saw a blur coming out of Randa's office, heading for the parking lot, so he called her name. Not stopping, she turned to look at him then ran out the door. He ran after her, but wasn't fast enough. By the

144

time he got to the door, she was already in her car and driving off.

"What the hell?"

Jack appeared at his side just in time to see Randa driving off. Neither of them could even begin to guess what the hell just happened.

"I take it she didn't react well to your gesture?" Josie came out, still in scrubs and holding a bottle of water to her lips. She was about to take a drink, but instead dropped it down to her side. "What the hell happened? Kitty called me, telling me that you two were jonesing for my friend, even had a dinner date with her— which she didn't tell me about, mind you—but that you had screwed things up. You realize now you won't see her for a few days? She goes off with Baby when she's upset. She has never told me where she goes, but I think she tells her sons, at least one of them."

"Okay, so can you give us one of their numbers? I'm assuming they live in the area?" Chase impatiently asked her.

"Well, one of them lives in the area, yes. The other lives in DC. I can give you Colton's number, though," she answered.

"Wait, what? Colton? Her *son's* name is Colton?" Chase asked, feeling sick to his stomach.

"Hey, buddy. What's going on? Why are you suddenly looking green around the gills?" Jack looked concerned.

"Is Colton about five foot eleven, early twenties?" he asked in a low voice.

"Yeah, he is. That means you've met him already, and I'm thinking due to your reaction it wasn't at his restaurant, but at Randa's. And I'm also guessing the boy led you to believe that he was some kind of a date?" Josie shook her head but had a slight smile on her face. "They are both extremely protective of their mom. She doesn't have a great track record for good guys flocking to her. They do what they can to look out for her, but Colton may have gone too far this time."

Chase was furious and grateful at the same time. If the kid hadn't purposely led him to believe other-wise then he and Jack wouldn't have been motivate to express themselves the way they had. But why had she reacted like she did? Was it too soon for them to tell her how they felt?

Before they left work, Jack had called the son with the number Josie had given him. Chase didn't trust himself to talk to the kid without getting into it with him. Their shift done, they headed home to change and wait for Colton to come over.

***

Jack heard a car pull in next door and peeked out the window. The Lexus he'd seen the night Randa went out without them pulled into next door. He watched the young man, Colton he presumed, let himself into the house. But he wasn't in there for long. Soon, he was making his way over to their house. Ringing the bell, Jack opened the door and stood there with his eyebrows raised waiting to see what the kid wanted. Colton wasn't aware that Jack knew who he was. A bit of a pissing match ensued with neither saying a word for a couple of minutes. He wasn't happy with Colton for misleading Chase the other night, but Jack introduced himself then stepped back and let him come in. Chase came into the hallway looking pissed off and ready to rip Colton's head off. Before anyone could say anything, Max came around a corner and couldn't stop in time, running right into Colton's legs. He laughed and knelt down to scratch behind the dog's head, trying to avoid a tongue determined to lick.

"Max, down! Come lay down, big guy," Jack called out to the dog.

Jack motioned for Colton to follow him into the kitchen and handed him a beer. Colton took it, looking a little nervous, and swallowed back about half the bottle before setting it on the counter.

"Okay, first off, Chase, I want to apologize. I should have told you who I was, but I wanted to make sure you knew my mom was a special lady and she wouldn't be alone long. And yeah, I know about both of you. An asshole she used to date was kind enough to tell me—in my own restaurant—when I wouldn't give him a break on the meal he and his anorexic date had been served."

"Glad the elephant in the room has been ousted," Jack joked. "And yes, both of us are interested in dating your mom, if she'll have us. But what I don't get is why you would think we needed to be warned? We know your mom is an interesting, beautiful, kind lady. So, tell us, why the warning?"

Jack could tell Colton felt uncomfortable and didn't know what to say to them. Colton began to talk about Randa's past boyfriends. Though there weren't a lot of ex-boyfriends, his mom had explained the breakups to her boys when they happened. How every guy she had dated in the past treated her like she was only good enough until a thinner woman could come along. Like she was only good for one thing, and once that was given up, she could be cut loose. Apparently, Randa was very close to her boys and never had a problem talking about her life to them.

"My mom married my dad after divorcing her first husband. Bradley was born a year later and then I was born three years after Bradley. Though mom never bad mouthed our dad, she wanted Bradley and me to know what kind of man our dad was."

Jack and Chase listened as Colton shared what she had told her boys. Only recently they found out that when their parents first married, their father was attentive and loving, but as the years went on, he became less and less interested in a sex life with her. She had also explained she had been full figured when they had met, maybe not as much after the babies were born, but still a plus size. After Colton's birth, she tried so hard to lose the weight, but most of it stubbornly stayed on. Eventually, arguments started because Randa thought he was cheating.

Then he spoke about the night his father died, how there had been a woman in the car, a younger, slimmer woman who had survived. When the police had asked Randa if she knew who the woman was, she couldn't answer. The last conversation she'd had with James was him saying he had a meeting in Oceanside and wouldn't be back until late. The woman in the car, when she awakened, said James was her boyfriend and they had been heading to Oceanside for an anniversary dinner. Of course Colton hadn't known any of that at the time, but had gotten the information out of his mom bit by bit over the years.

After weeks of court dates, the girlfriend was finally informed that she had no legal claim on any part of James' life insurance policy, no matter how many times he had promised her she would be taken care of. That was seventeen years ago and his mom's self-esteem had never fully recovered. She had never thought herself worthy of any true passion.

Colton went on to explain he was only six at the time, and hadn't understood anything other than his dad died, and *that* was barely comprehended at the time. As he got older, his mom taught him and Bradley to hold out for someone special to come into their lives, but to respect all women, no matter their size or shape. Their mom had always had a "pleasantly plump" physique, never obese. The boys watched as she agonized over what she had wanted to weigh, but seemed was unable to reach. Colton had always thought his mom looked great. But then again, he was a bit biased.

"Colton, this ex that you recently saw, was his name Philip, by any chance?" Chase spoke low and harshly.

"Yeah, he was the last guy mom dated. It only lasted a couple of months. About a week after the pool was installed, he broke it off with her. Said he couldn't date her anymore. That she was too big for him and he was having a hard time getting passed the fact. Mom had figured he had only dated her to get the commission on the pool his company installed for her. God, if I had known, Bradley and I would have hunted him down and beaten the shit out of him." Colton looked at the men standing before him. "He made my mom feel fat. She's not fat! She deserves so much better than to be treated like that!"

Chase and Jack looked at each other, then at Colton. They had to admire the fact the kid took defending his mother so seriously. Not that they didn't agree with him. His mother was fucking hot. But they had plenty of time to convince him how attracted they were to his mom. First, they needed to find out where she was so they could convince her of the same thing.

***

The Cabrillo Tide Pool trails had always been the place she would go to get in touch with herself. When James died, she had brought the boys here and they were able to deal better with their grief. After each of the breakups she'd been through, she had come here. She'd even 'borrowed' a dog or two on a couple of trips. Kind of like a field trip for dogs. It was her way of not only relaxing, but to give those dogs hope that their forever homes were coming, that their new mamas and daddies were just lost.

She adjusted her backpack. Thank god she'd always kept it stocked with basics. That way if an unexpected trip came up, only water and some food would be left to pack. She always carried water, six bottles to be exact. Plus a collapsible water bowl for Baby. The cookie that was on her desk that morning was in the pack, along with some granola, dog food and dog treats. If they got stranded, which had only happened once, her and Baby would be okay for a day or so. But she also knew the locations of a couple of natural springs, so even if they lost track of time and ran out of water, there was a clean source to refill her bottles.

She thought about that cookie again. It was truly the sweetest thing anyone had ever done for her. Well, outside of her boys that is. It was totally unexpected. And the roses? They could have done the dozen red ones, as per the usual for men, but to pick the two colors she loved, and only two? Genius. She already knew where they got the cookie. Kitty. She was the only one who knew about how, as a child, Randa's grandmother would make them when she was sick or depressed. She should be upset with Kitty for helping them, but couldn't bring herself to be. Kitty was one of her best friends. When she wanted to open her own shop, Randa had bought a ten percent interest. That investment had paid off, several times over.

The colors of the roses didn't go unnoticed either. Yellow roses were her grandmother's favorites, and became hers also. The deep purple? It had always been a favorite color of hers. She had always said that she could look at a deep purple rose and get lost in it. Now, that bit of info had come from Syun.

Syun Alvarez was another friend whose business she had a stake in. They had met when The Haven had wanted to spruce up the landscaping of the land the clinic stood on. They had wanted to give the business to a woman, and to an unknown. When the announcement went out through local media, there were many bids submitted. But the only one that stood out was from a one woman operation. Not only was she the lowest bid, but her proposal of what would be done was the best. She planned on repurposing, and drawing out what was already attractive about the location.

After she had been awarded the project, she had begun immediately and had ended ahead of schedule. The community was one hundred percent pleased. Randa had been so impressed that when approached for the name of the business, she was pleased to pass on the name of Syun to Grow. Soon after, Syun actually had to turn down work, but from that point on, she never had to worry. Work came looking for her.

Syun also did the landscaping for Randa's house. There were two rose bushes—of show quality—in her front yard, one yellow and one a deep purple. She had planted them as a thank you for the help Randa had given her, and for the investment she had put into Syun to Grow.

Syun was able to get top of the line equipment, including the custom modified Dodge Ram 2500. Her good friend, Luna, had taken the brand new truck—the investment that Randa made—and tricked it out, including a custom hitch to be able to pull the custom built trailer.

Luna had just been released from prison. They met when Syun's old truck broke down alongside the road. Luna had got it running and then helped Syun with her job. Since then, she had helped when other work came around, but her probation officer was working on a deal with a local car shop to get her in.

But that brought her back to the roses. They were the exact colors from *her* roses. She wondered if they took them. Syun would be the one to tell them those colors were her favorite. Damn, were all of her friends helping them? They were certainly smart in getting her friends to help. Since the three of them hadn't known each other long, the men would need help on simple things such as flowers and desserts.

But they wouldn't find her here. None of her friends knew this was her place. They knew she went somewhere, just not where exactly, so it gave her time to think. She would stay at the motel close by—that allowed dogs—for the next two days, and then head home Sunday sometime. She would be in no rush since she lived close.

As she hiked the trails, she contemplated her possible relationship. She wasn't sure what Chase and Jack wanted out of their seeing each other. Did they merely want to date her out of convenience? Figured when they were done they could send her home? Or were they looking for a relationship of sorts? How was that accomplished? Did they want children? Randa panicked. Marriage? She was too old to consider either.

Well, maybe not too old to marry, but children? Not only was she too old, but she was unable to have any more kids. *Whoa*, she chided herself. She was getting *way* ahead of herself with those thoughts.

***

Chase and Jack had gotten out of Colton that his mom liked the Cabrillo Tide Pools. She liked to take Baby for the exercise and it was a great place to go to think. There was only one trail, but it ended at the edge of the water. Baby loved running through the water. Colton had said he was always surprised when he saw the huge dog romping around like a puppy.

Colton explained to them he thought it better if he did not go with the two men to find his mother, though. As much as he didn't care about her love life as long as she was happy, that didn't mean he wanted to see two guys rubbing up on her.

Chase and Jack left in Chase's truck. Even though it was worth more due to it being rarer than Jack's Porsche, people tended to react more to Jack's car than the truck. Fairly soon after leaving, they came upon the parking area, even found Randa's car. They parked and saw the sign had park rules stating all visitors must be out by 5:00pm. They wouldn't have too long to wait. It was now three forty-five. They had stopped on the way and picked up subs and drinks, so they ate slowly, hoping to pass some time.

They had asked Trace to doggie sit Max, as they weren't sure how long they were going to be gone and they didn't need him in the way of trying to win Randa over.

Chase noticed they both kept looking at the time on their phones nervously. What if she wasn't feeling the whole relationship with two guys thing? What if she didn't want anything to do with them? What if, what if, what if...they could play the what if game all day and come up empty.

Chase sat behind the wheel of the truck. He had his eyes closed and he was thinking of the look on Randa's face the night she had dinner with them. She had a glow about her when she spoke. It didn't matter what she talked about, it came from within and could blind anyone if they didn't know she could do it. And when she came? Chase wanted to be one of only two men who could see her face when she climaxed. He wanted her face to be the last thing he saw before his eyes closed at night and the first thing they opened to in the morning. God, he sounded like a sappy greeting card. But shit, it was so true.

***

Jack had totally different thoughts running through his head. He was thinking of the night that douche, Philip Conrad, had stopped over. The look she had given them as she had went up the steps into her house—she had looked at them as if they believed what had been said, and that she believed it too. That look would be imbedded in his memory always.

They both must have dozed off waiting for Randa to come back to her car because both of them jumped as they heard a very loud bark close to the truck. Coming up the path toward them was their favorite Irish Wolf Hound, her mama not too far behind and looking not so happy. They got out of the truck and waited for her to get closer. She continued to glare at each of them, then looked at her watch. They all had about fifteen minutes to leave the park before the park rangers came to boot them out.

"What are you doing here?" she snapped through Chase's open window.

***

Randa was irritated. They had invaded the one spot she always thought of as hers. Her eyes caressed them when they stepped out of the truck. Both dressed in jeans, t-shirts, and boots, they looked like an ad for Cowboys 'R Us. She wanted to lift their shirts and lick their chests then unbutton their jeans and go further south. Damn it, she was not happy with them. She needed to stay irritated.

"You know what, never mind. We need to get out of here before Bruce comes and kicks us out. Just follow me; I have reservations."

She got Baby in the backseat then got herself situated. She backed out of the parking spot and headed to the exit gate. Seeing Bruce, she waved and drove through. She slowed down slightly to let them catch up, but was she really ready to confront what was going on between the three of them? She drove to the motel she had arranged to stay in. Even though she had not been there in a while, the clerk recognized her. They talked for a bit and then the clerk's voice lowered.

"I got you in the biggest room we got, for the usual price. I know Baby needs more room to walk around...*and* it's on the floor level so no complaints this time of a noisy dog." She winked at Randa, handed her the key card, and looked toward the men. "Can I help you gentlemen?"

Randa nodded her thanks and dug out a business card/coupon and handed it to the lady. She'd taken to giving them out when she needed to thank someone or if she saw an animal in need. The business card stated the coupon was good for one free checkup for any reason. The lady smiled at Randa and tucked the card away. As it turned out, her poodle needed his annual soon. That was one of the reasons they had pet owners willing to drive over an hour to have their pet seen at Haven. Their pricing was very reasonable, and the staff truly cared about the animals. It didn't matter how big the owner's wallet was, all animals and owners were treated the same.

Chase walked up to the counter, grinned and asked for a room close to Randa's. The clerk, Molly, looked at the two men and then at Randa, who just smiled at her and nodded. Setting them up in a room with two full size beds, she gave them their key cards and they all walked out into the fading sunlight.

With Baby out of the car and politely walking next to her mama, Jack and Chase followed. No need for luggage, as Randa had everything she needed in her pack. Chase and Jack would have to either go more than two days in the same clothes or leave the next day. So that meant the three of them would have that chat tonight, or tomorrow at the latest. Just to get things figured out. She really didn't want to drag it out and she was sure they didn't either.

Chapter Ten

The guys had eaten, but Randa had only snacked on granola, wanting to save her cookie for that night. So, she ordered a large pizza from a place close by. Their pizza was so good she had come here on a Friday or Saturday and brought it back home. It was the best around, cold or hot.

She ordered a six pack of beer to go with the pizza, and for the guys to drink. While they waited, Randa wanted to get Baby taken care of. She didn't need exercise, but did need to do her business, and then she would be set for the night. Since Chase and Jack had nothing better to do, they went with her.

After they returned from the short outing, awkward silence filled the room. Randa knew what was causing her discomfort. What did you say to the two men you had the best sex in your life with, not once, but twice in one night, only to have an ex call you fat in front of them? Her quietness was justified to her, but theirs? What would they have to be uncomfortable about? They couldn't be looking to break things off with her. If that were the case, why would they take the time to track her down? For that matter, how *did* they track her down?

Randa was the first to see the delivery car pull up. She reached into her pocket to pay for the order, but Jack beat her to it. Apparently, there was no way was he letting her pay. He handed the kid thirty dollars, telling him to keep the change. Chase took the beer, Jack the pizza, and they all walked back to Randa's room. Randa went to the closet and pulled down the extra blanket she knew would be there. Folded in half, she laid it on the floor for Baby, who immediately lay down and rested her large head on her paws, watching to see if they would drop a pizza crust. As Randa ate, the men sat there drinking beer and watching her. Yeah, wasn't that a situation every woman wanted, to have the man—or men in her case—she was attracted to see her eat?

"All right, I can't take this anymore. You eating that pizza is so fuckin' sexy. I need to talk to get my mind off it," Chase threw out. "Before you start in on what that douche, Philip said the other night, or anything else you might think we believe, let's lay it on the table, yeah? I'm only speaking for myself here, but I have a sneaking suspicion that Jack, here, either feels the same or is damn near close to it. Randa, I love you. Do you get that? I do not agree with Philip's assessment of your weight. In fact, I don't want you to lose weight unless *you* want to. I love you the way you are now. I want you in my life. As your co-husband, or a co-boyfriend. Hell, I don't care. I just want—no, need—to be in your life any way I can."

With the half eaten slice of pizza part way to her mouth, she stared at him. Shock reverberated through her whole body. She looked from Chase to Jack, who was nodding his head in agreement. She felt scared to death, ecstatic and nauseous all at the same time.

Jack got up and went to kneel down in front of her. "Everything Chase just said is true, baby. I love you. *We* love you. And you would be doing yourself a huge

160

favor by wiping anything that insinuates that you are overweight out of your mind and vocabulary. We both hate the word fat, or even heavy. Your body is perfect because we say so. However you want us in your life, we'll take it. We're not looking for kids, unless you want to adopt." He turned red with his next statement. "We wouldn't ask you to have a baby. We know the older the woman is when she gets pregnant, the higher the chance of problems. Neither of us have kids, but, and I'm only speaking for myself here, if I don't have any, I'd be okay with it. We can get another dog, or when our friends have kids, we can spoil the hell out of theirs."

Randa tried to swallow what was in her mouth, but it went down the wrong way, making her cough. Chase jumped up and thumped her on the back and Jack handed her a bottle of water to clear her throat. She opened her mouth to say something, but nothing came out, just a croaking sound. She raised the bottle of water to her mouth again and drank, feeling the last of the pizza crust go down. Hell, she couldn't sit with them staring at her like a bug under a magnifying glass. She got up and paced the room.

"Holy shit, do not do that to me again. You can't be talking like that when a person is eating," she said to them sternly.

She wasn't sure what she was going to say. Did she love them? Could she handle a relationship with both of them? A child? She knew the answer to *that* one. Even if she *wanted* to get pregnant, she wouldn't at that age. As it was, she couldn't have kids because of the partial hysterectomy she'd had to have after Colton was born.

Then, as the thought of adopting hit her, she could almost picture herself as a mama again with the two men standing in the room with her.

"Oh my god...I need to sit down. My brain is fried right now. I'm not sure what to think and what to believe. That was the reason I came here. Not to run from you or how I thought you felt, but to have the time to myself to get my head on straight. You guys are asking me to believe that in the short time you have been my neighbors and co-workers, you have developed feelings for me that normally lead to a relationship. And, oh my god, a child?" She looked at Jack and his red face and couldn't pass up making him squirm. "My age is an issue only when it comes to giving birth. I am not embarrassed about my age. See, forty-six is not old, and no, I was not insinuating that you called me old."

The red in Jack's cheeks deepened. He opened his mouth, but Chase cut him off. "Babe, I can speak for Jack by saying we are in no way misled in thinking you are old. True, you are older than us, but that is in years only. All of that is immaterial. What matters right here, right now, is how you feel about us." He walked to her, took her hands, and brought her to the bed to sit on the edge as they stood before her. "We've just told you that we love you, woman. We're not asking for you to go out and buy a wedding dress or choose furniture for a nursery. What we're asking from you is a reaction." He knelt down to be face level with her. "How do you feel about us, Randa? Is there any chance you might want to date us? And I do mean *us*. We are a package deal, sweetheart. You dating just one of us is not going to happen."

Jack grabbed her free hand, so they now each held a hand. "He's right. I could never solely date you knowing that my best friend is also in love with you. And it would devastate me if I knew you two were exclusively dating. We've done the three-way relationship before, and found out after, that the woman was only interested in one of us, but thought she could handle the emotional involvement with both. I won't be put through it again, and I won't let my best friend, my brother, deal with it either." He smiled at her sadly. "So our question is: would you be interested in a relationship with both of us? If you need time, just tell us and it's yours. You are so worth the wait."

Conflicting emotions and thoughts ran through her. One part of her mind was saying take a chance, don't let them get away. She opened her mouth to follow that advice. But then that little devil on her shoulder was whispering to her to walk away. She couldn't keep the men in her past happy so what made her think she could with these two? Just as she was getting ready to tell them she needed time, she heard her voice say something different.

"I'm going to slip up. I'm going to be self-conscious. I'm going to doubt myself and definitely doubt you. It won't be easy with me. I'm just warning you. I am in no way saying this to get you to work harder to pay attention to me or for any other ulterior motive; it's just how I'm wired. Past experiences have jaded me on men, no offense." She seemed to say all of this in one breath and sounded winded when she paused to inhale. "So, if you're willing to put up with all of that crap, I'm up for dating you both."

Slowly, both men smiled at her, then looked at each other in silent communication. When they turned back to her, they each had a look of pure, hot sex in their eyes, but they cooled slightly when Baby chuffed in her sleep.

"Uh, Randa, has Baby ever seen you in a romantic situation? And by that, I mean will she bite an ass if someone is inside you?" Chase asked nervously.

"No, and I'm not sure how she'll act if or when she does. *That* was a situation I never trained her to see." She laughed softly. "Would it be okay if she went to your room? She won't want to be there all night, since she checks up on me when I'm sleeping, but when we, uh...umm..."

Her voice trailed off as she blushed. She was forty-six years old and yet she had blushed more in the last couple of weeks than she had in the last fifteen years. And she had a sneaking suspicion that it would happen a lot with them. She called Baby over and got up to get her leash. Clipped on, Baby could barely control her excitement, ready to go for a walk. Randa felt bad that she was going to disappoint her, but she had to use the leash in public places.

Randa knew what was going to happen the moment she got back to her room. She was just glad the only room that shared walls with hers was the room Chase and Jack were given. She knew she could get loud. In fact, she remembered the other night when her ears rang after the first climax they had given her and it had

164

only gotten louder with the many more they gave her. She shut the door to their room and went to open the door to hers. It was confirmed; she had a dirty, filthy mind. All she could think about was they had better not have all their clothes on when she came back. And there they were, shirtless, pants unbuttoned but not unzipped. She sent a silent thanks to whatever cosmic being arranged hot sex. She closed the door and locked it. Her hands went to the hem of her shirt, but they both held up a hand to stop her.

Silently, they came to her. One set of hands pulled her shirt up and over her head, the other at the waistband of her pants. They made quick work of her clothes, then her lingerie. Before long she was standing before them, not a stitch on, with her arms crossed over her belly. Jack went to stand behind her. He took her hands and brought them up and around the back of his head. "Leave them there." That is all that Jack said to her. Still behind her, he cupped her breasts. Just that simple touch and her nipples went diamond hard.

Randa was sure Jack would be doing more than the hands on soon, but Chase had sat on the floor, back against the bed, and then motioned for Jack to walk her to him. His mouth was right even with her womb, but he dropped his head to begin at her knee and tortured her by slowly licking his way until he reached his final destination.

"Look down, baby. Watch him as he shows how much he loves you. I'm so fucking jealous that he gets to taste you right now. But I'll get my turn. I'm perfectly happy with what my hands are holding. For now." As he spoke, her head bowed and goose bumps formed on her arms as though a chilly breeze washed over her. "But as soon as you are on your back, I plan on fucking these tits as you hold them together. I've been thinking about it a lot."

Randa had thought her mommy porn books were exciting, but the sound of Jack's voice instructing her to watch Chase and then telling her what he was going to do, sent her flying. So, watch him she did. She watched as Chase looked up at her, never stopping the motion of his tongue. She'd needed this, they'd needed this.

***

Jack had to release a breast to wrap his arm around her to hold her upright. As he spoke to her and Chase licked and nipped her labia and clit, he watched as she was thrown head first into an orgasm that buckled her knees. If he hadn't been holding her in his arms she would have collapsed on the floor, her body still shaking from aftershocks.

They had plans for her to come many times over before the night was complete.

Jack laid Randa down and stared at her. She looked torn between watching him and closing her eyes to savor the aftereffects, but she kept them open, her expression glazed and her lips parted slightly as she watched him. He smiled at her as he pushed his shorts down and off. His cock stood at attention, pointing straight at Randa. He was about to follow through with the promise he'd just made her. She lay there, trying to catch her breath. They didn't want her to come down from the high too soon, though. Chase was already positioned between her thighs. His tongue, teeth, and lips already had her thrashing, her hips lifting then lowering, then repeating. Jack watched as first one then a second finger thrust into the wetness that waited for Chase. He had always loved how Chase got a woman going, but with Randa it was different. This was the woman they both loved. Her pleasure was the only thing either had on their minds. They ignored their raging hard-ons, blood filling their cocks to a painful ache.

Head lowered, Jack took Randa's lips as another climax ran through her body. Her lips slightly parted as the wave rolled through her, and his tongue dove in and tangled with hers. Her moans filled him and made his cock get harder, if that were possible. His hands went to her breasts again, squeezing and pulling her nipples.

***

Chase groaned as her sex pulsated around his fingers and another climax tore through her. He wasn't sure how much longer he could hold out. He stood and stripped, watching Jack now roughly kissing Randa. Between watching his hands on her breasts and his taking her mouth, Chase was ready.

He tore open a condom wrapper and quickly slid it on. With his gaze still on his friend's hands, Chase slowly entered Randa's pussy. She was so wet and hot. He could feel her channel pulsate around him. God, she felt so fucking right. He couldn't stop the growl that seemed to ooze from deep inside him. Chase alternated between watching as his cock entered her and Jack's hands still cupping, squeezing, and pinching her breasts and nipples. He couldn't wait to see her mouth wrapped around Jack again. To see them both inside her somehow. Randa greedily wrapped her hand around Jack and began to stroke him. He knew what would be coming next. He chuckled a bit when Jack bit back a curse but didn't stop her.

His hips slowly began to move as he watched Randa look up at Jack. He could almost feel that wet mouth, but the lifting of her hips rerouted his attention. The temptation was too much. He couldn't have kept still if someone had a gun to his head. The room filled with the sounds of the three of them. Jack growled as his cock disappeared into her hot mouth. Chase moaned at the feel of her. Randa's muffled groan upon taking Jack all the way into her mouth was fuel for both he and Jack.

With his cock buried deep inside her wet core, Chase watched and moved his hips in time to Jack's. Every time he pushed forward into Randa, he saw Jack would do the same into her mouth. His rhythm picked up and he saw Jack position himself to be able do exactly what he promised moments before. He pulled from her mouth and straddled her chest. He instructed her to push her breasts together. When she did, he slipped his cock in between and pushed toward her chin. Her tongue would come out and lick the head each time it got close to her mouth.

"Just like I thought this would feel. Everything about you is perfect, baby. Never doubt that. You were

168

made for us. You are our one. Do you understand that? You're the love we've been waiting for."

The sound of Jack's voice seemed to spur Randa on. Chase would have loved to see as Jack fucked her breasts, but the position was less than cooperative. The only view he had was of Jack's ass. It didn't take long, however, for Jack to decide he wanted more. He slowed his movements and could hear Randa whimper not to stop. His thumb went to her clit and rolled over it to keep her going but not to the point where she would lose it.

"I think she's ready, man. Damn, we have no way to lube her and I don't want her hurt. Want to take over here?" Chase spoke softly to Jack.

"Yeah, let me suit up."

**

Jack had surprised himself when he was able to speak to Randa coherently. The only thought in his head was to continue with his rhythm of push and withdraw from her between her twin globes. He couldn't tell which he liked better—the pushing through her softly rounded flesh or the tongue and mouth action. Luckily, he hadn't had to choose, as both happened. He lifted off her, smiling at her protests, and leaned down to kiss her.

He pulled out a condom and slipped it on. As he got closer to Randa, Chase pulled out and slipped his condom off. He walked into the bathroom and cleaned off a bit then came back in the room, still very hard. She watched as Jack stalked to her, and he liked the way her eyes hungrily tracked him. The need to be inside her was pulling at him. She placed her feet flat on the bed and let her knees fall over to show him how ready she was for him.

His eyes stayed locked on her and his breathing sped up as he watched her. He could see her outer lips glisten with her arousal and just begging to be filled. His hand came down and his fingers played with her, coming away almost dripping. He palmed himself with the same hand and stepped close to position himself right at her entrance. He held on to her knees as he slowly pushed forward until he was fully seated. Her body arched off the bed and she moaned, feeling every bit of his satiny steel length join her. Jack held himself still. He reached out with a hand and squeezed her breast as Chase joined them and lay on the bed next to Randa.

**

"Do you know why Jack had to stop, baby? You are so fucking hot that you're making his normal control slip and he doesn't want to go off yet. We want to come with you, all of us at the same time."

Chase took her lips roughly; needing that contact with her as Jack slowly pulled out and then pushed himself back in. Randa's hands were clenched in the bed sheets and she was trying to get him to speed up. But Chase wanted in her mouth. He looked up at Jack and saw the glassy eyed look from his friend and beads of sweat forming on his forehead. Chase knew it wouldn't be long.

"I got an idea, buddy. Let's turn her around. I need to be in that mouth while you're fucking her pussy."

They turned her so that her head was at the foot of the bed. Then Jack again took his time coming back into her, drawing out the pleasuring. Chase knelt down at her head and lifted it slightly, letting her watch as Jack began to enter her again. She watched his hardness pull out until she could see the mushroomed head, and then slowly disappear. Her breathing was coming more rapidly now and her hips rising to meet him. Chase knelt there, whispering to her.

"I love watching him take you. Yeah, I know his cock is bigger, but you can take him. I would love to be in your ass right now. I know how tight you are. Do you remember, baby? A cock in your ass and one in your sweet pussy. No worries; we will be doing that again. Very soon, I promise."

***

Randa let her head fall back as she listened to Chase. Positioned as she was, her mouth was primed for Chase as he stood and placed the tip of his cock at her mouth. Eagerly, she opened her mouth and took him in. She hummed in enjoyment and he pushed a little more until he was at the back of her throat. She swallowed, allowing him to slip further. She smiled inwardly when he groaned and grabbed her head to hold her still. She imagined they were quite the sight for Jack. She knew he would see as her neck bent slight backward, her mouth taking Chase in completely. She looked up and caught the almost imperceptible nod. She guessed that they would begin fucking her in earnest now. No holds barred, as it were.

Slowly, they began to time their movements perfectly. When one was pulling out, the other thrust in. Randa loved she could please both of her men at the same time, just as they were pleasing her. She could feel herself reaching that edge where she needed to go over and take them with her. She tightened her lips around Chase and sucked as hard as she could to get him to join her. He thickened in her mouth and then went still as he exploded. She felt the hot liquid fill her mouth and she rushed to swallow. Moments later, he pulled almost completely out of her mouth, resting just the tip against her lips. She leisurely licked and kissed the tip.

***

Chase looked down at her and rubbed his thumb along her cheek. God, she was so beautiful and she still wasn't convinced. He pulled out and away from her, but bent down to play with her breasts since she and Jack still had not come. As he pulled, pinched, and then leaned down to take her nipples in his mouth, he watched as Jack moved faster. Chase reached down to strum her clit, and sucked as hard as he could on her nipple as he plucked the other. Not too longer after, Jack thrust into her one last time then held himself still as Randa cried out and lifted her hips off the bed.

Chase leaned down and kissed Randa deeply. Her arms came up and curled around his head. Jack pulled out, with a slight protest from Randa, and pulled her up his body to drape her over his chest.

***

Randa slipped off Jack and lay curled to his side, giving Chase the chance to press against her back and ass. She closed her eyes and concentrated on the feeling of two men who expressed their love for her. She was pretty sure she loved them too, but she was scared. What if they got tired of her? She was not sure that she could get down to a smaller size. Years of trying had kind of forced her to accept her weight. And she was slowly beginning to like herself. Though still a little insecure, she knew she was a good person and she felt if they, or anyone else, didn't like her size then they could leave her life.

She wasn't sure she could take another rejection, especially from these two. They had wormed their way into her heart. Their kindness, their passion, their acceptance. Maybe her weight wasn't an issue for them, but she'd had this happen before with James and with other men she dated. They had shown how they truly felt towards the end and maybe these two men would do the same. *No!* Her mind was telling her Jack and Chase were different. That they wouldn't do that to her.

***

Jack had watched intently as Chase fucked Randa's mouth. Watched as her lips swallowed him and then released. When she swallowed then cleaned the tip of his cock, it sent Jack over the edge. His hips were quickly moving forward and back and forward again. At the last thrust in, he had held himself still as he felt her inner muscles begin to throb and milk him. He hadn't even noticed that Chase had been manipulating her nipples or her clit. He had closed his eyes and just gone with what he was feeling. And his feeling was to come and bring Randa with him. Which she did, and did so hard.

He moved off the bed and disposed of the condom. When he got back to the bed Chase and Randa were spooning. He stood there for a moment and just watched his best friend and their love, still in awe that no inclination of jealousy crept in. He had been worried their one past relationship may have ruined their trust that it could actually work. He was glad he gave it another shot. Randa was proving it was indeed possible. He lay on the bed facing her, pushed a lock of hair behind her ear, and smiled at her.

Jack couldn't help but stare at her beautiful face. He saw a look come over her that made him draw a breath. She looked so serene and happy, but as if a switch were thrown, she suddenly looked sad. He looked over her shoulder at Chase, trying to convey his concern because he had a good feeling where her thoughts drifted to. He really shouldn't have been surprised when Chase reacted the way he wanted to, but he still was. It was crazy how in tune they were with each other.

Jack nudged her until she was flat on her back, Chase having moved to accommodate. Jack could see the fury on Chase's face but was glad he steeled his features so she didn't think he was upset with her.

"Whatever is in that pretty head of yours, better fly out now. Can you doubt how we feel, how we see you now? Baby, we love you, all of you. Every last beautiful, fucking sexy inch of you. And since you've said you will slip up, we will just have to convince you some more when we get you back home, huh? Hell, I don't mind repeating our methods every single day just to reinforce it to you."

Jack listened as Chase spoke to her in his soft Texas drawl. He looked down at her and nudged her hip with his ever thickening cock and smiled. "Miranda Michaels, I love you. *We* love you. No one else matters. No matter what anyone else says, you are our one. So let's go back home and work out the logistics...like where to sleep tonight."

She looked from one to the other, and then seemed to accept it. They were hers. They were her men. The only thing left to do was to meet the only other men in her life that mattered—her sons. Oh yeah, and her friends. Jack knew how women were. A lot of times, if the friends didn't like the man, or in this case, men, then it could be rough. But then again, three of her friends already knew about Jack and Chase, so the rest couldn't be too bad. Could they?

Chapter Eleven

After a couple of weeks, Randa and her men had gotten into a bit of a rhythm. Work, home, swim, dinner, and then time together. They weren't all about the sex, although they couldn't keep their hands off each other. Since Chase and Jack had tracked her down at the Cabrillo pools, they had gone there quite a few times. Normally they would take the dogs, but they also went a couple of times without.

After dinner one particular evening, they decided to go back in the pool, Randa in her normal one piece and the men in their trunks. The dogs had worn themselves out from swimming already, so they were curled up together in the grass. She gave her men a look over her shoulder as she climbed down the steps of the deck to the ground below. Chase and Jack got up from their chairs and went to the railing.

Slowly, she walked down the steps of the pool into the shallow end. She turned to face them and brought a hand up to dribble water down the front of her body. The water, cooler than the air temperature, made her nipples bead and harden. She looked up, and with both of her men watching, she cupped her breasts, bringing her thumb and forefinger to her nipples and pinching them slightly through the swimsuit. Her lips parted and her eyes glazed over and she smiled seductively up at them.

They descended the stairs leading to the backyard and then entered the water. Within moments, they were standing on each side of her, right where she wanted them to be. Jack's hands joined hers and were cupping and caressing her breasts. Chase's hands were running down her body to cup her ass and then move to the front of her suit. His fingers nudged her suit aside and began to play with the soft skin guarding her sweet channel, drawing a deep sigh from her.

Jack pulled a strap down and lowered his head to take a nipple deep into his mouth. Her skin cool from the water, Jack's hot mouth made her gasp and grab his head. Not one to be left out, Chase thrust two fingers into her heat. Randa's head fell back and she allowed her men to take her to the edge. She needed them badly and couldn't care less that anyone could come upon them and see. That just added to the excitement.

The sun was starting to set, the bright light slowly starting to change colors and then fade. The colors in the early evening sky ranged from different shades of gold to pinks. It really was very romantic to have her two sexy men pleasuring her under the setting sun. It seemed time stood still, just for them. She was the luckiest woman in the world to have these two men focus all their attention on her. She would have to make sure she kept her men happy.

Randa wasn't interested in being just on the receiving end of the pleasure, though. Her men needed to feel pleasure along with her. Jack worked his magic with his tongue and lips on her nipples, while one of Chase's hands held her lower body still as two fingers from the other were slowly pumping into her very needy passage, his thumb brushing her clit on the in stroke. She knew they would keep her steady and didn't need to worry about keeping her balance.

Smaller hands were currently threaded in the hair of each man. Since Jack was obviously a breast man, she wondered if his nipples were just as reactive as hers were. She smoothed and caressed down his cheek and jaw line, to his earlobe, giving it a quick pinch and tug. At his neck, she could feel his heartbeat. The quick thud told her that he was definitely enjoying her hand on him. Down further she approached his nipple and could feel and hear his intake of breath in anticipation.

***

Jack was concentrating on Randa's nipples. The skin around the little bud crinkled eagerly. His head kept moving back and forth, trying to give equal attention. The feel of Randa's fingers in his hair, tugging and sifting, nails occasionally digging into his scalp was enough for him to growl and want to take her, but then her hand moved. He wondered what she would do, but only briefly. She caressed his skin, but when she pulled on his earlobe, he felt it shoot right to his cock, hardening him even more. Her fingers were now at his neck, pressing on his carotid, confirming his rapid heartbeat, then moving down again. The closer those digits got to his nipple, the heavier his breathing got. At the first tug and scissoring between fingers, he groaned. He had never considered his nipples sensitive, but in her fingers they tightened immediately and he suddenly knew how Randa felt when he did the same to her.

***

Chase was enjoying the scalp massage Randa was giving him, but then she moved south, down the back of his head to his shoulder. She continued to press and massage wherever she touched. His muscles tight at first, slowly loosened, eliciting a groan from him as she worked from his bicep to his forearm then back up to his chest muscle. She coasted down past his nipples to his upper abdomen causing his breathing to speed up. With the direction of her hands, from his chest to his lower belly, he had to hold back his need to urge her on. He noticed her teasing him a bit when she stopped her hand, then with a low laugh continued. Oh yes, she knew exactly what she was doing to him. She skimmed past the barrier of his suit and wrapped around his cock, right at the base, and began an up stroke to the tip which she circled with her thumb before smoothing down his shaft to the base again. The feel of her slightly cooler hand against his hot flesh felt so good he couldn't help the growl that came from deep within.

***

Silently, he opened the gate, knowing that if they were out here the dogs were too. He wasn't scared of the little dog, but the larger one made him a little nervous. He stayed close to the side of the house, sneaking toward the backyard. He peeked around the corner to find them in the pool. Well, he couldn't see *everything* they were doing, but shit, if the dots couldn't be connected then he'd have to be an idiot.

He watched as one man lowered the straps and bent his head to her chest. He couldn't see what the other man was doing, but a Harvard diploma wasn't needed to know what was going on below the water. This just solidified his decision that she was a whore. He had thought to hire the best in personal trainers for her, to trim her down and make her the perfect politician's wife. She was pretty enough, but it was her way with winning people over that he needed for his next campaign.

Damn it! Despite his anger at her for her actions, he was fucking turned on and it sickened him. What kind of woman allowed two men to paw at her out in the open where anyone could see? He was going to have to show her the error of her ways. But for now? He had to put a stop it. No way was he going to let this continue. She'd been tainted. What if her neighbors knew? Her behavior could affect his campaign, he just knew it.

But what to do? If she was going to act like this, how could he make it clear that her behavior was shameful? He continued to watch them and could not help his hand from going to the front of his pants and rubbing his cock. It sickened him when he realized what he was doing. He slapped the bricks on the side of Randa's house. Then the proverbial light bulb came on. Something to show to everyone what a dirty slut she was and maybe teach her those two men—obviously fucking her—would probably lose interest.

For now, though, he needed to do the entire neighborhood a favor and stop their actions. He let go of himself and looked around. He found just what he needed. Making his way back to the front yard, he debated whether or not to damage her car or her house. He figured the car would be a good choice, but might not require the immediate attention. A single woman in this day and age was more likely to have an alarm, so if he were to break a window the house alarm would go off.

He stood there looking up and down the block. It was the time of day that families were indoors as the sun had just about set and it was getting too dark to do much but water plants. The perfect time to do a little damage. He stood in front of her living room windows, and with a final glance around, he brought his arm back. He looked like an amateur pitcher as the rock left his hand and crashed through the window with a loud pop, immediately setting off the alarm he guessed she would have. He jogged to his car, got in, and left quickly, not drawing attention to himself.

***

The sound of the house alarm going off startled the trio in the pool. The dogs weren't too pleased with the sounds as Baby tore off for the gate opening, Max trying to keep up. Jack was the first out of the pool. He ran up the few steps and went after the dogs. Chase had not been too far behind his friend. Both men were trying to corral the dogs into the backyard.

Randa pulled the straps up onto her shoulders and got out of the pool. She watched as each of her men had a dog they were bringing back into the gated yard. That was strange. She knew the gate had been closed when they had all come outside. So, someone had to purposely leave the gate open for the dogs to get out. She walked to the front of the house and that was when she saw the glass on the ground. She looked up and saw the hole in the window and couldn't move. Partly because where she was standing, she was surrounded by broken glass. It was a wonder that she hadn't cut herself already.

She saw Chase come back out front. She couldn't bring herself to move anything but her head to look at him, then down to her feet. The moment he saw the hole was obvious as he swore and, with no regard for his own feet, came to her and picked her up, making sure she was far enough away from the glass so she wouldn't get hurt. She wanted to protest him carrying her, but she had to be honest with herself that his arms around her were comforting.

"What the fuck just happened?" Jack asked

Jack had come to stand beside them, surveying the scene. Randa was wringing her hands, Chase looking ready to beat the shit out of someone. The dogs were at the gate whining to come see what was going on.

"Damn it, man, someone busted out one of her windows. Could have been a kid throwing rocks or someone being an asshole," Chase ground out. "Let me find out who the hell did it and I'll beat the shit out of them."

Randa didn't know what to say. She *did* know the neighborhood kids and knew they wouldn't do this. They were all a great group of kids, not mischief makers. Neighborhood kids had never done anything like this before, so that left a vandal. The question now was who did it?

"Randa? We're going to figure this out, baby." Chase had his arms around her and his chin resting on her head.

"Do you think we need to call Trace in?" Jack asked quietly.

"I don't think the cops can do anything, buddy. No witness, and if the window was broken by a rock, it will be hard as hell to pull a print from it. We'll just have to keep an eye out."

They walked back to the back deck and inside. Sure enough, in the middle of the living room floor was a rock the size of a man's fist. The edges of the rock were jagged and one side was even covered in mud. *Definitely not going to get a print from that.* Jack went and picked up the rock as Randa turned off the alarm and called the alarm company. After explaining the situation, she directed the alarm company not to send the police as they were not necessary, and they agreed. Randa knew Chase was looking at her and Jack, and he looked angry. Jack approached and held out the rock. The two dogs sat by the sliding glass door; Baby looking like she was expecting to be chastised for running out of the backyard. Max was just being a sheep and following his lady friend.

"Okay, so we need to keep an eye on things. Anything weird, the three of us need to all be in on it," Chase said tersely.

***

After being told twice to go upstairs and soak in her whirlpool, she decided to let them handle the situation. She knew they were making sure that the repair of the window would be done first thing. Seems their friend, Pac, would be over in the morning to figure it out since he had connections. For now, she would just do as they wanted and let the tub melt away her worries. Hell, she'd take a page from Scarlett and worry about it tomorrow.

Chapter Twelve

Days turned into weeks and they had yet to do any introducing to any of their friends. Chase and Jack knew that Josie was the pack leader of the circle of ladies, but it seemed like Kitty was a close second in command. Whenever either of them worked with Josie, she busted their balls. She was definitely a tough nut to crack, but they knew that they needed to get along with Randa's friends if they wanted to stay in her life. Would she give them up if a friend didn't like or approve of them? Probably not, but it would make for uncomfortable situations. Besides, they pretty much *had* to get along with her since she was the head vet at Haven. They could take the ribbing from her because she really was a great vet, friend, and all around great person. They kept thinking they knew the perfect guy for her.

Kitty, on the other hand, was just as her store suggested—very sweet. They had called and thanked her for her part in getting past Randa's barriers and they even bought pastries from her shop quite often for Haven. The pet owners and rest of the staff had come to expect sweets, and despite good natured complaints of weight gain, loved the treats.

In fact, the men had this grand idea to fix up their friends. The small group all had a love of full figured women and they had, of course, noticed the two friends of Randa's that they had met were exactly in line with what any of the guys would be interested in. They just hoped Randa wouldn't have a problem with their brilliant idea.

So, with the weather getting warmer, they had decided on a combined BBQ/pool party to get all their friends together to introduce them. Randa's son, Colton would be having his chef get some dishes together, but mainly Chase would be doing the grilling. And Chase was thrilled whenever he had a reason to. It would be the perfect time to see if any of her friends had an interest in any of their friends. So far, Syun was the only one that would not be able to make it. She had a family thing to do, but she was very disappointed. For that matter, Luna wasn't one hundred percent sure she'd make it, but she was going to try. So that left Kitty and Josie as definites. Randa was checking to see if her eldest son, Bradley, could get leave from his Air Force position to come visit.

They had planned the party to take place in a few weeks, figuring that if anything in the meantime allowed for anyone to be introduced, then so be it. But they would officially be introducing themselves as a couple, or trio rather, at their party. And as luck would have it, there had already been one meeting that had already taken place.

***

To look at Sam Jensen anyone would think he was antisocial and the world's biggest asshole. It was just the dominant vibe and how he carried himself. So, when he walked into Haven carrying a tiny, shaky Chihuahua, Jack couldn't help but grin. Chase wasn't in yet and Josie was finishing up on an emergency surgical procedure. He had checked in with reception and requested either Chase or Jack.

Jack came out into the waiting area, stopped and stared at his friend holding the tiny animal as though it would break in two just by being held. He smothered a laugh and came forward.

"Hey buddy, whatcha got there? Come on back and we'll have a look at your little one."

Sam followed Jack into an exam room. "Man, am I glad to see you."

As soon as Jack closed the door, Sam placed the dog on the exam table with the utmost care. He had never seen his friend so worried about anything before. Though Sam didn't have a dog, he seemed to like them well enough and hated seeing one suffer. So to see him fawning over the dog was touching yet amusing. Sam seemed to know what Jack was thinking as he looked up at him with a cross between a smirk and chagrin on his face. His expression would have made a lesser man cringe and a woman unsure of how to react.

"So, tell me about this little, um," Jack cocked his head slightly to see the sex of the animal, "yeah, guy."

He gently placed his hands on the animal's abdomen, palpating and feeling to see if he could detect anything to be concerned over. Sam stood back and watched like a hawk to make sure that the dog wasn't hurt. When a sore spot was found, and the dog softly yipped, Sam glared at Jack.

"Hey there, little man, sorry about that, but we gotta see what's doin' with you," Jack crooned to the small, obviously petrified dog, and then spoke to Sam. "Where did you find him?"

"I don't know how the hell he did it, but he was in a truck when I got to work this morning. Probably went up a ramp when no one saw and curled up in the blankets. Is he okay?"

Jack had never seen his friend like this, but it didn't surprise him he was getting the little stray looked at. As a Dom in the BDSM lifestyle, Sam took it very seriously to look after things whether it was a male or female sub, or in this case, an animal that was naturally submissive to one more dominant. From what he could tell, the dog was healthy, but he wanted some blood work to make sure there wasn't anything internal they should be aware of.

"Yeah, he seems to be okay, but I want to take some blood to make sure nothing hidden is going on. Okay?" Jack looked up at Sam. "Are you planning on keeping him?"

"You know, I never thought of myself as a pet owner, but since this morning I've already grown accustomed to the little guy." Sam gently pet the dog and it seemed to preen for him.

"Okay, well, when we get the blood, I'll have them give him all the necessary shots and you might want to think about getting him fixed. He'll be marking everything if you don't."

Sam cringed and looked uncomfortable. Jack chuckled at his friend's reaction, but couldn't blame him.

What man wants to think about something like that? Damn, here the dog was just trying to survive and now the threat of losing his balls was almost a reality. But if Sam was going to keep him, he'd accept the procedure and become the alpha in his home. It wouldn't be any fun dealing with a dog trying to out-man him.

"Yeah, do the shots, absolutely. And let's get the snipping done. Would you or Chase being doing it?"

"Well, if you want it done right away, no. Our surgery schedules are full up. The head vet could do it, though. But you've got to talk to her. Let me go see if she's done with her surgery to be able to talk to you, okay?"

Jack left the room, put in the order for the blood to be collected and the round of shots the dog was to receive, then went looking for Josie. He found her in the break room, still in scrubs, grabbing a bottle of water out of the fridge. He had to admit she was a very attractive woman. Her long blonde hair up in a messy ponytail, almost like she didn't take any time to brush it, was kind of sexy. But then again, she seemed like a confident woman, no matter her size, so she probably knew how she affected men.

"Hey, Josie. I got a friend of mine that just brought in a male Chihuahua, approximately two years old, needs neutering. Can you talk to him and let him know if you have any slots open anytime soon?"

Jack waited as she turned to him and cocked an eyebrow.

"Snip some more balls? Save the bitches out there from another baby maker? Hell yeah." She laughed as she opened the door to the exam room.

Jack stood back as Josie walked into the room. Josie went to the exam table and was running her hands along the body of the little dog. Its body was shaking, and it cowered at first, but calmed at her gentle touch. For a woman who comes across as such a hardass, she always shows her love of animals with her patience and tenderness.

"So who do we have here? A soon to be non-Romeo, huh? Poor little guy," she cooed to the little dog.

"Hey, Doc, that's a great name for him. Romeo. I like it." Sam looked over the female vet and Jack could tell he definitely liked what he saw. "Can you fit a neutering in? If I'm to keep him, I don't want to worry about him living up to the name."

Jack stood quietly, watching their interactions. Since there were no patients waiting, he figured he would stick with Sam. He knew the man could be a little intimidating, even if Josie more than likely would give back as good as she got. He watched as Sam stood with his arms crossed over his big chest. Josie was trying to make it seem like all of her attention was on the newly named Romeo.

"Yeah, I can do it in a half hour if you like. I'm free the rest of the day. Are you sure though that you want to do this now? If this is a stray, we could find him a home if you don't want the bother. He, uh, doesn't quite look like your type of dog."

Jack cringed when Josie spoke to Sam like she did. He knew Sam would take it wrong and wondered if Josie intended the words to be about dogs or something else. He saw Sam's eyes narrow in irritation and made to move between them if necessary.

"Doc, how do you know what type of dog is mine? I found the little guy in one of my trucks and I will take him on. He seems to like me, and I'd been thinking of getting a *pet*." He smirked when he said the last word.

Jack had to cough to cover the laugh that almost burst from him. He wasn't sure Josie would pick up on the term, but he would love to be a fly on the wall when it finally hit her. He had a feeling, though, that she *did* because she froze and looked up at him. It was almost as if she recognized the alternative meaning behind the word and instantly responded to it. He was fascinated by the change in her posture and breathing.

"Well, a responsible pet owner is a good thing. Nice of you to take one right off the street," she commented breathlessly.

"I am always responsible. I take care of what's mine. Protect it and care for it," he growled. "So, do I need to fill out any paperwork or just go wait in the lobby? I want him to be fully vaccinated and to be neutered. Is there any way he can be groomed; teeth cleaned and nails clipped too? I want the little guy to leave here best he can."

"Yes, sir, there are some forms we'll need from you. Let me get the tech to take Romeo to prep him then we'll get that paperwork for you."

Relief washed through him when she merely walked out of the room with Romeo. She returned briefly to hand a clipboard to Jack then left again. Jack handed the paperwork to Sam to fill out.

Sam turned to Jack and pounced, filling out then signing the papers as he interrogated Jack. "What the hell, man? Why didn't you tell me that you had a submissive working with you? I'd have adopted a dog long before now."

Jack held his hands up in defense. "I swear I didn't know she was. You know I'm not into kink and she's a tough lady. How the hell was I supposed to know? I don't have the dommy-sense like you do." He laughed.

"So what's her name? Shit, man, you didn't even introduce us. I can take it from there, but you gotta give me a leg up."

"Her name is Josephine Stuart. She goes by Josie only. In fact, when we tried to call her by her given name, she cold-glared us until we caved. Like I said, tough nut, man."

Josie chose that moment to come back in the room. She held her hand out for the clipboard, turned, and walked away again. Sam, closest to her, made to catch her but she brushed him off. Jack continued to watch them, finding the exchange very entertaining. The stunned look on his friend's face made him decide to throw him a bone. He opened his mouth to speak when he was interrupted by the speaker system.

Jack was paged to the lobby, so he turned to leave, but he couldn't help the last shot he got in. "She has a thing for gummy worms." Laughing, he left the room.

***

Chase came in to work and saw two things. Jack was sitting laughing quietly and Josie was scowling at Jack. They didn't share an office, but they did all congregate in the same large open office to complete paperwork on surgeries. When Josie noticed him, she got up and stomped out, mumbling something about checking on Romeo.

"Okay, what is her problem and who the hell is Romeo?" Chase asked.

"She met Sam. Sam saw something in her, if you get my meaning. And Romeo is Sam's newly neutered Chihuahua," Jack laughed.

"What the hell? Where did he...? You know what? Never mind. I don't think I want to know. And you said he saw something..." His words trailed off as the only thing Sam could see in her that Jack wouldn't come right out and say would be if she were a submissive and Sam recognized the signs.

Oh shit, Chase thought, chuckling. So, Sam would probably be making a play for the sub in Josie soon. He hoped that she was okay with it and that it worked for them. It would get weird quick if they had to work with someone Sam broke things off with.

Before he could say anything else, Randa came into the office and sat down. She looked like she was going to bounce. The three of them sat there not saying a word, just looking at each other like they were all starving. Had it only been a couple of nights since they'd all been together? Chase and Jack could tell she had exciting news to tell them, but she had lost her train of thought when she saw them.

"Babe," Chase spoke to her softly, "did you have something to tell us? Or did you come to just sit there and watch us work? Cuz you know we won't get anything done if you're sitting there looking good enough to eat and we can't touch you."

***

"Huh, what?" Randa tore her gaze from their faces and her vision cleared. "Oh yes, um, Bradley called to let me know that he's going to make it for the party. He said he was coming in and renting a car, so no need to pick him up from the airport, and he's going to stay with Colton."

"Sweetheart, that's great! We know how important it is for you to introduce us to both of your boys. Then the three of us can sit and discuss where we want to go with this." Jack smiled at her and then got serious. "You know we love you, we know you love us. All we need to do is work out the dynamics. True?"

"Yes, dynamics. That is important," she answered breathlessly, still overcome with the hows and whys that were in her life. She just couldn't wait for her boys to officially meet both men.

They had talked about her past and what her exes had done to her. She didn't think she could do marriage

196

again, but neither of them had truly cared about it since they all believed it was just a piece of paper. Chase and Jack had talked to her about a collaring ceremony they had seen once at Sam's club. They all kind of liked the idea of giving each other tokens of love, but the actual marriage ceremony? None thought it truly important. If they decided to do the family thing, then whatever child they adopted would be raised by all three.

"Okay, so tonight I have kabobs marinating and thought we could eat poolside, if you two are okay with it?"

"That sounds great. That way I can get my swim in and the puppies can play in the water."

"Definitely. Sounds like a great idea. I'll be heading out soon, gotta hit the market and then I'll head home to prep some things. Okay?" Jack said.

She got up, and after making sure no one was around, she gave them each a quick kiss. "I'll see you both at home."

She knew as she walked away that they were smiling. She was too and that was a big deal. She had kissed them, at work. She suddenly realized that she no longer cared what people thought. They were well on their way to officially being a three-way couple.

Chapter Thirteen

Miranda knew Jack would be home and Chase was due to arrive soon. She needed to take a hot shower to freshen up. Maybe get in a few laps before they came over. Then she could do more laps later. She hadn't heard the car pull up and park across the street, nor was she paying any attention when she got out of her car and went up and into her house. Baby greeted her and Randa gave her treat for guarding then walked upstairs. In her shower, she ran the water as hot as she could manage then slipped in, standing under the spray for a few minutes and letting the hot water melt away all her work stress. Feeling refreshed after her shower, she got out, dried, and put on her swimsuit. As she stepped out on the deck, she could smell the grill next door heating up. A clear indication that Chase was home.

At first she floated through the water. The wet silkiness caressed her skin like lovers' fingers. The need to blow off the tension, to relieve her body of stress took over. She began to lift and lower her arms, cutting through the water and moving towards the deeper end of the pool. Lift, push, kick. Lift, push, kick. The motions not needing thought, they were instinctive. Slowly, she felt the tension start to leave her body. After a couple more laps along the length, she started thinking of what waited next door.

Her body tingled from her head to her toes at the thought that her men and her would be together. She stepped out of the pool and pulled on her cover. She left Baby in her yard to run and then bask in the warmth of the sun. She went around to the front of Chase and Jack's house and rang the doorbell. When Jack answered, she practically jumped him when he smiled at her and told her to come in.

"Hey, babe, come on in. Chase is just getting ready to grill. I'm going to go change into my trunks real quick. I'll be right back." Jack kissed her hard and quick, and jogged up the stairs.

She walked in the direction of Chase's voice. She heard him talking to Max. It was almost like he was having a conversation with a human, the way he talked to the dog. And when she saw Max's face, it was uncanny how the dog acted like he understood—same as how Baby looked at her when they had conversations. She walked up behind Chase and wrapped her arms around his waist. As she leaned in to lay her cheek on his solid back, he turned in her arms and pulled her close for a kiss. Her legs were about to give out when he picked her up and sat her on the counter. She gave a squeak in protest, but then forgot about it as he deepened the kiss and wrapped his arms around her waist to pull her close to him.

"Well shit, if I knew you two were going to start without me I wouldn't have gone to change." Jack came in and lightly punched Chase on the arm. "Go back to what you were doing. I'll take over."

Chase chuckled low and released her, turning to get the platter ready to take outside to grill. Jack moved between Randa's legs and began to kiss her as deeply as Chase had. Randa could definitely tell whose kiss was whose based on technique. But if she were ever asked which the better kisser was, she would not commit to an answer. In her book, they were both excellent kissers, just in their own way.

"Don't get her riled up, Jack. It won't take long for dinner to get done, and then we'll go for a swim. I've been thinking about how her skin feels slicked from the pool," Chase said as he went outside to the grill.

Jack ignored Chase, lifted the cover up and off her, and pulled the straps of her swimsuit down until her breasts were exposed. Since the suit hadn't dried completely, the cool air pebbled her nipples. Jack murmured his approval and bent his head to lick and suck on them. Her hands came up and threaded through his thick hair. Chase came back in and chuckled, seeing them still going at it. Jack raised his head smiling, pulled the straps to her suit back up, and lifted her down and off the counter.

"Sorry, buddy, I just couldn't resist. Do you not see what she's wearing? Damn! Too tempting." Jack gave Randa a look that said they would definitely have to pick that up later.

"Man, if I trusted you to actually work the grill properly, I'd have put you on grilling duty to give me the opportunity to do the same," Chase complained good-naturedly.

They laughed and went out the sliding glass door. Chase ran next door to get Baby so Max could continue his wooing of her. They sat down and ate dinner, talking about work and what was new. When Jack started the story of Josie and Sam meeting, Chase laughed, but Randa was concerned. She had yet to meet any of their friends, as the timing was off for all of them. Either that or they were all waiting until the party.

"So you're saying that Sam is into the whole dominant-submissive thing? And he thinks that Josie is a submissive?" Randa laughed at this. "No way. Have you met her? She's more in charge than anyone I know."

"Babe, did you know that it's common for people with high pressure or managerial type jobs to have submissive tendencies in the bedroom?" Chase said.

"Really? I didn't know that. But then again I don't know anything about that lifestyle. Not too many would want to see me tied up, I'm guessing," she casually said.

"We didn't know either. And if I were in the lifestyle you'd definitely wear ropes a lot. Even Sam said you had the body for it. We've been to Sam's club and he's told us that most of their subs are from fields like medicine, legal, and the police force," Jack said.

"Wait, Sam owns a club? There's a BDSM club in this area? I never knew there was," she said confused.

"Of course you didn't, that's the way they want it. Do you know how much protesting would go on if the general population knew where a sex club was?" Chase laughed. "And he doesn't own it outright, he's a part owner."

"And Josie knows he's a Dom?" she asked.

"From what Sam was saying when he called me? Yeah, it's something each side learns to recognize after time," Jack said.

"But she's never even talked to me about it. Never so much as mentioned having gone to a club..." Randa just couldn't believe it. One of her best friends was into an alternative lifestyle and didn't feel comfortable talking to her about it.

Her curiosity appeased, Randa didn't want to talk about their friends anymore. They had planned on movie night at Chase and Jack's house. She couldn't wait to curl up between her two hot guys. They alternated between her house and theirs for movie watching. The type of movie wasn't as important as their need to spend time down time together. The guys loved that she enjoyed their action movies just as much as her chick flicks.

With the dogs given their bones, they sat with the popcorn in Randa's lap. It was amazing how many times the two men "missed" the bowl and cupped a breast by accident. Randa knew the following day she would not remember anything about the movie, but since they had it on DVD they could watch it again anytime. There were moments, though, that they completely ignored the movie. It was like they were all back in high school. Jack would turn her head his way and kiss her as Chase would nuzzle her neck. Then Chase would kiss her as Jack nuzzled. Then the straps of her swimsuit came down and she felt two pairs of lips on her nipples. Her head fell back against the couch and she panted. Her hands came up and pressed both of their heads into her.

"Please..." She wanted them to make love to her.

They were all for answering her plea, but it was late and both men had surgery the next day. Randa was to have a full day giving tours for prospective donors, trying to raise more money to make some improvements at Haven. She was about to stop them, knowing time was not on their side when she felt their hands continue.

Chase brought his hand to the juncture of her thighs and pushed her bathing suit to the side. He moved first one, then two fingers inside her. Jack moved a hand down and did the same to her ass. With their tongues and teeth working her aching nipples, they began to thrust their fingers in and out of her until they hit a rhythm and were pumping at the same time. Randa knew what they were doing and was upset that they wouldn't join her. She began to fight them, but quickly lost the battle as her inner muscles were throbbing and milking their fingers. She was well on her way to a massive climax and she couldn't stop herself from crying out their names, begging for more.

The sound of her breathing sounded harsh in the now silent living room. She looked up at them and narrowed her eyes in irritation. If she'd had more control, she could have made sure they'd had pleasure too. She was tempted to just get up and leave, but her knees weren't working, and they were both throwing her smiles they knew she couldn't resist.

"You do know you're both in the doghouse now." She glared at them.

"Babe, if we had told you that tonight was just for you, you wouldn't have gone along with it," Jack explained with a slight chuckle. "You do so much for us that we wanted this just for you."

"We'll make sure we're selfish next time, if that's okay, darlin'," Chase teased.

"Not funny, Chase. If we didn't all have to get up early then we'd have it out. It's not right that you two are making decisions like that without me." She was frustrated. Sure, she'd had an orgasm, but she'd needed to be filled by them too. And she needed them to be satisfied. "Okay, who's walking me and Baby home? Or am I going at it alone?"

Chase got up and put his arm around her waist then whispered to her. "Go give him a kiss. You know we hate sleeping separate from you, but until we get the house situation figured out, it won't be an everyday thing."

Jack had sat back on the sofa, arms at his sides, eyeing her with a slow grin. She went and straddled him, pushing his head back against the sofa and lowered her head to kiss him deep and long. Her tongue pushed past his lips and began to duel with his. When his hands came up and moved to cup her breasts, she playfully backed up and got off him. He looked like he was ready to follow her, but she pushed him back down so he was sitting again.

"Welcome to my world, big guy." She laughed as she grabbed Chase's hand and they walked away. She didn't expect to hear his shout of laughter as they walked out of the house.

Chase unlocked her door with the key that she had given him and he pushed her up against the door frame. He grabbed one knee and pulled it up and around his waist so she could feel his erection straining against her. He assaulted her mouth with his and groaned when she kissed him back just as hard. She answered with a moan of her own and pulled his head closer to hers. When his hands went to her ass and pulled her closer to him, she had to pull away.

"If we don't stop now, we'll have to call Jack to come join us," she whispered. "And you two didn't want to go there, remember?"

"Sweet thing, it's not that we didn't want to, but we all would be up way late to do your body justice and we can't afford that. Surgeries and paperwork and all that."

***

"I know, and that is why you're going to say good night, turn, and go home to your big empty bed," Randa said with a smirk.

"Fine, but I'm not leaving until you close the door and I hear you lock up."

He gave her one last kiss and then gently pushed her in the house, patting Baby on the head as the door closed and he heard the lock click. He walked back to his house and did the same, closing and locking the door. Jack was still on the couch, barely paying attention to the movie as it rolled credits. Chase joined him and let his head fall back.

"We gotta get this figured out, buddy. This separate bed shit is frustrating. I miss feeling her next to

206

us, between us. I like sleeping all night wrapped around you two." Jack blew out a breath of frustration.

"I know, Jack. We'll work it out very soon, I promise," Chase consoled him. "By the way, do you know anyone that owns a silver Cougar?"

Jack frowned slightly. "No, not that I know of. Most of the families on this block lean towards cars of the soccer mom or family roadster variety. Why?"

"I'm betting it's just someone who's visiting a neighbor late, and we've just never seen the car before. It was just weird, parked across from Randa's house."

"Well, keep an eye out. It could just be nothing."

Chapter Fourteen

Randa was just getting home after a long meeting with some potential donors. They wanted to bring in some local celebrities to get the word out again about Haven. She had been through this before, but on a more national level when a pro sports athlete had volunteered. It had brought in so much awareness that donations poured in for months, allowing Haven to be very successful when other no kill 'last chance' shelters buckled under the pressure of day to day operations.

Her men had a poker game at one of their friend's house—apartment, whatever. So she hadn't rushed home. Colton had asked her to come by Flavour just to say hi. The sun was almost down when she pulled into the driveway and cut the engine. As she got out, she saw the gate to the backyard was open. *Weird*, she thought, she always made sure it was closed when she left in the morning. But maybe Chase or Jack had come over to swim before they left. She'd have to talk to them about making sure they closed it after. She closed the gate then and walked back to the front of the house. That was when she saw one of her rose bushes partially dug up and mangled.

With a cry, she looked around to see if maybe she could see any dog prints or something similar. That could be the only reasoning for this. Maybe a neighborhood dog had gotten loose and came into her yard to dig? As upset as she was, she was more upset because of what the roses meant to her. She needed to call Syun and see if the bush could be saved. As she pushed the key into the front door's lock, she heard a car's engine rev and then pull away. She couldn't see the make or model. And due to the lack of light, wouldn't be able to even pin down a color.

She hurried into her house, crouching to hug Baby as she came running to the door barking. This was unusual behavior. Normally, she was sitting by the front door waiting as Randa came through the door. Tonight, she must have been occupied in another room and heard the door open. Protective as ever, she came running to find out who was coming in.

"Baby, house okay? Where were you, girl? Did you see what happened to my roses? And damn it, I wish you could talk to tell me."

After taking pictures and texting them to Syun, she quickly changed into her swimsuit, grabbed a towel, and headed to the pool. She decided to work out her anger and the rose bush issue by giving herself five extra laps. She knew if she didn't tire herself out she wouldn't be able to sleep. She was so engrossed in her laps that she didn't notice that Baby wasn't lying within sight. She reached the steps and looked around for the dog. Maybe she heard something while Randa was swimming and went to check it out. A strange feeling came over her. One she had no rhyme or reason for.

The feeling of unease persisted despite the fact that the area was a relatively quiet one. It was a dream neighborhood to move into because everyone quickly made her and the boys feel at home. The problems with the burglar a while back seemed to end when Baby assisted the local police department. Maybe it was one of the local teens looking to use the pool as they were known to do, no permission needed.

She knew if she didn't get out of the pool when she did she wouldn't be able to eat. She always made sure that she didn't eat too close to when she went to bed, knew it was not good for the digestive system. They walked up the steps to the deck and went inside. Baby toweled off to get the remaining moisture out of her coat, Randa opened the fridge to take out three eggs, cheese, mushrooms, and roasted peppers. Not really interested in a heavy dinner, she put together a quick omelet. She remembered fondly, when her mom would make breakfast for dinner a couple of times a month. It was good for their dad since he was in the military and for months on end would have to work the swing shift, so dinner time was his morning.

She sat at the kitchen table, eating as Baby calmly did the same. She kept thinking how much she missed her men. She understood the nights away, poker night or some sporting event on pay-per-view. But it didn't mean she missed them any less. Dinner complete, she cleaned the few dishes, turning the light off as she left the room. She checked to make sure the locks and alarm were all set, and then headed upstairs. In her spacious bathroom, she turned on the hot water, adjusted the temperature to just slightly less than scalding, added her favorite scented oil, and stood back to begin undressing.

She just couldn't shake the weird feeling she had. She debated telling her men about the roses and whether or not to ask about the gate. She just didn't want them to worry. She was getting the feeling both were connected somehow. She heard her cell ping, announcing that she had received a text. She picked it up and hoped it was either Chase or Jack checking in on her. Slightly disappointed, she saw that it was from Syun. She said she would be by sometime the following day to take a look at the bush. She would be bringing a replacement in case she couldn't save it.

With a heavy sigh, she climbed into the huge whirlpool tub and turned the jets on, moaning low as the tension instantly started melting away. Not all of it drained from her, though. Her instincts were telling her to be mindful of her surroundings. There was just something off, but she couldn't pinpoint what it was. She lay in the bubbling water, trying to relax. When a soft noise sounded, she sat up straight in the tub, turned the jets off, and just sat there.

She waited for the longest time, expecting something to happen, or another sound to hit her hearing. Baby had risen and walked out of the bedroom, only to return a few moments later. Randa knew that *if* something was going on, Baby would protect her fiercely. When the massive dog lay back down, laid her head on her paws, ears still perked and alert, Randa relaxed a little. She turned the jets back on and closed her eyes. She tried not to drift off, but between the hot water and the massaging water jets, she dozed.

***

Chase and Jack had a key to Randa's house, as she had one to theirs. They had all been known to come into each other's houses at weird hours, or even if they missed each other. They arrived home and figured since it wasn't too late to pop in next door to see if Randa wanted to either have them sleep at her house or maybe she would sleep in their huge custom bed next door. Baby came and stood at the top of the stairs, chuffing a greeting. She wagged her tail then went back to her mistress.

They looked at each other, wondering where Randa was. Maybe she was already asleep? Chase started up the stairs, Jack following behind. Once in her bedroom, and not seeing her, they both headed to the bathroom. They knew she loved her tub as it was the one thing they knew she had splurged on for herself, well besides the pool.

Chase grabbed a big, fluffy towel, folded it, and then knelt beside the tub, just watching her. He could do that all night. He looked up at Jack standing in the doorway and smiled slightly. He knew if she was using the whirlpool then she had a bad day. He wanted to be one of the ones to help her through her bad days. He stood and removed his shirt, looking at Jack and beckoning him over with a nod of his head.

***

Jack stood in the doorway and saw the worry on Chase's face. Randa had a long, and apparently stressful, day if the whirlpool was being used. He came forward, pulling his shirt up and over his head as he moved. As he drew closer to the tub, he kicked off his shoes and looked down at the woman they loved. The water moved over her lush body like a lover's caress.

Her breasts bobbed on the surface gently, nipples not soft but also not hard, almost as if starting to wake. One hand rested between her breasts, trying to decide if it wanted to cup or not. Her other hand was between her knee and her inner thigh. The sight she presented to her men was alluring and seductive.

They both stood there looking down at their love. If they could, they would make it so she never felt stress again, but that just wasn't reality. The only thing they could truly do was be there for when she needed them. Like now. But neither of them knew their presence was adding to her anxiety. She sat up and screamed, her vision unfocused as she was looking their way.

***

Randa had been dreaming of Chase and Jack. Unconsciously, her mind and body needed them. She heard a thud and sat up in the bath, screaming, at first not recognizing the two figures that stood next to her. Baby jumped up and growled, not understanding why her mistress would act as she was toward the men she had grown used to having around. When Randa heard

214

the dog, her head turned and looked to see its teeth bared, ready to defend with her life, if necessary.

Both men backed away from Randa, hands up, knowing even though Baby knew them, she wouldn't hesitate to attack if she thought Randa was threatened. Chase held his hands out to Baby and spoke low to her. He was almost saying nothing that made sense, just stuck to the tone of voice. Randa, her mind now clear and her vision taking in her dog acting aggressively, stood and firmly spoke to Baby.

"Baby! Down, girl. You know them. Everything's okay. You're such a good girl for protecting me, but you know them. Come. See, I'm okay." She kept her voice firm, but started to soften her words.

With a whine, Baby approached, acting as though she knew she was in trouble. She came to them, head close the floor, shame filled her body, begging forgiveness. She planted her bottom next to the tub and laid her head on the side. She looked up at the two men and whimpered. Then she lifted her head and nudged one leg then turned to the other man and did the same.

Chase took pity first and rubbed her head then kept his voice gentle, "You are such a good protector. Your mama is so lucky to have you."

Jack joined in and was rubbing her back and making murmuring sounds of agreement. She soaked up the attention then turned back to Randa. Randa was smiling at her men cooing and coddling the dog. Yes, she was glad they loved Baby so much, but they did tend to spoil her. She waited a few more moments for them to stop. She stepped from the tub, allowing Jack to wrap her in a towel, and then they went into the bedroom where she sat at the end of her bed.

Randa sat still as Baby skulked her way over and sat in front of her. Jack and Chase sat on each side of her, allowing her the time to deal with the dog. She glanced at them long enough to see the curious expressions on their faces. Then she spoke to Baby to praise her, after which she stood and settled the dog in another room. She came back to the bedroom and shut the door then stood there, arms crossed over her chest and waited.

When she returned to the bedroom Jack and Chase sat on the bed, still shirtless, but now grinning at her. Jack crooked his finger at her, wanting her closer. She stayed where she was, letting him think she wouldn't move. When he frowned, she laughed softly and stepped closer until she stood between them. Her heart raced as Jack calmly pulled the towel off her and coaxed her down on the bed between them. Lying next to her, his head cradled in his palm, Jack softly ran his fingertips from her neck down her body as far as his arm could reach.

"What made you scream like you did, babe? You said you were okay with us using our key to come in at any time," Jack asked her.

"Okay. See it from my point of view. I'm dozing in my own bathroom and don't hear you come in. When I open my eyes, I'm half asleep and see two men standing in front of me." She frowned at them. "How did you expect me to react?"

"We're sorry we scared you, honey. We just missed you when we got home." Chase tried to smooth things over with her. "We came over to try and convince you to come home with us. We have that big bed just waiting for all three of us to crash in."

Randa debated whether or not to say something about what she had found when she first got home. She decided it was probably nothing and concentrated on them. She would worry about the other stuff later.

"So, now that you've scared the crap out of me, got my dog in trouble, and have me naked, how on earth will you make it up to me?" she teased them.

Chase lowered his lips to her ear and whispered to her. "Well, if you dress in enough clothes to be decent and return with us, we would love to make you scream a few times before you pass out." He followed his statement with a nibble on her earlobe and swirling his tongue along the shell of her ear.

Randa's head was turned in Jack's direction. She loved that he watched them, knew it excited him. The feel of Chase's mouth on her, hearing him whisper to her as Jack looked on turned her blood hot. When he picked up the hand closest to him and pulled one finger into his mouth where he sucked on it slowly, then ran his tongue along the length, she gasped.

Randa was on sensory overload with one hot mouth working her ear, down to her neck, then up to her lips. And the other mouth surrounding her finger, sucking and licking as though her finger were a cock? She so wanted them to continue with their ministrations, but knew that tomorrow would be a headache to get through if she didn't get to sleep soon. The donors would be in again. Today was just the beginning of a three day process she went through with every potential donor.

With a moan, she raised her head and took Chase's lips. He growled at her and deepened it. But when he left her mouth again and began to move to her chin then down her neck, heading toward her chest, she grabbed his head and held him where he was.

"As much as I want this delicious torture to go on, I can't. I have donors to give tours to and spend the day with. If I don't get to sleep soon, I'm going to be so punchy tomorrow," she said disappointedly.

***

Despite his knowing she couldn't stay too late, Chase couldn't seem to tear himself away from Randa. But then again, he definitely didn't want to do the "quickie" route. It was just not in him to rush perfection. And she certainly was exactly that. Not just in the bedroom but in every aspect of her life. What she did for The Haven and how much of herself she put into it, made him love her even more. She was very passionate about it and protective like a mama bear. Haven was lucky she was in their corner. He dropped his head to her chest and just rested his forehead there, trying to slow his breathing. Never had a mere kiss or a simple nuzzle taken him as far as it did with Randa.

Her skin was so soft, and begged for his attention. Chase put all his energy into coming down from what seemed like constant arousal whenever he was around her. He and Jack joked all the time that the mere thought of her and they were both ready to pound nails with their dicks. As she ran her fingers through his hair and Jack's they both groaned. As Chase mentally shook his head to try and clear it, Jack spoke.

"Babe, we understand, really. But do you want to grab your stuff for the morning and stay with us anyhow? We missed you tonight. If we can't have you the way we want you, then give us what we can have. Please? You know Baby loves it when we have a sleepover," Jack teased her.

As she laughed, she responded, "Fine, you got me. I need that, too. I love being tangled in both of your arms and legs. Let me get my clothes for tomorrow figured out and one of you can bring Baby."

* * *

Randa got up and walked to her closet. She knew her men were lounging, watching as she moved around the room with not a stitch of clothing on, and loving it. They had done wonders for her self-esteem. A few months ago she never would have done this. Philip had continually asked her to cover up. He had never allowed her to fully undress when they had sex. Sure, it hurt at the time, still did in fact, but since she thought she should have tried harder to lose the weight for him, she'd had no right to complain. She knew better now.

She wondered what they were thinking as she gathered her things. It was as if she were seeing herself through their eyes. She could almost see her own skin as the light in the room made her glow. She laughed to herself when she thought of those sculptures in a museum of the goddesses. She reminded herself of the

Goddess of Fertility. The roundness of her hips gave no doubt that she was a lush woman. Her breasts may not have been the breasts of a twenty year old, but they were lovely and firm. Her nipples were a coral brown shade, areolas perfect in size and made to be sucked on. *Now to see their reaction*, she giggled inwardly.

With the clothes she was to wear the next day in hand, she turned and saw them staring at her. Both of them had tents in the front of the trousers and a satisfied smile came over her face. Feminine pride that she did that to them overtook her. The thought that she and she alone, could affect them was empowering. She sauntered to the bed and laid the clothes out. Then she turned and grabbed sweats and a t-shirt to get her next door. As she pulled her boy short panties on, they shook their head. She assumed they didn't want her wearing any, so she took them off and decided to wear them tomorrow. Next came a bra and after they again shook their head, she tossed it with the panties. She pulled the t-shirt on and smoothed it down. With their eyes glued to her chest, her nipples hardened, begging for their touch.

Back in her closet, she grabbed the heels she would wear with the dress pants and blouse. As she stood there, they had not moved. Well, their hands had moved but the rest of their bodies were right where she left them. She watched both of them as they stroked themselves for her. She knew they weren't intentionally trying to get her to change her mind, but they were. She so wanted to rip their clothes off and make love to both of them, but they knew during the week, she had to be on her toes for Haven. There was just too much riding on her. Because they were unknowingly torturing her, she decided turnabout was fair play. She used one hand to cup a breast, pinching the nipple through her shirt while the other delved into her sweats and brought a finger to her clit and rubbed, making her knees weaken. When they each sucked in a sharp breath, she pulled her finger out and sucked on it. Then she calmly grabbed up her clothes and walked out of the room. On the way down the stairs, she called out that one of them should grab Baby and she would see them next door.

***

Chase and Jack looked at each other and laughed. They jumped off the bed and rushed out of the room after her. Jack called to Baby, clipped on her leash, and was at the door waiting for Randa and Chase. Randa grabbed her purse and keys and was about to grab the clothes on the hangers, but Chase beat her to it. She had her heels dangling from one hanger so there was nothing for her to carry. They left the house after locking it up tight, walked down the steps and, with Randa in between them, started walking to their house. She slipped a hand in the back pocket of each of them and gave each a squeeze. They both looked down at her and grinned, enjoying her playfulness, but warned her they would retaliate soon. They entered the house with laughter ringing out in the darkness.

***

He could not believe what he just saw. The meek Miranda he used to know was not the same. He remembered her as insecure and frumpy. It was amazing what a few years did for her. He guessed maybe she was so desperate for attention she had to throw herself at not one, but two men. What a slut. But he wasn't as convinced as he'd like to believe that she was desperate. The woman seemed confident, despite her size. And here he was thinking of giving her the opportunity of a lifetime of having connections. Connections she could use for that pathetic animal shelter she worked at.

He had liked messing with the rose bush out front of her house. If he remembered right—not that he cared at all—the two shades of roses meant something to her sentimentally. So, to maybe kill one, he found quite funny. Maybe he could come back and do the other one. He hadn't meant to leave the gate to the pool open. He'd been in the back and got pissed she had a great pool, but had not lost any of the weight he used to tell her she needed to lose. When he left the backyard, his only thought was to punish her by killing the rose bushes, but had only enough time to do the one before a neighbor could catch him.

He pulled on one of the gloves he'd brought and pulled out the envelope he'd done up special for her. He also grabbed the bottle of bleach he'd brought with him. With a last look around, he quickly walked up to her front door and stuck the envelope in her door so that when she opened the door the next day, it would fall to the floor. Then he went back down the steps, uncapped the bottle, and liberally poured the liquid around the base of both rose bushes. He knew enough about plants to be sure that by morning they would be dead. Just for the hell of it he tossed the bottle into the brush near her garage.

With a smile and a confident walk, he headed back to his Cougar, slipped in, and quietly shut the door. He wasn't worried about anyone hearing the engine. He took excellent care of the vehicle, since it was his proof he'd made it in society, and knew it would be almost silent upon starting and even when he drove off.

***

Randa's day had been stressful enough with babysitting potential investors. She took a quick break then went outside for some fresh air and to check her messages. She saw that Syun had left her a message to call as soon as she could. With a heavy sigh, she dialed her friend and then had to sit on the bench as Syun went into what she'd found. Her heart beat faster when she was told it was no accident, no animal digging. This was deliberate and malicious. When Syun said she had a strong guess that bleach was used to kill the flowers, all the blood drained from Randa's head. It would take some time for the bleach to render itself inactive. In the meantime, the surrounding area would be removed and treated with fertilizer and fresh soil.

Randa didn't give herself time to dwell on the situation. She couldn't. She had a job to do and investors to schmooze. Despite her heavy heart and confusion, she would put all of herself into getting the money that Haven needed. Too many relied on her to be professional and not allow her personal life to affect her job. She would dwell on it later.

Chapter Fifteen

Finally, they were satisfied with all of the numbers given, the day to day operations, and even the staff. Randa wouldn't know for sure if these high number donors would be writing a check for a couple of weeks, but for the amount they were expected to donate, she could be patient. If they came through, there would be more animals in the community that could benefit.

She walked into her office and collapsed in her chair. As she sat there and started going through the research information she'd put together for herself, she didn't see the heads that peered around the corner at her. Oblivious as she was, she didn't realize the alluring sight she made to the men that loved her. She certainly couldn't have predicted that they would see through her act that all was well. She picked up her phone, her need for any news. Then she changed her mind and set the phone down again.

***

Chase and Jack both finished with their patients almost at the same time. They knew they only had moments before another patient would need to be seen, so they hoofed it to Randa's office to check on her. They had both met the potential donors and, despite their gratitude, they weren't happy with how much Randa was stressed. They stood there watching as she looked at her phone as if she were about to make a phone call. They saw the tired expression on her face combined with a look of fear. They recognized it well from pet owners who hear bad news about their animals.

Jack moved forward to her side and crouched down to be eye level. "Randa? You okay, sweetie?"

"What? Oh yeah. I'm fine, Jack." The look on her face said otherwise, but Chase wasn't completely sure he could translate her expression.

Chase looked intently at her and didn't quite believe her. "Babe, you know you can come to us for anything, right? You know we're not just pretty boys," he teased.

"Pretty boys? You two are definitely not 'pretty boys', my loves. You are my hot lovers, my friends. And I cannot wait for the entire world to know you're mine and mine only."

They both looked at her, knowing she was changing the subject. There was something going on and she wasn't telling them, but they wouldn't press. Chase wanted to say something—hell, he was sure Jack did too—but they knew her well enough that she would pull away if they pushed. They would just have to exercise patience.

"So, what put that worried expression on your face?" Jack asked.

"It was nothing really. I had Syun check on my rose bushes and she found something wrong. So, nothing to worry about, just plants. Okay?"

***

Randa hoped they wouldn't ask her for any more details. She didn't want to tell them about how she thought someone had been in her backyard, or how she thought her roses were vandalized. She just had a bad feeling and now that Syun gave her the news, she was really worried. But since there wasn't anything else to go on, she didn't want to worry them. She needed to get all her info straight before she involved them. This was her problem, for now.

"All right, but you'll let us know if we can help, right?" Chase softly asked.

"Of course. Oh, by the way, have you two thought any about moving into my house? I think we'd all be more comfortable there, with the pool and all. My backyard is a little bigger than yours and my master bedroom is plenty big enough for that massive bed you have." She gave a valiant effort to change the subject.

The subject change was a weak diversion, but a valid one. Now that she brought it up she wondered if maybe one of their friends could be looking to move out of an apartment and the house could be rented to them. That way they wouldn't have to try and sell the house they just bought, because she had to admit she could picture their bed in her room. It might be a tight fit, but wow the fun times they could have would be endless.

"Why don't we go to Flavour tonight and talk about it over dinner? It would give you a chance to see Colton again, and none of us would have to cook," Jack suggested.

"Oh, I like that. You know how to win me over. Offer up a chance to see my son."

***

Randa and her men sat at a table that had been pulled off from the others. Sort of the VIP treatment. Big enough for four, but with plates only for three, they enjoyed a lovely meal prepared by Colton himself. He had even sat with them briefly to make sure they were being treated well and to chat about the party coming up.

After some long phone calls and in depth conversations Colton was slowly getting used to the idea of her dating two guys. He told her it wasn't so much the number of guys being the issue as it was the timing. He kind of laughed awkwardly and admitted he never would have thought that she would date them at the same time, literally. That he just had to keep telling himself that the only thing that mattered was that she was happy. And as long as those two guys made her happy, everything else could be bypassed. He teased her saying he just hoped that Bradley was just as easy going. As soon as Colton found out about the relationship, he told her he had called to warn Bradley. He knew she would be calling his big brother to tell him and to invite him home to meet them. And he basically learned from the conversation going around the table, they would be moving in with her soon.

When Ashley approached and asked to speak to Colton, she looked around the table at Randa and the guys and blushed. Apparently, Colton had told her about his mom's boyfriends. Colton had eventually told her how they had met when she began working for him just after her parents passed away. He had also explained that she had a medical condition and he'd known about it when she was hired, however it was something she didn't want the other employees to know about. Colton then admitted he had feelings for her. Though they had only been dating a few months and he could see a serious relationship forming, but he could feel her holding back for some reason. He had told Randa she insisted her past was pretty nondescript, but *something* was influencing her. All he knew was there was something very special about her and he vowed to himself to be patient. In the meantime, they were certainly going to have fun.

Colton excused himself and headed in Ashley's direction. Randa watched as her son placed his hand at the girl's waist and gave a slight squeeze. She saw Ashley look their way again, so she smiled gently. Randa could see Ashley was falling in love with her son. She was so proud of the men her boys had grown into. They were respectful of others, always had a cheerful smile on their faces, and were protective of those they loved. She wasn't sure Colton had even admitted it to himself yet, but he was falling fast. The way his body crowded Ashley signaled Colton was being territorial. But since she was an employee, he didn't make it obvious to the passersby that they were a couple. Just a boss having a conversation with a hostess.

Colton approached their table again to let them know he had another customer that wanted to meet the chef. His face was slightly pink. Despite the notoriety of his restaurant and the popularity, he had not quite come to grips with his celebrity status in the community. But he was taking it all in stride. Randa was so proud of all he'd accomplished. When he made a point of talking to their server and taking their bill, she knew what he was doing. Just as she suspected, he wasn't going to allow them to pay for their meal. And, by the looks on Chase and Jack's faces, they weren't happy about it. With a smile, she placed her hand on Chase's arm and shook her head. Neither Chase nor Jack were happy, but there wasn't too much they could do about it.

The trio left the restaurant with their decision made. The men would have a couple of friends come help them move the custom bed to Randa's house and then move her bed to their house. They decided to put their dressers in the small office room off of Randa's bedroom. In fact, if they put all three of their dressers in there, it would give them as much room as possible for the custom bed.

***

On the way home, Jack called Sam and asked him if he was still interested in renting their house. When he was told the amount the rent would be, Sam jumped at it. The condo he was currently renting was a few hundred more and he had no privacy. He had told Jack there had been times when he left the club with a submissive and could not even take her to his place due to the paper thin walls, so he ended up having to go to a hotel.

Off the phone, Jack turned to the other two and said it was set. Randa had said they needed to come up with a rental agreement to protect all involved. At first, Chase fought it by saying Sam was their friend and he wouldn't screw them, but after Randa re-worded it so that the rental agreement would be good for both parties, and Jack agreed, Chase lamented.

Back at the house, they had decided since they would be doing the moving into Randa's house soon, they would survive the living arrangements a little longer. It wasn't what they would like, but they were pretty sure they could handle it. None of them wanted to admit that to not be pressed against the body of your loved one was hell. Sure, they slept okay, but when you know more comfort is a house away it can mess with your mind and not allow you to get the quality of sleep your body needed. But then again, it wouldn't be too much longer.

They all knew if the men walked her to her door they would want long kisses goodnight and then it would get hot and heavy. That would lead to them not sleeping in separate houses. Jack was the first to say good night. He leaned back against the car, his hands framed her face, and he brought her lips to his. Gently, he sipped, feeling the silkiness of her lips against his, her soft breasts pressed against his chest, her hips pushing into the "v" of his own. Chase had stepped behind her and was pressing his front to her back.

***

Randa pulled her head away from Jack and dropped her forehead to his chest, trying to catch her breath. Chase, impatient for his turn, spun her body and his around so he was now in the same position Jack was in. His head dropped to assault her mouth. No gentleness, just taste. She could feel the urgency in his kiss. Jack immediately lined his body to her back and reached around to cup her breasts as Chase pulled her hips closer to his. He ground himself into her, making her moan. Jack went to press kisses to the side of her neck.

Randa's body was like dry tinder to the flame of her men. They knew exactly what to do to get her to lose control, knew how to make her mindless and turn to putty in their hands. But not tonight. Cold showers would be very popular in their houses this evening. Her lips released, Randa extracted herself from their embraces and looked at them one last time before whispering goodnight and walking to her front door.

The night out and the subsequent kisses had allowed her to momentarily forget about her roses. When she passed the holes in the ground, she stopped and stared. Her eyes welled up with unshed tears while she wondered who would do that. At the top of the stairs, she looked down to the men still standing by the car waiting until she was safely in her house. Key in the lock, she opened the door and a long white envelope fell to the floor. Curious, she stooped and picked it up. She waved one final time to her men, then closed and locked the door, envelope in hand.

Her name was on the outside of the envelope. With a fingernail, she ripped at the sealed seam. She pulled out a sheet of paper and gasped as she read the vicious words. Stunned, she sat on the floor as Baby came running to greet her. Before Baby could so much as sniff the paper, Randa snatched it up, folded it, and put it back in the envelope. She wasn't even sure what to do with it.

Baby sensing her mistress was distressed, lay next to her, and placed her head in Randa's lap. Randa curled herself into Baby's body seeking comfort. The words on the paper horrified her. She was scared there was someone out there who could write something like that about her, and then threaten her as they had.

***

He sat in his car a little further down the street. He was furious when she hadn't been home earlier to read his little note. When a car pulled up and they all got out, it incensed him even more. He had to sit there as the two men pawed at the woman he needed to make his career successful. The words slut and whore filled his head.

He'd arrived earlier, wanting to see the damage the bleach had done to the rose bushes. Infuriated that they had been dug up and the holes were now empty, he'd wondered how she'd done it. She'd obviously been working all day, so she must have had a landscaper take care of it for her. He had wished he could have seen her face when she read his little letter to her. She was sure to know now that her being with him was certainly not an option. How could *he* be associated with someone who so shamelessly allowed two men to use their body, at the same time no less? Well, he would have to make sure his next step was an eye opener for her.

He started up his car, drove by her house slowly, and smiled. He knew inside that big, lovely house was a woman that was now seeing the error of her ways, that now saw how much she would miss out on by playing the whore. Oh yes, she would see it, and maybe even beg him for a chance in the process.

***

Their moving day arrived very bright and early for Chase, Jack and their sexy as hell girlfriend. Chase got to stay in bed as Jack had gotten up extra early to make a quick run to town then go over to Randa's to wake her up with a hot cup of coffee and homemade cinnamon rolls from Kitty's shop.

Chase was just about to leave their house when his phone buzzed, letting him know he had a text. He had Max on his leash and knew the little guy was barely containing his excitement to see his buddy, Baby. He opened it up and saw the message from Jack. He chuckled thinking why couldn't the man just wait for him to come next door? That thought vanished when he actually read it. Randa's roses were gone? *Weird*. They both knew why the roses meant so much to her. He guessed Jack wanted him to ask Randa, since she was more receptive to his brand of pushing than Jack's.

He walked into her—soon to be *their*—house and headed toward the stairs, only to be tackled by Baby. He let Max off his leash and they both engaged him in play after a quick greeting. She was in a particularly playful mood. Chase had been playing rougher with her lately, without Randa seeing of course. Baby had taken it upon herself to play rough right back, as long as her mama wasn't anywhere around. Anyone who thought dogs weren't smart sure needed to meet Baby.

Finally, Baby's playful mood temporarily appeased, Chase was able to extract himself from her and head up the stairs. He got to the master bedroom and stopped in the doorway. Before him was enough to give him an instant erection. Jack was sitting on the bed, back leaning against the headboard, legs splayed out. Randa, nude as the day she was born, seated on his lap. Chase couldn't see Jack's hands and assumed they were very attentive to her breasts. What he *could* see made him lick his lips and walk toward them, undressing as he went.

***

Randa had woken to the smell and sight of three of the four things she loved most: Jack, a steaming cup of coffee, and a plate with Kitty's cinnamon rolls. The coffee and rolls could be re-heated. What had her licking her lips more was Jack. She didn't say a word, just sat up and pulled her t-shirt over her head and dropped it to the floor. Then she delved under the covers and pulled her boy shorts down her legs and dropped them too. When

235

she leaned back and braced her body on her arms, she looked at him and just smiled. She was so proud of herself. She didn't even hesitate to initiate and strip in front of him. In the daylight was even more impressive.

She was hoping he would take her up on the offer, and he looked like he was sure to not disappoint her. Her eyes tracked him as he placed the plate and mug on the bedside table and slowly undressed. The moment he climbed onto the bed, she told him to sit up against the headboard. Then she proceeded to climb on his lap and lower herself onto him. A recent trip to the GYN doctor negated the need for a condom. With Jack and Chase she felt incredibly sexy and confident. She was slowly coming to terms with the fact that they loved her few extra pounds and the softness of her belly, that her being a size two was not necessary.

Jack pulled her down to his mouth and kissed her hard, tongue seeking out and dueling with hers. With her chest now resting on his, he had her in the perfect position for Chase to join them. She made a small sound as she felt cold on her rosebud entry, then Chase's hands on her hips, holding her still as he slowly pushed past the tight ring of muscles. Inch by powerful inch, he worked his way into her. She felt Jack's hand at her entrance, working her clit to keep her excitement going, not that she needed it. She seemed to be ready all the time around them.

Simultaneously, Jack and Chase began to move their hips. Jack's moved up then down. Chase's pulled back then pushed forward. Randa was not given a moment to think as she was bombarded with multiple zings of electricity. She loved the feeling of fullness she got when they were both inside her, loved their give and take thrusts, always filling her. They all knew this couldn't be dragged out, but they were definitely going to make it an awesome time, that was for sure.

As if they were dancing partners, the two men moved in perfect synchronization. Randa was getting closer to falling over with their movements and Jack's hand making her twitch because of his pressing on her clit. She wanted to make sure her men were taken care of and yet they stubbornly held out for her. Every time she was out voted when it came to her climaxes.

Steadily, the pace they set sped up. Randa was trying to prove she was just as stubborn, but Jack wasn't having it. He pinched her clit, which rushed her climax even more and soon after had her cry out and tighten in their arms. She knew her reaction would spur them on and when Chase's hips began to piston, she was not disappointed. Jack's pushed up and then came down. She could feel them thicken and knew their bodies were rushing to the point of no return. She loved the sensations they both evoked in her and couldn't get enough. Their twin shouts triggered Randa again and she joined in with another climax so powerful that she fell on Jack's chest and couldn't move.

Chase gingerly pulled from her and Jack did the same. Randa moved slightly so that Chase could lie down and sandwich her next to Jack. The trio was breathing hard, trying to calm their racing heartbeats. Randa could feel the sweat on her body begin to cool, keeping her nipples pebbled hard, which Jack continued to play with.

That, in turn, kept sending jolts of energy to her core, eliciting low whimpers.

"Now *that* is the way to wake a girl up. So, do you plan on doing that every morning?" Randa teased and huffed into Jack's chest.

"Baby, we are definitely out to keep you happy," Jack murmured.

Chase followed up with, "And if *that* is what it takes to keep you happy, then absolutely we will have to engage that tactic whenever possible."

They lay there for a while, recovering, until Randa caught sight of the clock. She knew Sam and Pac were due to arrive in half an hour, and there was no way she was going to get caught with her pants around her ankles. Or rather, all her clothes off and her body draped over their friends. She frantically got out of bed and rushed to the bathroom to take a quick shower and yelled to them to get dressed. She heard them chuckle, but guessed they wouldn't take the chance of banishment to the couch on their first night living with her.

With maybe about ten minutes to spare, Randa made it downstairs to see both men drinking coffee and eating a cinnamon roll. They had kindly heated her coffee up and had it waiting for her. She was sipping the coffee when Chase asked her about the roses.

"Randa, what happened to your rose bushes? There are huge holes where they used to be," he asked nonchalantly.

"Syun is bringing new ones. For some reason the other two had died. She's not sure how, but she said

238

she'd let me know," she answered off handedly. She hated lying to them, but worrying them was less desirable.

At that moment, the doorbell rang and she rushed to answer it. Baby was already there, hackles raised in preparation of protecting her mistress. Randa told her to back up and sit. She did so, reluctantly. When Randa opened the door, Baby made to move, but Randa just put a hand up and said "sit" sternly, so she did. Better to listen to her mama, than to get no treats.

Randa watched to make sure Baby kept her manners. Sam said not a word, but brought himself to Baby's level and slowly extended his hand for inspection. There was just something dark about the man. Not that she would ever think he'd hurt an animal or her, but it was almost as if she could see the power oozing from him, like he had complete control and never lost it. She relaxed when Sam smiled at Baby and when the dog licked his hand and sidled up next to him. It was almost as if the she was flirting with him.

Randa let her gaze travel from his wonderfully thick hair down to the biker boots he was wearing. His jeans were well worn and just tight enough. He hadn't shaved, so he had a sexy, just-out-of-bed look about him. When their hands met, he didn't let go, holding hers slightly longer than he should have. She couldn't seem to make herself let go of his, and he chuckled low when he finally did release hers. He looked at her with just a raised eyebrow, causing her to blush.

"Sam! Knock it off. She's not into that, and you know it," Chase growled at him.

Randa looked behind her and saw Jack and Chase were now standing a few feet away and both of them were frowning at their friend, who still had not said anything and was looking at them with a smile in his eyes. She suddenly remembered them mentioning he was into kinky sex and something about submission? Her blush deepened and she backed away until she had backed into her men.

"Don't worry, little lady, I know who you're into. I'm just messing with you," he continued as if his friends weren't in the room. "But if you ever feel the need to be spanked, you'll let me know, yeah?"

Jack stepped around her and made to swing at Sam, who ducked and then they good naturedly punched each other. Chase stepped up next and they unabashedly did the man-hug routine, slapping each other on the back. The playfulness relieving the tension. When Sam walked around them toward her, she stepped backward until she almost tripped on Baby, who was now growling at Sam in warning. Sam stopped where he was, unsure what to do. Max had entered the room and meekly sat next to Baby, not impressed by Sam since they already knew each other. Randa stood in front of Baby and spoke to her in a firm voice, which brooked no argument from the canine.

"Baby, this is Sam. Be nice, or there will be no swimming for you any time soon. Got it? Sam is a good guy."

***

Jack watched as Sam looked at the large dog with a bit of unease in his eyes. It was kind of humorous really. He knew once Baby accepted someone she would behave just as her name suggested. Plus, looking at how Randa, this tiny slip of a woman, ran roughshod over this massive dog and the dog seemed to understand and obey.

"She expects you to scratch behind her ears to show your gratitude for not eating you," Randa teased him.

"How did you do that?" he asked incredulously. "She is obviously much larger than you and yet she treats you like it's the exact opposite."

"Randa's dad used to train dogs for the military," Chase spoke up.

"Yeah, man, you should see how much Max has changed in his behavior since she's been around him," Jack laughed.

"You think you can help me with Romeo?" Sam looked down at the tiny woman in front of him. "He's not as big as this pretty girl, but he is having issues right now."

"I love dogs, big and small. Maybe after you move in, we can have him come over to play with Max and Baby?"

"Holy shit! The play on the name is classic," he laughed.

Jack led the way into the kitchen where Jack gave Sam a cup of coffee and offered a cinnamon roll. Sam took a bite and moaned loudly. The others laughed at him, only because they had felt the same way when they ate theirs. He devoured the one and reached for a second, which he practically inhaled. Then he spoke.

"Where the *hell* did you get these?" Sam could not contain another moan. "I have never had a cinnamon roll this awesome."

"My friend owns La Dulce and Jack made her open shop early this morning to make them for us," Randa explained. "I'll be sure to let her know you liked them."

"Wait, you know the owner of La Dulce? I love that place. The snicker doodle cupcakes are ones my drivers cream over when I buy a dozen assorted. They actually do rock, paper, scissors to see who gets them."

"Yes, they are amazing," Randa laugh.

Jack's phone buzzed with a text. "Pac just arrived."

In the living room, Jack pushed the curtain aside and watched as Pac stepped out of the truck and raised a hand in greeting. Jack couldn't believe his friend still drove that rust bucket. He remembered Iain saying that the engine purred like a kitten, but Pac refused to have any body work done to it. He watched as Pac swaggered his way to the house, not in any particular hurry.

***

Randa, having joined Jack at the window, watched the big man. He looked like he was in his mid forties, even though she had been told that he was only forty. Randa figured since he was in construction and outside a lot it would be a plausible explanation as to why he seemed older than he was. His hair was prematurely grey, but looked full and thick. He looked very commanding, but when he stopped in front of them, his craggy face broke into a smile that truly changed his entire look. She hoped never to be on the receiving end of his non-smiling look.

Randa was a little self-conscious as Pac came into the house and they joined the others in the kitchen. She knew his friends would all still be wondering about her. She tamped down her insecurities and the urge to defend herself against what she didn't know. Pac was making it pretty obvious he was assessing her. She didn't get the feeling, though, that it was in a negative way. She tried to convince herself she should be flattered, but being looked over—even in a good way—was a bit uncomfortable for her. It really was new to her to be admired.

She remembered Chase and Jack telling her all their friends liked curvy women too. That common desire was part of what brought them together. However, that was still something Randa was having a difficult time comprehending fully—or maybe it was believing—but she definitely wasn't going to argue about their preferences.

Pac was a large man, bulky almost. Though his muscles weren't as defined as her men's, or as Sam's appeared to be, Randa decided that Pac's strength was achieved by working hard at his job. Here was no physique by fitness club design.

She stood within the circle of Chase and Jack's arms, one arm around her waist, the other along her shoulder. It was as if they were still staking their claim on her. Totally unnecessary. Their friends—no matter their looks—were not Chase and Jack. And she even got the sense none of them would ever act inappropriately towards her. True, she could find other men attractive, but she felt not even a twinge of anything to even be slightly tempted by them. She couldn't wait to see how many of her friends fell for her men's friends.

She couldn't figure out why she was so nervous with their friends around though. Pac was a gentle giant. And Sam? Any man that let Baby cuddle with him was okay with her. Maybe it was just a case of her being the only woman in a room full of attractive men?

"Randa, you cannot believe what 'Chatty Cathys' you've turned these two into," Pac drawled, smiling.

"Pac, I will have to take your word for it. By the way, it's awful nice of both of you to give up time to help them move in here. Uh, have you had coffee, Pac? Are you hungry?" Randa rambled, her nerves got the better of her.

"I've had my breakfast, yes, but wouldn't turn down a cup of coffee."

***

Chase stared after Randa as she practically rushed to get the coffee. The four friends didn't say a word at first, but then Pac asked about the holes in the front yard. Were they putting in new shrubs or had some just been removed? This got Chase concerned again. The last time he remembered seeing the rose bushes they seemed fine. Why, all of a sudden, did they need to be replaced or whatever her friend was doing to them?

He and Jack would have to get her to talk to them later, much later. For now, they walked into through house so that Pac could do his measuring. The man was a whiz at taking mental measurements. They would need to make sure that when they dismantled the custom that it could actually fit in the master bedroom.

***

Randa followed the sound of the deep voices up the stairs into her room. She blushed knowing not too long ago they had been in that mussed bed having sex and she had to wonder if the other men were guessing what had happened. She handed the mug to Pac and he smiled in gratitude, sipped, and nodded. Apparently, he took his coffee black and lightly sweet like her guys.

She decided to get Max and Baby from their confines and let them outside to work off energy they built up while sleeping. Besides, they would need to be kept out of the way when the moving got started. At first, Chase and Jack had been worried about Max and the pool, but after a few words with Max, and him watching Baby, he caught on the pool was only allowed when one of his owners was around. No person, no pool. Her men were amazed at how quickly the wild dog took to the rule.

She stood staring out at the two dogs running and playing while she thought about the letter that was in her door the other night. She had been wracking her brain to think of who could think such vile things about her. Sure there were plenty of past relationships that ended badly, but she just couldn't convince herself any of them capable of the things done. She had been so floored she hadn't shown anyone the letter, but hadn't gotten rid of it either. She didn't want to think about it. Today was a day for new beginnings.

Arms wrapped around her waist from behind, making her jump slightly. She must have been so deep in thought she didn't hear Chase come out onto the deck. His head settled in the curve of her neck.

"You okay, babe? You still want this, right?" he asked her in a low, soothing voice.

"What? Of course I do. I want nothing more than to have you and Jack with me every day and every night," she answered with a smile, her voice husky.

"Something is rolling around in that pretty head of yours. I know you're not ready to talk, but you need to tell us what's going on."

Randa turned in his arms and looked up at him. She had pegged Chase as the more perceptive one of her two men. Not that Jack didn't notice things, but it was Chase that seemed to catch the deep down things. She didn't want them to think she was hiding anything from them or that she didn't trust them, but resigned as she was, she would not get into it today. Tomorrow would come soon enough.

"I know, love, and I will. I just have to work something out in my head. Okay? As soon as I do, I promise the three of us will talk about it. It's not anything bad, just something puzzling right now."

"Okay, I'll let you have your time to do your thing, but I can't promise to stay out of it indefinitely," he warned her.

They went back into the house, leaving the dogs outside. Jack was coming toward them with a bucket of water for the dogs. Since they would be locked outside for the majority of the day, they would need a lot of water, and drinking the pool water was out of the question. Chase held Randa still so Jack could press against them and take her lips in a quick, but satisfying kiss. At the sound of a throat clearing, the trio pulled apart, both men chuckling as Randa felt her cheeks burn and ducked out of the room. Why she was so skittish she didn't know. It's not like they were caught in a more compromising situation. She admonished herself she should be more laid back. Two gorgeous, hot men loved her and wanted her. No more playing innocent virgin.

She was still giving herself a pep talk about her men as she climbed the stairs to her bedroom. Pretty soon, this house would be filled with not only her things, but theirs. A warm glow spread through her body. No more coming home and spending lonely nights watching movies alone, or making meals for one, or sleeping alone. Baby went a ways to providing companionship, but it just wasn't the same.

In the master bedroom, Randa was busy stripping the bed with the plan of taking all the linens to the laundry room to run them through the washer. She wasn't sure, but thought maybe Sam could use the bedding—if he didn't mind that they weren't new.

Sam walked into the room, and for some reason, the room got very small. He helped her gather up the bedding, their hands meeting when a pillow case fell to the floor. She knelt down to gather it up, and he chuckled. From her knees on the floor, she looked up at him, wide-eyed. *What was he...Oh no!* Was he thinking she was..? Getting to her feet quickly, she made to leave the room. Sam grabbed her arm to stop her.

"I'm sorry, Randa. I didn't mean to embarrass you." He sounded contrite. "I have a hard time looking at such an attractive woman without seeing the possibilities. It won't happen again, I promise."

"Sam, I know what you're into. Chase and Jack told me. I also heard about your meeting my friend Josie at Haven. Remember? Can I ask if you're interested in her?" She crossed her arms over her chest and took the stance of a protective mama bear.

Sam looked down at her. "Randa, as I will not intrude on your personal life with Chase and Jack, I would ask the same courtesy. I mean no disrespect. Am I interested in her? I do not know. I am interested in getting to know her better to see if there is a mutual interest. Does that answer suffice?"

He had looked down at her with such a stern look on his face, she had almost felt like she had disappointed him. She was tempted to apologize for her behavior for some reason. Damn it, he must be using his Dom powers on her. She laughed and then covered her mouth. He looked at her again, this time crossing *his* arms over his massive chest, along with an eyebrow raised.

**

Jack found their standoff amusing. He and Chase watched as Sam came to the conclusion he wasn't going to be able to influence Randa, that she wasn't as submissive as he may have thought. Randa stood there looking scared, yet determined not to show it. Finally, a reluctant, easy-going grin crossed Sam's face. He had met his match. With no warning to Randa, Sam gathered Randa into his arms. She stood there stiffly until she listened to what he was saying to her. Chase and Jack couldn't hear his whispered words to her, but a relaxed look came over her features. She returned his hug and then jumped away from him when she noticed her men standing there watching.

"Hey don't mind us. We're just going to be moving things around so that we can move in with our woman." Jack tried to act nonchalant, steeling his features to not show his amusement.

"Absolutely, you just let us know if we get in your way." Chase mastered his expression too.

"Oh no, it's not what you think at all!"

Jack saw how Randa reacted and remembered her telling them about boyfriends in the past that tried to act possessive—put any and all blame on her—then would try and say that she couldn't stay faithful and break up with her, followed by the insult directed at her weight. So here she reacted the only way she knew, which was to come to them, wring her hands, and start to explain.

Jack knew Randa would have walls they would have to tear down. She had warned them relapses would happen. When he looked at Chase, Jack could see the same sadness mixed with anger he was sure was in his own expression. Jack wanted to get the names of every man she'd ever dated and rip their tongues out for anything they said to her to convince her she wasn't worthy of being treated anything less than a goddess. Then he and Chase could lock her in their room and go through every supposed flaw those men pointed out to her and show her they were not flaws but things that needed to be treasured, paid homage to, loved until she couldn't speak because her voice was hoarse from screaming in pleasure. Sam looked at Jack and Chase, nodded his head in Randa's direction then left the room wordlessly.

Chapter Sixteen

Chase and Jack turned back to Randa. She was standing there, very upset and for once speechless. She looked like she had so much to say, but wasn't sure how to word it. Her hands were entwined and were alternating between red and white with how tightly she was wringing them. She had convinced herself they were upset with her. Instantly, they rushed to her and gathered her in their arms. Jack wrapped his arms around her shoulders to drag her close to his chest, Chase's around her waist to hold her still between them. She started to say something, but Chase interrupted her.

"Baby, you didn't do anything wrong. We saw what happened. We know what we saw was perfectly innocent," he reassured her.

"He's right, Randa. We trust you and Sam implicitly. We know you're not the type to act like that. And Sam? Just because he's in that lifestyle, doesn't mean he'd jump anything that comes across his path," Jack said.

"Really? You believe me? I would never do that, ever!"

"Randa, the men you dated in the past were losers. They didn't know what a great woman they had and when they gave you up, we're sure they suffered. No way could any woman compare to you."

As Jack was talking to her, Chase's hands were running along her arms. He could feel her body loosen and begin to relax. Chase just couldn't believe those other men had let her get away. She was absolutely the most beautiful woman he'd ever met, and with her real curves the most sexy he'd ever gotten involved with.

"You two are a dream come true. Do you know how much I love you both?"

"We know, babe. We are the lucky ones, though. How you can take on two men is amazing. Most women would think it a novelty, but you? You are so up for the challenge of us." Jack pressed his mouth to her cheek.

Chase did the same to the other cheek and teased her. "Definitely. You are such a brave lady."

***

Pac and Sam came into the room and started clapping and whistling their approval loudly. Randa had come to the conclusion she would have to stop the blushing and being embarrassed about being caught in their arms. She might not be a Dom like Sam, and may not be intense like Pac, but she was proud of her relationship. She turned toward the men in the doorway, Chase and Jack positioning themselves behind her.

Randa stepped close to them and then realized she would have to look up, so she stepped back just a step or two. With her arms crossed over her chest, she gave the same look she gave her boys when they were teens and trying to get an attitude with her. She hoped her bravado stayed strong.

"Okay, so you've been entertained. Pac, you have your mental measurements—will the custom fit in this room?"

"What? Oh! Yes, ma'am. You'll have plenty of room as long as you keep the dressers out." He looked surprised a woman could talk down to him while looking up at him.

She turned to Sam, who didn't look quite as stunned as Pac, but stunned nonetheless. She knew enough about the BDSM world to know that Doms weren't used to being talked down to at all. It was in their alpha nature to instill respect and fear, not mouthiness. She kind of liked seeing Sam speechless.

Chase and Jack had already taken the dressers out, and the only thing left in the room was the flat screen TV on the wall and a small couch. The couch would need to come out to see what room was left over.

"Okay, so if you know the bed will fit, how about we get started on dismantling this one and figuring out if we donate it or maybe...Sam, would you want it for a guest room?"

"Well, uh, yeah, I guess it could just go into the room the custom comes out of." Again a rattled Sir Sam amused her. Maybe she had a little—*what was a female Dom? Domme, yes that was the word*—in her after all.

Randa saw the look in his eye and shook her head. No way was she going down that road with him. She had no interest in his kind of sex and was damn glad her men weren't into it either. She liked it rough from them, but not in a 'spank me, Daddy, I've been a bad girl' sort of way. No thank you.

"Well, let's get to it then. I have plans for my men and you two are just holding them up." She couldn't believe she just said that, but she certainly wasn't going to back down now.

That being said, she breezed out of the room to go and check on the dogs. She left the four men standing in the bedroom with what she hoped were stunned expressions on their faces. It was definitely empowering and she would have to remember this feeling for future reference.

***

Chase was ecstatic she was starting to come around to not caring what others thought and even becoming more confident in herself and their relationship. Not that their friends would ever think badly of them. Hell, according to society, they all should think twice for being attracted to heavier women. In fact, most of them had dated thinner women at some point of their lives until they reached a point where they couldn't deny it any longer. Add that to the fact that ménage relationships were taboo and the public definitely wouldn't approve. Not that they were looking for anyone's approval.

He looked at Sam and had to choke back a laugh at his expression. He guessed Doms weren't used to being spoken to like Randa had just done. From how Sam and Iain talked about the women at the club, if they were assertive like Randa had just acted, they were the

Dommes. He liked that his lady gave Sam something to think about.

When Chase looked at Pac there was a similar look on his face, but with one difference. There was admiration mixed in. When Pac's wife, Carla, had passed, Pac became a single dad and had put his love life on hold. Since he was surrounded by construction workers all day, he didn't have much call to interact with too many women. And when he did it was brief and business related. He could see Pac approved of how Randa was handling herself and Chase had to admit he was a bit relieved to know their friends liked her.

They worked at taking the couch out of the bedroom and out to Randa's garage temporarily until they could donate it to a local charity that helped homeless furnish the apartments they move into to get off the streets. It would be picked up the following day since Pac knew the director and they would use his truck. Next, was taking apart Randa's bed and getting it set in one of the rooms of Sam's new rental house. The custom was already in pieces, waiting to be brought next door and be put back together.

The custom did indeed fill up most of the room once it was re-assembled, but there was still room to move around comfortably. When Jack handed her the other half of the bottom sheet, she asked them where they got them. The company that made their bed had a side business of custom making sheets to fit. With the bed made and all their pillows ready for the three heads to rest on them, Pac and Sam quietly left the room and went out on the porch to talk for a bit.

Jack sat on the bed and pulled Randa between his legs. He wrapped his arms around her waist and pressed his face into her belly. Chase stood behind her and put his arms around her until his linked hands were resting on her breasts. Randa put one hand on top of Jack's head and one rested on top of Chase's hand. They stayed like that for quite a while until finally someone had to break the silence. They just didn't know it would be the dogs running into the house looking for their owners.

Chase laughed as Baby came barreling into the room with Max right behind. Pac and Sam were pulling up the rear since they hadn't meant to actually let the dogs in. They were both speaking at the same time explaining when the door to the deck was opened, Baby had pushed her way through and took off for the stairs. And Max had merely slipped between Sam's legs and followed Baby. While Baby may have held off jumping on anyone or anything, Max had other ideas. He ran into the room and jumped up and tried to tackle Chase.

**

Jack watched as Randa stepped away and knelt on the floor. Baby stepped forward cautiously. He knew their move into her house would be an adjustment for Baby, but he figured with the help of Max, things would work out just fine. He had seen how Randa was with dogs and knew if any problems came up she could handle it, effortlessly. He was sure there would be bumps in the road for them all to acclimate themselves to, but the end result would definitely be worth it.

He and Chase stood by while their lady hugged the big dog. A massive paw came up and settled on Randa's back, as if to comfort the human, when the dog was the one needing reassurance. Jack was shocked when that massive hairy head bowed and came to rest on Randa's. Owner and dog now meshed together in a moment of affection they had never witnessed before. In unison, they walked to the two females, knelt down, and wrapped their arms around human and dog. Max just sat by, panting, and looked like he had a huge grin on his face.

***

Chase looked at Pac and Sam as they stood in the doorway. His friends said not a word, but they did have grins on their faces. He could almost predict what was about to happen. Sam was going to make a wiseass comment. Out of the corner of his eye he saw Pac elbow Sam, trying to get their friend to curb his mouth, but they all knew Sam just couldn't control himself. The guys were used to it, but he didn't want Randa to get upset.

"So, now that all is well in threesome land, what do you say we fire up that grill in *my* backyard," Sam said with a wicked smile, "and build up our strength to finish this day off? Or are we going to head towards tissues and tampons? We still have dressers to move from next door to here. And that other bed needs to be put back together."

Chase and the other two men jumped when Randa, peeking from around Baby, had laughed. Sam looked at her and smirked then turned and left the room. Chase went to Randa, kissed her gently and then after clapping Pac on the back, headed downstairs in Sam's wake. He heard Pac shuffling behind him. When he and Pac got outside, they found Sam standing waiting for them.

"Chase, would Randa normally have empty containers littering her property? This bleach bottle and those holes in the front are just not adding up. I think something's going on." Sam turned to Chase. "Has Randa mentioned anything about any vandalism? I'd recognize it anywhere. When the club first opened, we had some issues similar to this."

Chase looked at the bottle of bleach that Sam pointed out to him, and then thought back to the now empty holes where the rose bushes used to be. Randa had said she had to work something out. He wondered if something had happened and she didn't tell them to not worry them. Hell, now he was worried more. He and Jack would have to address this right away before she tried to keep anything else from them. When he saw her and Jack come out of the house and begin to walk toward them, he stepped up to them and decided a diversion was needed. He nodded to Sam and knew his friend would give Pac and Jack a heads up. He swung Randa up into his arms and pressed his lips to her.

She laughed loudly, "Chase Fargo! Put me down!"

He laughed and did, pulling her into what would now be Sam's rental. But for now, their stuff was still in there. He had steaks marinating and cold beer in the fridge.

***

Jack, Sam and Pac were still outside. Sam was going over what he had found and Jack was getting upset. They didn't want to touch anything. Jack got on the phone with Trace and explained what was going on. He was told to not touch anything and he would be there shortly. Jack paced away from his friends and was tempted to go in the house and confront Randa, but he didn't want to ruin their day. Once today was done, the three of them would sort it out. Randa came out to see what was going and Jack calmed himself so he could hopefully enjoy the rest of the day.

"Randa, babe? Can you go check with Chase to see if there's enough food for one more? Trace is on his way over."

She gave him a quick kiss and turned to walk away, but Jack pulled her back and kissed her deeper and harder. After she left he happened to see a Cougar drive by. He couldn't see who was driving since the windows were tinted. Was this the car Chase had mentioned? As the car drove off, he got the first three digits of the license plate number. If the driver had kept up the slow speed, getting the plate number wouldn't have been a problem, but it was almost as if the driver knew someone was watching him.

Jack and Sam explained to Trace about the bleach bottle and the missing rose bushes, as Pac listened. They talked it over and decided they would need to keep an eye on things and Trace would only get involved if the situation progressed to more damage or if anyone got hurt.

"So, now that you've called me over unofficially, you're gonna have to feed me. I don't work for free." He took a swing at Jack, who nimbly sidestepped his advance.

"Don't push it, cop. Can't believe you're trading in doing your civic duty for steak."

"Oh shit, man, Chase is grilling? I'd whore myself out to have him feed me his steak. He is a master."

They were all laughing as Trace walked to the house. They all knew where to find Chase, at the grill working his magic. Jack asked Sam and Pac if they wouldn't mind getting Baby and Max from next door. They agreed and headed over. He and Trace passed the living room and fireplace, and was almost to the kitchen when he heard low voices. He came around the corner and saw Chase standing, facing away from him, his hands caressing the arms wrapped around his neck. Her skin was creamy and blemish free. Her fingers interlocked and clasped behind Chase's neck.

He leaned back against the opening in the room and watched as Chase lowered his head to kiss Randa. As much as he wanted to, he couldn't make himself move to interrupt their moment. He watched as Chase moved closer and ended up between her thighs. It seemed like every drop of blood in his body suddenly dropped and collected in his groin.

Graceful hands came up and threaded through Chase's dark hair. When he saw Chase's hands move down and a leg come up and wrap around Chase's hip, he cleared his throat to announce his presence. He allowed a big grin to come over his face when he heard Chase swear and thought he heard a squeak come from Randa.

"You have exactly two seconds to leave the room. Preferably out with the others, or I swear, no steak for you," Chase threatened as Randa laughed softly into his chest.

"Leave? Pal, I was just making sure you knew you had an audience. Besides, the party isn't complete until I join you. Right, baby?" Jack's voice was rough with desire.

"Damn, Jack. You had to go and say something? That was quite the show they were putting on for the rest of us. Besides, you two are the sharers of the group. Don't you want to share your pretty lady with me?"

***

Chase swore under his breath. Trace was walking on thin ice with a pick ax in his hand, but Chase knew he was harmless. They all got a kick out of razzing him and Jack at every opportunity. They would stop soon. He hoped. In the meantime, he stared daggers at Trace as he stood where he was, arms crossed over his chest, watching them with one eyebrow raised and clearly baiting him. He knew Randa wouldn't catch the meaning in Trace's expression, but Chase knew him well enough to know he was just busting balls. And it was lucky for Trace that he did know.

"You're very lucky you're my friend and I know you're screwing with us." Chase was about to say more when he heard the front door open and the other two men come in.

Chase poked his head around the corner to see Pac and Sam come in and shut the front door. They each held a dog on a leash and released them as soon as the front door was closed. Baby went running for Randa, but stopped short at the sight of Trace, her nails not finding any traction, and slid like a baseball player making a run for home base. She ended up sweeping him right off his feet and even landed on top of him when she eventually stopped. With a loud 'oomph', Trace wrapped his arms around the big dog, and then froze when she growled low in her throat, looking down at him.

Chase was glad Trace knew enough not to make any sudden moves. When Baby attempted to get off Trace, she stepped squarely on his balls. Chase and the other men in the room involuntarily reached down to reflexively protect their family jewels. He muffled a laugh as Baby immediately stood over Trace and growled longer and louder, until...

"Baby, to me. Get off him and come to me."

Randa didn't have to raise her voice, not in the slightest.

***

Much to Trace's surprise, the dog's ears dropped low on her head, her tail slunk between her legs, and she hesitantly went to her owner and slouched at her feet. She even seemed to have a look of shame on her doggie face, but it didn't stop her from glancing back at him and shooting him a dirty look. Randa had jumped down from the chair she had been in and stood in front of the dog with her hands on her hips.

"Trace, please stand slowly. Would hate for my girl here to hurt your man-bits." Randa looked down, smirking at him.

"I'd appreciate that, ma'am..." Trace couldn't begin to explain why he called her ma'am, probably because he didn't want to get the dressing down like the dog was getting.

"Okay. Well come over here and let me introduce you to this rude girl." Randa spoke impatiently, clearly not liking the 'ma'am'.

When he got closer, the dog—*shit, was her name really Baby?*—narrowed her eyes and looked at him with distrust in her canine face. Randa began to talk to the dog like she was a human. She was explaining who he was and that he was another one of 'hers', as in another member of Baby's family. Trace stood there in total disbelief when she took her paw and extended it to him as if gracing him. He looked at her, then at the others in the room, and lamely shook her paw.

Duty completed, Baby went to Chase and sat at his feet, nuzzling his hand. Chase dropped his hand to the top of her head and began to scratch behind her ears.

Since she was such a tall dog, he didn't have to reach down, she fit perfectly against his side.

Trace looked at Randa, then at the dog. Never would he have thought this tiny slip of a woman could control a dog like she just did. Especially one so much bigger than her. He didn't have any problems with Jackson, since he was trained by the police academy, but he'd heard Sam just got a little dog. He wondered how she'd do with little ones. Shit, maybe he should see if she was looking for a side job. He knew plenty of guys back at the station had talked to the department canine trainer about personal lessons, but that douche was too good for non-police dogs.

"So, if I were to come into your house again, invited of course, would she now welcome me?" Trace crossed his arms over his chest and looked down at Randa.

"Oh yes. Once she knows someone is one of 'hers', she gets it right away and has never forgotten." She laughed and went on. "She still treats my boys like brothers. Bradley isn't home as much so when she sees him she tends to be a simpering mess for a couple of hours after he comes in the house."

He looked on as Chase went around the kitchen getting together what he would need for the steaks. Unabashedly, Trace watched the trio as they did their thing. Randa went to the fridge and got the salad fixings out and started working on it. Jack, knowing Chase would need the grill as hot as he could get it, went outside to fire it up and get it ready. Randa got out two beers and a water, popped the tops off, handed them to Pac and Sam and the water to Trace, and then walked outside to check on Jack.

Trace joined Pac and Sam at the sliding glass door and watched as she went up behind Jack, slipped an arm around his waist and leaned into his side. He smirked as Jack pulled her closer, then he leaned down and she raised her head up and kissed him softly. When the other two looked at him, they all smiled at each other. Sure, they felt like voyeurs, but it was so nice to see their friends happy, finally.

Trace nudged Pac, who in turn smacked Sam upside the head. They definitely didn't want their friends to think they would no longer bust on them, so all three of them went out to join the kissing couple. With chairs pulled out—noisily—they sat to enjoy the show. At first, Jack and Randa were oblivious to their gawking, or at least Randa was since her back was to them. Trace knew Jack had never been a shy guy so he couldn't care less if they watched.

"You know, you three need to get a life. Better yet, go find your own woman and get laid, repeatedly," Chase said as he came out the door with a platter full of raw meat.

***

This caused Randa to jump out of Jack's arms and turn toward Chase. Neither man cared if she kissed one when the other was busy, or vice versa, but hearing Chase's voice startled her. When she saw their friends sitting there drinking their beers, she blushed. Again.

She saw four sets of masculine eyes staring in her direction. When she looked at Jack, he just shrugged his shoulders and smiled at her. She narrowed her eyes at him causing him to glance away, but he continued to smile. She knew then he had known they were watching and didn't tell her. With her hands on her hips, she walked away from the men to go play with the dogs. A tennis ball in hand, she started throwing the ball for Baby to lope after and for Max to try and keep up. Since they weren't going into the pool just now, the exercise would be good for them both.

***

Jack took advantage of the short time they had alone as she had walked away. Pulling a slip of paper from his pocket, he gave it to Trace. Even with only a partial plate, they should be able to find *something*. There couldn't have been *that* many Cougars out there with partial plates like what he saw. There was just something off with that car and its owner. Now that Trace had everything needed to check things out, the five friends looked out at the backyard as Randa worked the dogs. Jack knew they all saw the potential of a business for her, with how well both dogs were behaving.

He watched as Chase grabbed up the tray he had carried outside and started manning his grill. The four of them sat and waited patiently for Chase to do his thing. The friends knew better than to razz on him. What he could do to meat was pure genius. Randa would come up behind him and press against him from time to time, making the others groan. They feared that their steaks would be delayed in being served. But Chase, the master griller, was able to juggle soaking up the loving from his lady and manning his grill. Finally, to appease the others, Jack got up and grabbed her around the waist. He sat and pulled her down to his lap.

The group of friends sat around the table, eating, laughing, and engaging in several conversations at once. Seemed like when there was a lull in the talking, Jack would look up from the whispers and grazing touches he and Chase showered on Randa, to find the others unabashedly watching. By now, he could see Randa was getting used to them not even attempting to look somewhere else. He rewarded her with another kiss, as Chase kissed her hand.

**

Chase got up to walk Trace to his car when it came time for him to leave. Typical goodbyes were given out. The handshakes, bro-hugs, and of course, a regular hug for Randa. The dogs sat calmly by her side and allowed him to pet them before he and Chase turned to walk out to the front yard.

"I'll give you a shout when I get any info on that partial plate Jack gave me. Okay?" Trace promised.

"Yeah, man, that'd be great. Jack said something about just getting a weird feeling about it is all."

Chase shook his friend's hand and waited until he had driven away before he turned to return to the backyard. Coming down the sidewalk was a very well dressed man. He kept looking at Randa's house next door, but when he noticed Chase looking at him he cleared his expression and coolly walked past with a friendly enough grin. The face was familiar, but he just couldn't place it. It would come to him, though.

Back with the others, Sam was next to leave. He was explaining with it being a Saturday, he needed to get showered and changed to go to Rapture. He was on the schedule to dungeon monitor that night and it wouldn't set a good example if the boss showed up for work late. He never asked anything from his employees and volunteers that he, himself, could not perform or accomplish. He gave the guys each the usual bro-hug and then he pulled Randa into a tight hug. Chase saw she held herself stiffly in his arms, probably still not used to men being open about being attracted to her.

"Randa, it was a pleasure to see you. You really are a good influence on these two jokers."

"Sam, it was great seeing you too." She stepped out of his arms and backed into her men, who each put an arm around her.

***

Randa wasn't attracted to Sam at all, but there was just something about him she was drawn to. She couldn't explain it, but she knew it wasn't right for her. She felt safe, less threatened. No, that wasn't right, but she couldn't put her finger on the feeling he elicited from her. All she knew was that Sam was a very intense man, though she had no doubt he could please a woman well.

He was built for it and had an air of confidence about him that shouted sex.

Pac was the last to leave. He too, gave Randa a hug and did the bro-hug routine. True, he was bigger than the other men, and in excellent shape, but he was more of a gruff teddy bear. Though he looked like he frowned all the time, when he looked down at Randa— wayyy down at Randa—his eyes had a sparkle of humor in them and his mouth even cracked a smirk.

Everyone gone, they started to clean up. They left the dogs outside to play and get fresh air. Randa had to admit a yard with no pool was convenient. Once all was cleaned up, Chase and Jack began the task of packing their things to take to their new home. They had talked to Sam and they agreed that over the next few days Chase and Jack's belongings would be moved to Randa's house. Also, anything in the way of furnishings that Sam did not want or need would be packed up and stored in Randa's garage. By the following weekend, Sam would be moved in completely.

Iain, Pac, and Sam would be over the following weekend to move Sam's stuff in and help move the grilling monster next door to the pooled backyard. Sam had already called and talked to their friends to see if they wanted to bring their dogs over so it wouldn't matter how long they were gone. They could use Sam's new backyard as a giant doggie pen. That way Randa could meet their dogs and see what magic she could perform.

Chapter Seventeen

Randa woke with Baby's muzzle lying on the bed beside her, just watching her sleep. With a laugh, she kissed the tip of the dog's nose and stretched. *Today is going to be a good day*, she thought with a sappy smile on her face.

Bradley had come in from Washington D.C. a couple days ago and Randa had yet to see him. When his closest friends had found out he was due in, they had all grouped together and they did the whole catching up routine the night before. She wondered if he and Ayden would mend their friendship. It was such a shame that something in their final two years of high school ended their friendship. They were so close, inseparable and then suddenly nothing. Bradley had refused to talk about it but Randa figured it had to be major to end a friendship that begun in Kindergarten.

Randa had originally planned on having time for just her and her two boys, but it didn't happen. Another local shelter had an unfortunate fire, rendering the building unfit for habitation. Haven had kindly taken in as many of the animals as it could with emergency donations and funding from the community. This caused every available employee and a massive amount of volunteers to help get each animal checked in and settled. This, of course, created tons of paperwork for Randa.

But that was yesterday and today was the day she would see her boys and all of her friends. She couldn't wait to see if there were any other potential connections besides Josie and Sam. She shook her head, wondering how that would start. She already knew Sam was interested in Josie. She never would have thought Josie to be—*what was that word?*—oh yeah, a submissive. She wondered if her other friends would be interested in any of Jack and Chase's friends. As she got up and went into her shower, she started laughing. It would be hilarious if they all hooked up.

With all the food pretty much prepared—with the exception of the meat Chase would be grilling—and all the drinks on ice, there wasn't anything to do except wait for everyone to arrive. Colton would be bringing some dishes from Flavour. That food would arrive shortly before they all ate so it would be hot.

The day went by slowly with Randa constantly looking at the clock. She was expecting her boys to come over before everyone else. They had figured to get the awkwardness of their mom dating two men at the same time, literally, out of the way before their friends came over. She heard a car door shut and jumped up. Finally, they were there. Her boys were there.

She ran out to the top step of the house and didn't have to wait for Bradley. Colton had driven and apparently Bradley didn't give the car time to stop before he was out and had jogged to her. She went down the steps and barely got off the bottom one when he grabbed her up and swung her around. Colton stood not far away, smiling at their antics.

***

Jack and Chase came out of the house behind Randa. Down the steps he watched as a tall, very muscular young man was hugging her like he hadn't see her in years, when in fact, it had only been about six months, from what Jack heard. But he was glad of the close relationship. She stepped back, but stayed within the circle of his arms, then looked in the direction of Jack and Chase.

The young man glanced in their direction and sized them up. Chase and Jack stared right back, not in the least bit intimidated. Despite her son being a good thirteen to sixteen years younger than them, they were probably in just as good, if not better shape than Bradley. The military had been very good for the young lieutenant and physical fitness was obviously very important to him.

They approached mother and sons and waited as Randa extracted herself from the embrace of her oldest to turn and slip between her men. She wrapped her arms around their waists and looked at her boys.

"Bradley, this is Chase Fargo and Jack Benning. Your brother has already met and accepted my relationship with them." She turned to her men. "Jack, Chase, this is my oldest son Bradley."

***

Chase extended his hand first. The challenge was given. At first, no one said anything. Chase got a sense from her son that any sign of weakness would be preyed on. So they had a Mexican standoff, of sorts, for both sides to show they weren't a pushover. Chase could tell he made the right move. Bradley started to relax, but didn't back down all the way. Randa, on the other hand, was visibly relaxed and had a huge smile on her face.

"I talk to Colt often, so do not even think I won't hear if you have hurt our mother. I may not be in a very physical type of a career field, but if I can't take care of you, I'm sure any one of my buddies in the SEALs would be happy to help me out. Got me?"

Chase and Jack looked at each other and had to hold back smiles. The young man was entirely serious, and probably *did* have those contacts, but he needed to understand his mom was theirs, and they would beat the hell out of each other before laying a hand on her. However, it would be better to stay in 'yeah, I got you' serious mode and not belittle his love for his mother.

"Bradley," Randa admonished.

"No, it's okay, hon. We know he's just looking out for his mom." Jack turned back to her son. "Bradley, will we ever hurt your mother, physically or mentally? Believe me, we hope not, but we can promise you something," Jack looked her son straight in the eye, man-to-man, "it will never be intentional."

Jack spoke for both him and Chase, and with Bradley continuing to stare, Chase was about to speak up until the younger man stepped closer and held his hand out. First Jack, then Chase shook his hand. Randa looked on with eyes beginning to well with happy tears.

"Okay, the only other thing I ask is that you do not call me Bradley. My mother is the only one who refuses to call me Brad. Something to do with not liking to shorten names." He looked down at his mom to gently tease her. "Yet she insists people call her Randa. Kind of hypocritical, huh?"

Colton chimed in, "Please, since Brad brought it up, call me Colt. Mom really has a thing for nicknames, but we gotta make our own way."

After much talking and hearing Baby practically howling her displeasure they were taking so long, they went into Randa's house, where both young men were promptly bowled over and then sat on as she licked their faces and whimpered how much she had missed them. Max was quick to realize the two young men were family as he pushed himself close to them to receive rubs and scratches.

By the time Randa's sons had the dog calmed down, they had decided a swim was in order with Baby. At the mention of the pool, both dogs went nuts. Quickly, the young men changed and brought the dogs out on the back deck. Down the steps they went. Bradley began to roughhouse with Baby, as per usual, causing Max to go into hero mode and begin to growl at Bradley. For such a portly dog, the deep growl sounded menacing enough to stop the rough play and make Bradley stand still.

Randa, at the top step, admonished Max. "Max, no growling." She called out to the boys, "He's a bit protective of Baby."

The look they gave her hinted they thought she had lost her mind. It always amused her when people forgot the instincts animals had to protect their perceived mates. Once Randa gently, but firmly reminded Max that they were family—and with a few more rubs and scratches—Max chuffed his approval of them petting his 'girl'. Their friendship solidified when they called Max into the pool moments later. Chase looked on from his poolside chair as the four of them were had so much fun they didn't notice the other guests showing up.

***

Randa was dumbfounded to see Chase and Jack's friends arrived before hers did. Of course, only two of her friends were coming. She was kind of curious to see how Sam and Josie were going to act. After what she'd heard happened at Haven, she had a feeling if nothing else, there was an attraction there. Hopefully, Josie would be open to it.

After everyone arrived, the men headed next door to Chase and Jack's old house. Since the pool took up so much room, the grilling and eating would take place over there, with the pool open for swimming. Randa was changing into her swimsuit and then covering with shorts and a cute top when her doorbell rang. Since the boys and Baby were still outside, she went downstairs to see who it was. When she opened the door, an envelope fell to the floor. She looked outside and saw no one coming or going.

There was no writing on the outside of the envelope and when she tore it open with her fingernail, there was only a piece of paper inside. Curious but hesitant, she pulled the sheet out. She gasped as the words 'dirty whore' and 'gangbang slut' jumped out at her. She looked around, as though expecting someone to be standing on the sidewalk pointing a finger at her.

She slammed the door shut and backed away. Her fist pressed to her mouth. Bile rose in her throat, so she ran into the kitchen and hunched over the sink. She dry heaved for a bit then straightened and splashed cold water on her face. Who left that letter? She couldn't fathom who or why they would.

Another knock on her door startled her and she cautiously headed in that direction. A second knock came quickly after the first, and then she heard a female voice. In relief, Randa opened the door to see Kitty standing on the top step with a bakery box. Her wide smile was like a balm to Randa's nerves. She was dressed in a cheerful sundress that complimented her skin tone and put a shine in her eyes.

"Hey girl. So today's the day your men are coming out of that closet."

"They were not in a closet, Kitty." Laughing, Randa pulled her in the house and hugged her. "What did you bring? You realize you're gonna make those men— not mine but the others—fall in love with you?"

"Girlfriend, if Chase and Jack's friends are even half as hot, they're in danger."

Since Randa had met the men coming to the party, she smiled a little private smile. From the way

Chase and Jack spoke, a bit of matchmaking might be planned. She couldn't wait for her friends to meet the other men. She knew Kitty was a huge flirt and would have no problem pursuing any of the men that would be there. She tried to think of who would be a good match for Kitty, but without knowing them it was difficult to even guess. Since Sam was into the alternative stuff, she didn't think he would be a good choice. Besides, Josie and he had already met and she couldn't wait to see how they acted. But the others...

"Kitty, you may wrap any of the other men around your little finger. I say you go for it."

They laughed as they went out the sliding glass door to the deck. From there, they could see the boys still swimming. Apparently, the dogs had been worn out and were lounging. Since Iain, Syun, and Luna couldn't make it, they were waiting on Pac and Josie to arrive. However, Josie had called to say she'd be running late. Randa hoped that it wasn't her way of avoiding the Sam situation.

Sam was making use of his new backyard, throwing a ball for a tiny dog. Randa laughed and had to wonder whose little one it was. Neither of the big men seemed the type to own a bitty dog like that. Not very masculine.

Randa went to where Kitty was leaning on the railing. Her cinnamon toned hair was pulled back into a ponytail that curled elegantly along the back of her head, almost reaching her shoulders. There were times Randa was envious of Kitty's beautiful hair. A cross between her black father and her very Sicilian mother, she made a striking figure. Her skin had a honey tone to it that made her look tanned year round. Most people thought she was Hispanic—minus the red hair.

Kitty turned to smile at Randa. "Come here, girl, and stare at your men. I see a couple of handsome specimens that are just calling out to me." Kitty waved her over, "I see one in particular that I'd love to see laid out flat for me to feast on."

Randa laughed, "Kitty, you may ogle any of the men that are not taken. I do believe since I licked them both I have staked my claim."

"Lady, I cannot believe you just said that. And while I whole heartedly approve of your territorial tactics, don't you think it was a little too much TMI?"

Randa could not believe she just said what she did. Normally, she should have blushed and been tongue tied over her reaction to a man, but with Chase and Jack's love and devotion to her, she has adopted a 'devil may care' attitude.

They went next door to greet the other guests. As Kitty was introduced to Sam, and officially to Chase and Jack, Trace stood from where he had been sitting watching quietly. Randa watched him approach, his gait was catlike, almost like stalking prey. Randa heard Kitty suck in a breath like someone just put an ice cube down her bodice. Jack looked up with a smile and wrapped his arm around Randa's waist.

"Trace, buddy, this is her friend, Kitty Campanetti. She owns La Dulce and makes the most to die for desserts."

***

Jack stood with his chest pressed to Randa's back and Chase next to the both of them. As Trace walked away with a sly grin on his face, Jack watched as Chase fist bumped their friend and Randa shook her head at their antics. The dogs began to bark and run along the fence at Randa's house as they heard someone pull up out front. Romeo had taken to doing the same thing on the other side of the fence. Over Randa's shoulder, Jack watched Sam stop throwing the ball and was about to jog over and snatch him up, but the little guy was faster than expected and got to the gate just as Josie opened it. She reacted quickly and grabbed him up before he could escape.

"Oh no you don't," she scolded the tiny dog as he squirmed in her arms. "Not gonna let you go runnin' out and risk getting hurt."

Jack, Randa and Sam had walked over to Josie to make sure everything was okay. Josie put him down and he took off to run the fence again, the miniature mocking the larger ones on the other side. She stood and brushed the stray blades of grass from her legs. He had wondered how Josie and Sam would react after the first meeting. Tomboy that she was, she had on cutoff shorts and a man's wife beater. Over the fence, Randa's boys called out their hellos and she waved at them. When she turned she almost ran right into Sam. Jack watched in amusement as Sam grabbed her arms to steady her.

***

"Whoa there...Well hello, Doc. Josie, isn't it?" Sam cocked an eyebrow.

Randa watched as her tough as nails friend almost fell on her ass, but then plastered a stiff smile on her face. She remembered what Jack and Chase had told her about Sam being a Dom and Josie a sub, but wasn't sure how far the reach went for that lifestyle. Maybe she *should* talk to Josie about it and find out at least the basics. She made no move to leave, even if Jack and Chase had kissed her cheek and went to check on things. She wanted to make sure Sam knew no matter what she stood by her friend.

"You know very well who I am. I neutered your dog, remember?" Josie's voice shook.

"Listen, pet, we both know this is gonna end badly if you keep up with the bratty attitude." He pulled her close to him tightly. "If you like, we can correct this little issue somewhere more appropriate."

Randa stood there, mouth agape as she listened to how he talked to her friend. What *did* amuse her though was the reaction Josie had. She watched her friend lick her lips and close her eyes. *Oh yeah, there is major heat being thrown out here*. The show was too entertaining for her to even think of leaving. With her hands on her hips, she didn't even remind them she was still there and could hear the whole conversation. Maybe her education would expand without even having to talk.

Josie narrowed her eyes at him. "You have no authority over me. I do not have a Dom and am not interested in having you as mine."

"Oh really? So, I do not affect you in the slightest?"

"Not in the slightest. No."

"Then would you care to explain why your nipples are rock hard and begging for my mouth. And why are you rubbing your thighs together?"

Randa looked down and indeed Josie was scissoring her legs. She heard Josie curse under her breath. Randa bit her lips to stop herself from laughing at her friend's predicament. It was kind of a comfort to know the one person who she never thought could be thrown for a loop had been.

"Let go of me. Now, sir," she sneered the last word and waited.

"It's good you acknowledge what you know I am." He leaned close to her ear, "I hope to see you at Single Sub night again real soon, pet."

That was enough for Randa. Her face heated a deep red as she watched Sam walk away. She noticed Josie watched him too. With her arm looped around Josie's she led her flustered friend over to where Kitty had disengaged herself from Trace. While they all caught up on their circle of friends, Randa was very pleased to see Josie tried—and failed—to ignore Sam.

Chapter Eighteen

Chase was at the fence watching the dogs in Randa's yard. He'd just received a text from Pac saying he'd just pulled up. Pac had already warned them he couldn't stay long. His son, Ryan, had a track meet he was due to compete in and Pac never missed anything for his kid. It was hard being a single dad, but he had never had any problems with Ryan. Sure, when Carla died two years before, Ryan had acted out. What kid wouldn't when they lost their mom? But through lots of love and support, he had grown into a great young man.

Around the back of the house, the group of friends greeted Pac like Norm from *Cheers*, or rather the men did. A lot of fist bumping and bro-hugs were thrown around. Randa's boys were now out of the pool and drying off in Chase and Jack's yard and they had left Baby and Max in Randa's yard. After introductions were made, Chase got started on the grilling and the conversations were flowing.

***

Randa had gone into the house to get more drinks. With the fridge door open, she was hunched over trying to find the hard ciders she knew were in there. She felt hands reach down, grab her under her arms, and pull her up until she was aligned perfect to the front of a very hard body. Just to tease the man, she moaned and reached around.

"I'm not sure you should be doing this, my boyfriends are sure to come in at any moment."

Randa felt his arms tighten around her and heard Jack chuckle softly as he played along. "Baby, just a taste, that's all I need. Your men won't know and you're so fuckin' hot."

"Okay, just a taste, but then you have to go."

She turned in his arms and pulled his head down to hers. Their lips locked and Jack pulled her tighter to him until not so much as a piece of paper could fit between them. Neither of them heard the door, nor did they hear the fridge door open, close, and then the sliding glass door close again. Jack had, at this point, backed Randa into the wall on the other side of the fridge. He had lifted her, her legs circling his waist and arms around his neck. When a throat cleared, and a voice interrupted them, they pulled away from each other reluctantly.

"Well, hell, is this game open to all couples, or are the hosts the only ones allowed to play tonsil hockey while their guests languish away in thirst?"

Randa lifted her head and saw Kitty and Josie were standing there watching. Although Josie had the grace to look slightly embarrassed, Kitty looked on with no intention of turning her head. Behind them, the sliding glass door opened again. Trace and Sam came into the house and stood back. While the women were watching the couple, Randa could clearly see the interest the men had on her two friends. She wasn't shocked at all at the quick progression with Trace and Kitty. Trace smiled at Kitty when she turned and he crooked his finger. She made a low sound and walked toward him, every inch a runway model. She looked at Sam and saw he was watching Josie, who refused to turn and look at him. Instead, she turned on her heel and walked around him to go back outside. Sam chuckled low and made to follow, but turned back to the now slightly less panting couple.

"You might want to come outside and keep us company unless you invite someone in to join you," he said drolly. "Chase is outside feeling neglected."

With his hand still cupping her ass, Jack dropped his head into her nape and laughed quietly. Randa, a little peeved at being interrupted, and also upset for not including Chase, swatted him and told him to put her down, which he did reluctantly. When they returned outside, all but Chase and Randa's boys were clapping and catcalling. Chase wasn't upset, but shook his head at them. Her boys just looked embarrassed.

***

As they all sat eating and talking, Jack made sure that Randa wasn't lacking for attention, since Chase was busy manning the grill. It was only when it came time for Pac to leave that Jack left her side, if you could call draping his arm around her shoulder, as Chase's was around her waist. Pac had only had time for a quick burger and sampling of some of the foods Colton had provided. He smiled down at Randa when she excused herself briefly to make Pac a small plate to go of the desserts Kitty had brought along with a plate for his son.

After the bro-hugs and lady-hugs, Jack walked Pac to his truck, and with a final handshake, stood to the side as the bigger man got into the cab of his truck. Jack thought of Pac's son, Ryan. He had been glad to hear about him joining the track team. Not only was it keeping him healthy, but with the help of Pac, the track team, and all of his 'uncles', the kid had a great support system. But he wondered when Pac would get back on the horse. He had a feeling Pac was more than ready to move on.

***

Randa was in the house putting together some containers for everyone to take home. With so much food left over, the group would each be able to take food home and not cook for a couple of days. She got to thinking about the whole time they were all outside talking. She had witnessed Josie watching Sam the entire time. And she had seen the cozying up to each other Trace and Kitty were doing.

The connection Trace and Kitty had going on was kind of funny. A cop and a baker. Yes, she made donuts, but mainly cakes and other kinds of desserts. It was kind of cliché that a cop would have any kind of interest in someone who baked for a living.

Chase came in the kitchen and wrapped his arms around her waist. With his chin resting on her head they looked out the window at the dogs playing in the backyard. It turned out Romeo was a friendly little guy who got along really well with Baby and Max. It was like they had always known each other.

"So we came out of the closet, babe. Your boys accept us and our friends are thrilled for us. Can we talk now about the happily ever after we've all been heading toward since Jack and I moved in?"

"Happily ever after, is it? Like the knights in shining armor?" she teased him. "But this damsel hasn't even been rescued from the fire breathing dragon."

Jack walked into the kitchen and heard the last thing she said. He stood to the side so she could see him as Chase held her. The serious look on his face told her he wasn't taking what she said lightly, even if she meant it as such. Just the intensity of his look heated her from head to toes. She craved each of them equally, loved them both the same.

"Baby, you know we'd do a beat down on anyone or anything that would dare to hurt you."

She turned in Chase's arms and reached out with a hand to Jack. When he got close enough for them both to lay a hand on her waist, she looked at them. How in the world did she get so lucky to have met not one but two of the most generous, loving men? She wished she could see what they saw in her. She got that she had a great personality and she was a true friend, but how could *she* be attractive to such in shape guys who obviously could get any woman they wanted? And that was when she wised up. She didn't care anymore of the whys. She was finally going to listen and believe the words and gestures that they continually showered on her. These men were *hers* and she loved them.

***

The more he thought of her allowing those men to paw at her, touch her, and fuck her, the more he knew he should be grateful she wasn't—and hadn't—been his wife in a long time. What the fuck was he thinking even considering taking her back? His political reputation would go into the shithole if that fat skank were back with him.

Since the sun was going down, he knew now was the time to do what he had planned. He got out of his car, shut the door soundlessly, and looked up and down the street. Casually, he walked across the street, ignition key held tightly wedged between fingers. To anyone passing by, it looked like he was just out for an early evening walk.

As he stood next to what he knew was Miranda's car, he again looked around to make sure no one could see what he was doing. Starting at the front driver's fender and travelling down the side panel of the car, he applied a good amount of pressure to make the key gouged the paint. Because of the noise he kept checking for anyone watching. At the back bumper, he stood back and got a look at his handiwork. Since her car was a dark maroon, the metal underneath could be seen easily in the dying sunlight. With a smile and a low whistle, Simon walked back to his rental and drove off, satisfied she would soon know that someone was disgusted with her.

Chapter Nineteen

Monday again. After the weekend Randa had, and despite the love she had for her job, she just did not want to go to work. She would love to lay in bed all day with her men. She had wished that Bradley could have stayed longer, but he had to leave the day before, as he had a trial starting and needed to get back to DC. She had waited until he had promised to come in the summer then left with Colton, to cry. She wouldn't have long to wait to see him again.

Since Baby and Max were outside, letting loose their morning energy, Randa was able to get through her morning routine with no interruptions. She brought them back in and gave her instructions to guard the house. Chase was still in bed, and Jack's day began a lot earlier. Apple in hand, bottled water in the other, she grabbed her purse and keys and walked out of the house, locking it behind her.

Down the steps, she approached her car. As she got closer, she began to feel off for some reason. As she came around the back of her car, she gasped. Her hand went to the line dug into the paint. It extended from her rear bumper to the front. She knew nothing about cars, but she could tell this was bad. She covered her mouth and cried out. She looked around, expecting to see the guilty person standing there laughing.

She was tempted to just get the damn insurance company involved and have it taken care of without Chase and Jack knowing, but she couldn't hold back something like this. She didn't want to tell them about the letters or her roses just yet, though. Dread rushed through her until finally she admitted to herself that the time had come.

In her car, she drove to Haven, constantly looking around to see if someone was following her. She was starting to get paranoid and it pissed her off. In the years since James had died, she had never felt fear of living alone with her two boys. Never. So to feel it now enraged her. Sure, she felt like a victim, but she was a strong woman and refused to allow some asshole to make her cower.

The whole day Randa spent trying to figure out who could be vicious enough to terrorize her. Killing her roses, breaking her window, leaving two very nasty notes, and now vandalizing her car. She had a feeling they wanted her to find it the next day because of the side it was on. If they had keyed the passenger side, it could have taken a couple of days for her to notice.

***

Jack had been at work a couple hours before Randa. Chase would be in an hour after her. All day he and Chase did their rounds on their patients and saw the ones coming in for appointments. He had caught Randa spaced out more than once, but when asked she claimed she was fine. He knew something was up and he meant

290

to find out what it was. He would be getting to the bottom of it, whether she liked it or not.

Chase and Randa were in the kitchen having a quick break when Jack walked in. He saw the determined look on his friend's face and decided to keep quiet. He figured if need be he could always step in and get him to back up.

"Randa, what's going on with you today, baby? Now, with both of us here, I want you to tell me you're fine. You have been spacey all day and distracted. Never rude, always doing your work, but there's still something going on."

Jack could see resignation in her expression. He wondered if she were missing her oldest son? Or maybe something to do with Colton? Could Haven be having issues and she was trying to handle it on her own? Whatever it was, he needed her to know he and Chase would help her in any way they could. He watched as she closed her eyes and sighed deeply, as if she needed the fortification.

"I'm sorry, Jack. I kind of told a white lie to you earlier in the day. I just didn't want to worry either of you. I guess I want to believe that the whole situation that I'm worried about is just a bunch of teenagers acting out."

***

Chase sat up straight in his chair and looked first at Jack, who looked like he was about to blow his top. He then looked at Randa, who had turned white at the mention of what had been bothering her all day. He didn't want her to think—whatever it was—she had to go through it alone. He took one of her hands in his and he looked at Jack pointedly. Thank god Jack took the hint and sat down, gently taking her other hand.

"Darlin', come on. Tell us what happened," Chase softly said to her.

"It might be better to show you. Come on, let's get it over with."

He and Jack stood when she did. She led them to the parking lot and then stood back from the driver's side and just stared. Chase approached first and could not stop the stream of obscenities that came from him. He knew about the rose bushes and window, but now this? He was positive they were connected. A white-hot fury came over him and threatened to spill out, but he was able to rein it in before losing complete control. Someone was fucking with their lady. It was time for him to step out of his cool and calm and bring out the badass country boy he had been growing up.

"Jack, you got your phone on you?" Chase asked in a deadly calm voice. When he saw his friend pull out the phone, he continued. "Good, take some shots of the damage and make sure you get some close-ups for insurance purposes. Then please send them to me and Trace. I'm going back inside to get my phone."

Chase walked away without another word. He was taking a chance that Randa would assume his anger was directed at her. He also knew Jack would explain to her his mood right then. He would make it up to her later.

***

Jack had not been at all prepared for what he was looking at. There, in her dark maroon paint, was a line scratched so deep into the side that there was no paint showing in the marks. This was not something a teenager would do. From the viciousness and the depth, he would bet his ass she knew the person who had done the damage. However, he couldn't think of a good reason for anyone to do this to her. She was the kindest, most giving person he knew. Plus, the whole damn neighborhood loved her—including the local teens.

He and Randa stayed outside, Jack taking the pictures with his smart phone as Chase instructed. He waited until Chase was coming out of the building to begin sending the photos to Trace since Chase was still talking to him. He was probably explaining what was going on, but all he and Randa heard was the last bit of the conversation.

"...yeah, got it. I'll do what I can, but can't promise anything. Okay, man, and thanks a lot." Chase got off the phone and returned to Randa's side. "Baby, I'm so sorry this had to happen. I just need to make one more call. Okay? Jack's off work and I know you're about to leave for the day. I promise, I'm only an hour behind you both, and Jack here will stay with you until I get home."

Jack watched as Chase gave her a deep kiss, probably too deep seeing as they were both breathing hard when he pulled away. He was grateful when, with his thumb and pointer finger, Chase turned her head so that Jack could treat her to the same attention. With a tense chuckle, Jack brought her into his arms and kissed her deeply, almost as if his lips could pass on his strength and support. They broke apart as Chase cursed again. Jack kept an arm around Randa's waist as Chase stood staring at her car. When Chase turned and impatiently walked back inside, Jack had to tighten his arm around her waist to keep her from following.

"No, babe, let him go. He needs to calm himself down. You won't mean to, but you'll only remind him." Jack rubbed his hands from her shoulders to her hands to comfort her.

"I just hate to see him upset. This isn't his fault."

Jack held Randa tight in his arms, hoping the embrace would comfort her, even if just a little. He followed her home and was grateful again they lived close to work. Once home, Jack kept an eye on Randa as she wandered aimlessly around her house. She hadn't said a word to him, and once she tired of pacing, sat next to him on the couch curled against his side.

***

Jack and Randa were home, the dogs in the backyard stretching their legs. They were waiting for Chase to get home to figure out the next move for the car. Their buddy, Iain, would be coming over about the time Chase arrived. Since this was a stressful day, Randa decided on pizza and beer for dinner. She didn't want Chase to have to grill and she didn't want the hassle of cooking.

Randa was sitting with Jack out on the deck sipping their beers when they heard first one, then another car door shut. They heard two men talking and knew it was Chase and Iain. Jack got up and headed toward the front yard to join the other two. Randa went inside and grabbed two beers then met the others.

Iain Sinclair was a very tall, muscular man with chestnut hair, tattoos and scruffy facial hair. Worn jeans, a black form fitting t-shirt, and biker shitkickers rounded off his look. A first impression would make someone think he was a shady character, but Randa figured if he was a friend of her men, then he was good people. Especially since, when he turned her way, he had a big smile on his face. She could be imagining it, but once his eyes looked her up and down, she thought she saw a whole lot of appreciation staring at her. Now, normally her past insecurities would begin to creep in, but her confidence level has made her realize that she was indeed a catch. Besides, she wasn't concerned with Iain's attention, her men were the only ones she wanted to notice her.

He stuck out his hand and it was easy to tell he worked with paint. There were a few paint specks on his hands, but for the most part they were clean. She got a good glance at his nails—no dirt under them, which surprised her. She assumed all mechanics would have grease and grime under their nails. Not this one. He must wear gloves at work. In fact, he looked like he had recently had a manicure. She had to laugh to herself about that. No way would this very manly man go and have his nails done, even if he was looking to impress a lady.

"Randa, hey there. Great to finally meet the lady that has made honest men out of these two."

"Umm....thanks, I think?"

"Just ignore his humor, babe. The man is deluded in thinking he's funny." Jack stepped behind Randa, laughing.

Chase stepped closer also. "Iain Sinclair, this is Miranda Michaels. No funny business, she's not interested. Now, tell her what you were just telling us."

"Okay. So, yeah, whoever did this took their time and went deep. If I were doing an estimate for you to give to your insurance company, I'd say there is probably about two to three thousand dollars in damage here. You've got about a three foot area from bumper to bumper that will need to be worked on. From looking at the depth, I would say there was a grudge involved."

Randa remembered Chase and Jack explaining Iain's background. How he had grown up in a rough neighbor in Chicago, which exposed him to vandalism. Hell, as a kid he was involved in quite a bit. His father hadn't been in his life as a kid, due to constant stints in jail. His mom did all she could, but Iain just got in the wrong crowd. When his Uncle Mark had stepped in, he was given a choice: military training school or work in the auto body shop any and all days that he was told. He chose the shop. That was where he acquired his love of cars.

"I'd be happy to get this cluckerfu—uh, mess repaired for you. I can do it at my cost to help you out.

You may or may not want to submit a claim to your insurance. Up to you." He had gone on his haunches and was running fingers along the gouge in the paint.

Randa stood back, watching and listening. What should be the happiest days of her life were marred by ugliness of which she could not fathom. She began to space out as she thought about whoever had done this was probably watching and getting a kick out of her misery. They probably thought they had scared her. She tried to think what message the person was trying to get through to her. She was almost sure the roses, and now this incident, were to punish her for some reason. But why? Who was this person and what had she done to piss them off?

"Baby? Did you hear what we said?" Jack was speaking to her, his hand on her elbow.

"No. I'm sorry, I drifted for a bit. What was that?"

"Well, Miranda, I was saying that I've got a week before my next project comes in to start and other than small stuff to finish up... I can work on your car if you like. No pressure though, if you choose to take the car to a chain type body shop. But I can guarantee that they will charge you more than I will." He smiled gently at her.

She felt a little shell shocked. "Iain, that would be great. If these two trust you, then I trust you." She felt like she would start crying any moment. "How long will it take?"

"Shouldn't take more than a week, which fits in perfectly, right? I've even got something I can let you use as a loaner."

Randa had a feeling if it was going to take that long, there was a lot involved. She wondered if he really wanted to help since she was his friends' girlfriend. She would have to think of a way to thank him that wouldn't include money. She just got a vibe from him that he wouldn't do or offer anything unless he truly wanted to.

"You don't know how much this means to me." She walked to him and threw her arms around his waist and hugged him tight, but briefly, not knowing how he would react. At that moment, a delivery car pulled up and one of the neighborhood kids got out with a smile.

"Hey, Mrs. M...got your pie. And Mario says no charge. He says your money's no good at Salvatore's."

"Well, you tell Mario that the next time Guido needs a check up, he's to let me know. Okay?"

"Sure thing, Mrs. M. Have a great night."

***

Chase took the pizza boxes with the stereotypical black, red, and green lettering from the teen and turned to her with question in his eyes just as Jack and Iain did the same. She blushed and told them to just come in the house so they could eat. Iain waited until she was far enough away.

"You need to keep an eye on what goes on around here. Someone is going to hurt her if you don't stop them."

"Yeah, buddy, we know. We're on it. This new thing had to have been done at the BBQ the other night."

"Speaking of which, sorry I couldn't make it. A customer came from LA to talk to me and convince me to take on a new project."

They walked up the steps into Randa's house, still talking about cars. Iain, the first in the house, stopped dead in his tracks. A loud laugh came from Chase at the look on Iain's face. While Iain was used to big dogs—his own a Cane Corso named Ghita—he certainly wasn't used to dogs being able to just about look him in the eye. Chase had gone with Iain when he took ownership of Ghita to make sure she was healthy. Since Iain was a Dom at a local BDSM club, he had schooled his friend in animal politics, explaining there were protocols that needed to be followed. Once learned, he found Iain was a natural with dogs. The men stood still as Randa made the introductions and they all laughed as Baby sidled up next to him to allow him to pet her.

Chase was throwing away his garbage when the others finished up. His appetite was still off from the worry of Randa's safety. Moments later Iain announced he had to go. They all agreed he would bring one of his loaners over in the morning for Randa to drive and he would get back to his shop with her car. With another hug for Randa and the customary bro-hug their group seemed to favor, he left. Jack and Randa went back in, but Chase decided to just check out around both houses. That was when he saw what looked like a newer model Cougar drive by slowly. He couldn't see who was driving as the side windows were tinted so dark they bordered on black. His intuition just knew this car and the driver were involved somehow, but before he could formulate a plan to try and stop the car, Randa called him into the house. He looked at the car one last time then turned to go inside.

Chapter Twenty

Dogs on leashes, the trio decided it was such a beautiful day, they would go to the tide pools to have time to relax and let the dogs have fun. No matter how many times they went, to Randa, it was special. She had her men, her dogs and beautiful Mother Nature.

Supply packs were already packed with everything they would need for them and the two dogs, and they would each carry one for safety reasons. Jack and Chase had insisted the heavier items be put in theirs and she would be carrying a change of clothes and the dogs' paraphernalia. She had tried to insist she could handle it, but both men had agreed if she didn't *have* to, then why do it? They would be able to carry it easier and they just wanted her to concentrate on enjoying herself.

She decided to pack her camera to be able to get some pictures of her favorite guys at her favorite spot. The last time they were here she missed the opportunity to capture her men and the dogs being silly. She had regretted not bringing the camera then, and vowed to bring one every time going forward. It would be great to get photos of the four of them to maybe have framed to put on her desk at work.

They had decided to take the Infiniti EX37 the men had purchased together for times like that. The dogs loaded in the back, Randa buckled in the front passenger seat, and Jack in the backseat, Chase pulled out of the driveway. A short time later, the Infinity was parked at Cabrillo and they were starting off on the trail to the tidal pools. Max was doing very well in emulating the same behavior Baby did. Randa loved seeing the shocked looks on Chase and Jack's faces. It had taken a little longer to get Max used to walking on a leash like a little gentleman, but Randa was able to use Baby as a good example. In no time, Max was a pro. Now, he walked nicely beside Baby who had shortened her stride to accommodate him and the rest of the group. Jack held Baby's leash and Chase held Max's, freeing Randa up to take the random photographs she was wanting.

Twice, she stopped the group and was able to set up her camera's timer to take a picture of the five of them. For Randa, it was great practice for her amateur photography. She had done some photography for some local charities and had found out that she had a pretty good eye.

Once at their destination, the dogs were let off their leashes. Again, Jack and Chase were astonished at how well behaved Max was being. Not only did Randa know what she was doing with dogs, but Baby was the perfect example setting companion. A ball was pulled from a bag and they frolicked in the surf until both dogs were tired, Max more so than Baby, since he was trying to keep up with the much bigger dog. Bottles of water and snacks for them all were brought out. Randa and the two men sat on a large rock just off the shoreline; Max and Baby lay on the grassy banks.

She was tempted to continue to bite her tongue and keep the knowledge of the vicious stalker-like situation to herself, but since they were all now living together they had a right to know what was going on. She took a deep breath and figured the best way to get through it was to just start.

"My rose bushes were purposely destroyed. The next day there was a nasty letter waiting for me when I got home. I have no clue who's doing it and no idea when it is being done." She took another deep breath, waiting for someone to get pissed.

"Randa! Why didn't you say something? Do you know a bottle of bleach was found alongside your garage? We're guessing it was what was used to kill your roses." Jack sat on one side of her and took her hand in his. "Baby, Trace came over specifically to get the bottle Sam found and take it in to see if they could get prints off it."

Chase had her other hand and was rubbing the palm with his fingers. "Is there anything else we need to know, darlin'? You know we'd never let anything happen to you."

Randa sighed. She wasn't sure how bad it really was, but she needed to tell them all of it. "I received another letter. And there have been a couple of times when I thought I was being watched. In fact, that night you both were out playing poker? The back gate was wide open and that was the night the roses were killed. I thought at first the gate was from one of you. Now, with everything else that has happened, I know better."

"Okay. We've got Trace working a couple of things for us. Knowing him, he'll get it expedited. He's not one to fool around with his friends' safety. True, he just met you, but you're ours so..." Chase let his words drift off, knowing the implication was there.

It was getting close to the time the trails would close, so they decided to pack it up and head home. The walk back to the car was a bit more subdued than when they got there. Each in their own thoughts, the dogs were acting normal, but Baby was watching her humans carefully. Max happily sat back and watched the scenery on their way home.

***

Back at the house, they let the dogs in the backyard and would have turned to go into the house if Max hadn't stepped in front of Baby and started growling. Chase turned to him to admonish him when he heard it. The slight hissing could not be missed even a few yards away. He slowed his steps and approached the dogs slower, not making any sudden moves. Behind him, he heard Randa and Jack coming into the backyard. He didn't turn his body, but raised his voice only slightly so they could hear him.

"Stay where you are, both of you. I'm not sure what kind it is, but there's a snake near the dogs," Chase said in a monotone voice. "Jack, could you get that five gallon bucket in our garage and either a shovel or rake?"

Jack backed away and then took off for the garage. Within moments, he was back with the bucket and shovel. As Jack rushed to do as he asked, he knew Jack had never come up against any kind of snake before, poisonous or otherwise, and it had been a while for him too.

When Jack returned, Chase took the tool and bucket from him. He knew Randa was scared as she stood back in terror, but he had to keep his focus on the snake. Max continued to growl in protection of his much larger furry friend. The snake was making a loud racket, definitely pissed off its nap in the waning sun had been interrupted. Chase was circling the reptile, holding the shovel like the weapon it was about to become.

With a sudden strike, he brought the tool down and embedded it in the ground. The thrust was so hard that the handle was swaying back and forth like a metronome. He waited a moment, then scooped up both halves of the snake onto the shovel and deposited them into the bucket. As a vet, it bothered him to kill the snake, but when his pets or loved ones were endangered and there was no chance to safely catch and relocate the animal, he had to choose his priorities. He got down on his haunches and looked into the bucket. Although he was more familiar with snakes from Texas, he'd had to study up when he had moved to the San Diego area, just in case. He looked closely at the markings and called Jack over to see if his guess was right.

"Dude, this look like a Southern Pacific Rattler."

Chase reached in, and picked up the body to get a closer look. *Now, how the hell did this guy get here*? When he had moved to San Diego, he wasn't expecting to treat reptiles, but the last clinic he worked at insisted on at least being able to identify the local indigenous harmful animals, just in case a patient came in injured by one of them.

"Buddy, you're right. That's exactly what this thing was." Jack was dumbfounded. "But how did it get here? Not like they're common around here, right?"

***

Randa came over and looked at the headless snake's body. With a grimace, she looked at the serious expressions on their faces. She wondered why. When she really thought about it, she thought she had the answer to her own question. They were thinking this thing was poisonous. Her eyes widened with the realization that maybe someone purposely put this snake in her yard to either hurt one of them or one of the dogs. She began to shake and would have tripped on her backward step if Baby hadn't run to her. Instinctively, the dog knew her owner was upset and wanted to help.

Chase and Jack rushed to her, catching her as she balanced her weak body against Baby. An arm from each of her guys wrapped around her back made things a lot steadier. She didn't realize how close she was to falling on her ass.

"Who...why would someone do this? How could someone want to hurt my dog, or hell, me for that matter?"

Jack looked at her with concern. "Think, baby. Was there an unhappy pet owner that may hold a grudge? An ex that didn't want to break things off?"

With a laugh mixed with a cry, Randa responded, "All, and I do mean all, of my exes chose to stop seeing me, not the other way around."

"We already know they were idiots, darlin'," Chase soothed her. "But, for us it's a good thing they were idiots. If they hadn't been, you wouldn't be free for us to love."

They got her to a poolside chair and sat her down. Jack stayed behind her and was rubbing her shoulders, while Chase was kneeling between her wide spread feet, rubbing her calves and thighs.

***

"I'm going to give Trace a call and let him know what happened. I have a feeling he won't be able to do much since no one was hurt, though." Jack turned and walked away. He pulled his phone out as he rounded the corner to the front. Out of habit, he looked around and couldn't believe his luck and the balls of the driver he knew was looking back at him. The same Cougar that they had seen repeatedly was parked about three houses down.

As he waited for Trace to answer, he could hear the car start up. He wanted to drag the bastard out of his car and find out what the hell he was up to. He obviously didn't live in the area. Jack and Chase had never seen the car parked in a driveway, just on the street. And no one with a status statement like a fully loaded Cougar would willingly park that beauty on the street overnight. It was too much of a coincidence when shit happened at

Randa's place, the same Cougar was seen. Jack was beginning to think the driver was involved somehow.

Only getting voicemail, Jack cursed, waited, and nonchalantly began to position himself to be able to get a look at the plates on the Cougar if it went by. Tersely, he left a message for Trace to call him back as soon as he got the message. The Cougar was coming toward him and picking up speed. The driver had to know his plates would be seen. He would have been smarter turning his car around and leaving the street the opposite direction. It was almost as if the driver *wanted* Randa to know who was hurting her.

As the car went by, the driver slowed down, cocky almost in his speed. When Jack looked, he saw why the driver was not worried about getting caught. The windows were all blacked out except for the windshield, making it impossible to see inside, and the plates had been covered. No wonder the bastard wasn't worried with Jack seeing him. And Jack could almost picture the smirk on the face behind the wheel.

Chase and Randa came up to stand by Jack as he continued to look down the street where the car went. He turned to them and gave Chase a look. He caught Randa watching them and could see the concern starting to show on her face. She crossed her arms over her chest and stared them both down. Damn it, they were going to have to tell her.

"Okay, spill it. You two know something and you're going to tell me." She glared at them with her 'mom' look.

"We're just as guilty of not wanting you to worry. There's been a tricked out Cougar running the street and from what we can tell, they are focusing on your house only," Chase replied reluctantly. "We've got a partial plate Trace is going to check into. Will let us know as soon as he has something."

Jack stood there as Chase explained. He didn't trust himself to speak. He was so angry at himself for not getting the complete plate number the last time. He could have avoided the whole debacle of the snake situation. *Damn it!* He didn't know what he would have done if Randa had been hurt. Sure, he loved the dogs, but Randa was his main concern.

Randa went to him and wrapped her arms around his waist. "Jack, honey, it's okay. I'm fine. The dogs are fine. You and Chase made it safe for me."

***

Chase knew his friend was upset with himself and felt for him. Any man worth his salt kept his woman safe. This was something that, even though he didn't cause it, and couldn't prevent it, Jack felt he should have been able to make sure it hadn't happened. They would both just have to keep a better eye out for that Cougar.

"Okay, why don't we all go into the house and start packing our stuff? Might as well get a jump on that while we wait for Trace to call back, right?" Chase put one hand at the small of Randa's back then nudged Jack as he stood right where he was, staring down the street in the direction the Cougar must have gone. "Come on, buddy, let's go."

They spent the rest of the evening not so much packing as transferring the rest of his and Jack's belongings from their house to the one next door. Some things were packed for storing in the garage, but some, like dishes and other kitchen goods would be left for Sam to use when he moved in. By dinner time, they decided to stop. Mainly, because it was later than they would normally eat, and Trace had called to say he was on his way over.

Pizza ordered and beer in the fridge, they waited for both the delivery guy and for Trace to show up. Trace arrived first. They only had to wait a few minutes before the pizza delivery was there too. Plates of hot pizza with various toppings were handed out while beers were opened. They sat on the deck and ate while Chase and Jack went over everything. Randa listened in and chimed in about the letters she still had and the feelings of being watched.

Chase was glad Trace could come over. Hopefully he had some good news in this shitstorm of a situation. The food was good, the company was better, despite the reason behind it. They all came to the same conclusion that Randa was indeed being stalked. Trace had done a search in the DMV database for the partial plate of the silver Cougar that Jack and Chase had seen. The results showed that it belonged to a rental company for exclusive clientele, of which they didn't have to share the name of the said client unless a warrant was issued. They decided then and there they would install a camera system. It would videotape any activity on the property from several different locations. He could understand why Randa was upset because she suddenly needed one after years of not.

They waited while Trace made a couple of calls and set them up with a company who would install a very discreet system, undetectable from outside and would be installed with utmost care to not be noticed when it was done. There would be a video feed on the backyard *and* the front. He hated the system was necessary, but would do anything to keep Randa safe. Hell, he and Jack both would.

After an hour of talking, Trace told them that he needed to get going. He promised he would bring Jackson over to meet the other dogs and for Randa to assess his training. Chase would have kissed Trace for the security system help and the diversion tactic, if he could guarantee that he wouldn't get his ass kicked for trying to get Randa's mind off what was going on. True, he and Jack could comfort her and make her feel a little safe, but maybe with Trace's help she'll not worry. Soon after Trace left, it was just the three of them.

Chase's phone buzzed, and seeing Trace's number, he answered. He sat up straight and hung up. He turned to Jack and Randa. Quickly, he explained Trace had seen the Cougar parked close by and then told them what they needed to do. Trace was going to circle the block and they were going to take the dogs for a walk in the opposite direction. Trace wanted to see if the asshole would have the balls to do something a second time that day.

They put 'happy go lucky' looks on their faces, the men each holding a leash and Randa with an arm around each of their waists. They looked exactly like what they were, an intimate threesome.

***

Trace had circled the block and when he got to where he had seen the Cougar, he found it gone from its original spot, but brazenly parked directly across the street from Randa's house. Now all he had to hope was the asshole didn't have the plate covered like his friends reported seeing earlier.

Trace parked his cruiser three houses down from Randa's and radioed into the station about a trespassing situation in progress. Thank whatever gods were looking out for them—the plates were clean as a whistle and pretty as can be. Quietly, he rattled off the license plate number for them to run. His gut was telling him it was the same car, but fuck if he would assume. And now that it appeared the car was involved with a crime, they had cause to know the name of the person renting it. He pulled his Glock 9 out of his holster and palmed it, knowing it was fully loaded. Making sure his badge hung around his neck, he quietly got out of the car.

Since dispatch knew he was off duty, they were sure to send a road unit over, but in the meantime, it was up to Trace to check it out and make sure it was a legit situation of trespassing. He skirted the very bright street lights and made it to the house across from Randa's without being detected. He saw a shadowy figure go around to the side of the house where the driveway was.

He kept to the shadows and came upon a tall figure shaking a spray paint can. The bastard was so confident he wouldn't get caught that he never once looked around to see. He knew he would have to allow the male to actually deface Randa's house. There was just no way around it. The perp had to be caught in the act or it would be difficult to press charges. Unfortunately, to do so would be to allow the asshole to do more damage. He heard the sound of air whooshing and knew that the spray paint had connected with the house.

Chapter Twenty-One

He had seen Randa come home from wherever she and the boy toys had gone. They had been gone long enough for him to decide to put into play the punishment he'd come up with for her. He wanted her to hurt for not being her true self while they were married. Hell, if he had known she was into three-ways he could have brought in another female with a killer body for him to play with. But no, she had been the put upon fat wife that followed him around like a damn puppy. She had no clue how to keep a man. He just knew he was right these two were only with her for money, or something else he hadn't figured out yet.

He had gone to his car and pulled out the canvas bag. All the way to her backyard the damn thing inside hissed and rattled at him. With the metal grabber his supplier let him borrow, he opened the bag and grabbed the snake behind its jaws as he had been shown. With a slow pull, he brought out the venomous reptile he hoped would hurt one of them, badly. He flung the snake as hard as he could, to see it land in a sunny patch of grass. He knew it would calm quickly and not bother him as he backed up from it, but he still kept an eye out.

Later that day, he was disappointed to find out they had managed to kill the thing and had called over another friend. Simon had wondered if maybe the threesome was a foursome. Damn, he hated her. He had friends when they were married that had needed to get laid and wanted a piece of her—for whatever reasons— but she was too fucking prim to do it. Now, here she was doing three guys.

He was now forced to make sure her neighbors knew how much of a whore she was. He had a background in art and was pretty good with free handing simple pictures, no matter what he used. He had a pretty decent outline of her fat body painted along with a guy standing behind her body ready to fuck her. He was about to start with another figure when he heard a voice.

"San Diego Police. Drop the can and lay on the ground. You're under arrest for destruction of personal property."

Simon almost shit himself when the cop came out of the shadows. No way could he get caught now. He couldn't believe teaching that bitch a lesson might be the fall of him. He just couldn't let her think she was anything more than a fat lump. But he'd worry about her when he got the hell away from the fucking cop.

***

Apparently satisfied with what he had sprayed, Trace kept a good eye on him as he stepped back to admire his handiwork—not knowing he was surely caught with his pants around his ankles and cheeks spread. Trace hated the asshole felt it was his right to destroy someone else's property, and wanted to beat his head in, but he had seen too many cops do that and have their reps ruined or their careers suffer for it.

Trace allowed his suspect to dig himself a deeper hole. When the painting got real graphic, he decided enough was enough. With his weapon sighted, he confronted him. In a way, he was hoping the son of a bitch would run. He needed to work off a bit of aggression, so maybe the idiot would resist arrest.

"I repeat: San Diego Police. Get on the ground, hands behind your head, lock your fingers. I won't tell you again and I will not hesitate to shoot you."

Apparently, the idiot had that insane thought of running too, because he threw the paint at Trace and took off. Trace ducked to avoid the can and smiled evilly. *A wish about to come true.* What the runner didn't remember was with nighttime came dew on the grass. Oh yeah, and actually getting past a cop who had trained with S.W.A.T. just for the hell of it and to stay on his game would be no easy feat.

Crouched to avoid the can, Trace was able to throw his body toward the male trying to get past him. Not going to happen. He'd seen the tortured look on Randa's face, and for her and his friends' sakes, he was going to catch the asshole. He hated that Randa—whom he'd fast started to consider family—had that haunted, violated look.

As they wrestled to the ground, he could see the glow of the blues and reds of a marked unit coming their way. An elbow to the eye knocked him on his ass, but he quickly recovered and dove again to catch the other male around the knees, bringing him down hard. He pounced and leaned his knee into the lower back of the suspect, grabbing his thumb and wrist in such a way to hurt yet not truly damage him.

Quickly, he pulled out his cuffs and was able to get them on before he was thrown off. Out of the corner of his eye he could see two uniform cops come his way and his friends rushing to make sure he was okay. Randa's expression was of a fierce mama bear and Trace laughed. Unnecessary, but touching. He grabbed the suspect by the elbows and pulled him to his feet. When Randa saw who it was, she turned white and gasped.

"Simon! What the hell are you doing here?"

With Jack and Chase standing beside her, holding her protectively, the two officers started walking the man away while reading him his Miranda Rights. Randa turned to her men and Trace with a look of disbelief on her face, until she saw Trace's eye. Now swollen shut, he looked down at her as she gingerly touched it. He smiled and pulled her hand away.

"Randa, I'm fine. This is minor compared to the scrapes I've gotten into in the past." He suddenly frowned as he realized what he'd heard. "Who was that guy to you, Randa? I thought you said you didn't have any enemies?"

"Well, if I had known my ex-husband would want to kill my roses, break my window, send me nasty letters, try to hurt me with a poisonous snake, ruin the paint job on my car and then spray paint the side of my house, I would have told you."

"Randa, pardon my lack of tack here, but how could you *not* have known?" Trace ignored the dirty looks from his friends.

"Well, he's a narcissist, sure, and a Grade-A jerk, yes. Hell, he's even a dog. Oh wait, I can't insult the canine species. Trace, he was an awful husband, but I never would have thought him capable of being a stalker or vandal. The Simon I knew would have thought behavior like that beneath him." Randa sounded exasperated.

"How long have you been divorced, and can I ask the reason?" Trace was still off duty, but figured he would get the answers to questions he knew the officers would need.

"It's been a little over thirty years. We married young and divorced a year later." Randa answered stiffly.

"And the reason, Randa?" Trace hated to do this to her, he really did.

"To put it bluntly, I was fat. He said he wouldn't make it in the political scene with a fat wife and if I wouldn't lose the weight he'd divorce me and marry someone skinnier." Randa's voice was flat and monotone.

***

Chase looked at the tortured expression on her face. The thought of laying Trace out after he beat the shit out of him was so tempting. He almost did but felt Jack's hand on his arm. He'd known where this was going and hated she would have to relive it. But if they wanted the whole thing behind them once and for all, she would have to. He stepped up behind her and put his hands on her waist to pull her back against his chest. He just had a feeling the conversation would feed her insecurities and push her several steps back from the progress she was making. Her body was stiff against his.

"Darlin', you know how he treated you does not represent all men. Do you remember the day we moved in and we were all in the backyard relaxing? Do you know that same night we all talked about how sexy you were, how real women looked like you? Those luscious curves you have made all of us hard as a rock." He turned her so he could cup her face between his hands and made her look into his eyes. He waited as Jack turned her around so he could then talk to her.

"The point he's making, honey, is that not all men are shallow. You had six men practically salivating and all you did was come out of your house in a one piece bathing suit. You are so fucking hot. Chase and I wanted to beat the shit out of the others when they were eyeing you up like candy."

***

Randa knew they were telling her the truth. She now knew there were a lot of good guys who preferred full figured women. She had grown more confident in her size and in her looks, but it still tore at her heart to have a failed marriage due to what someone else perceived as attractive. Was she being vain? Was it possible there were more men like hers out there that did not favor ribs showing, and liked a little bit of a roll on a tummy?

"You needed to know why Simon divorced me. And I told you, but his humiliation of me didn't just end with him telling me how I looked to him. Oh no, he went and claimed in open divorce court that I misrepresented myself. He basically—*publicly*—called me fat. Let the whole world know what a hardship it was to be married to a fat slob of a wife. And when the divorce was finalized, he assured me that no man would want me because of the fat I was carrying around with me." She spoke harshly and with a hitch in her voice. "Is that what you needed for the report, Trace? Will it make it easier to put him in jail? Will it stop him from tormenting me when I did absolutely nothing wrong, nothing to him?"

***

Trace felt bad for asking the question, but he was doing his job. It needed to be asked. She needed to hit the epiphany of knowing that she didn't deserve treatment like she had received. That she wasn't the cause of her ex's psychotic behavior. She needed to know all of it was on that poor excuse of a man. He stepped close, but not close enough to be in her personal space.

"Miranda, your men are right. You are a beautiful, sexy lady. No, I'm not hitting on you, just stating the obvious from the vantage point of any man with a set of eyes that work." Trace looked at her in all seriousness. "From what your two men have said, and from what I've seen, you are a strong lady. Please do not let this piece of shit victimize you."

"All right, Trace, do you have all you need from Randa, at least for now?"

Trace knew from the terseness of Jack's voice what he was about to do could very well backfire on him. He looked down at Randa and then reached out to push her hair out of her eyes and behind her ears. Sometimes he hated his job, hated what he put the victims through. In this case, the victim was someone who was close to him, even if she was the girlfriend or lover of his friends, so he hated this shit even more. He rubbed the back of his neck, and even though he was very interested in her friend, and knowing he risked getting his ass kicked by one or both of the men standing next to her, he grabbed her chin in his hand and brought her closer to him. He kissed her hard and thoroughly. He needed her to see that she was exactly what a lot of men out there were looking for. When she pulled back with a gasp and slapped him, he laughed.

"There you go. Get angry, get riled. Know that if your men here ever fuck up and you aren't happy, there will be a line as long as a two block radius of men out there willing to do whatever it takes to make a lady like you happy."

That said, he turned and walked back to his car. Behind the wheel, he pulled out his cell and shot his friends a quick text to apologize. Quickly, Jack had responded that if he did a repeat of the kiss again, he wouldn't hesitate to fuck him up. With a laugh, he knew there would be some extensive comforting going on in that house.

Chapter Twenty-Two

With everything that had happened, Jack and Chase had wanted to do something special for Randa. They all lived in the same house now and things were exactly as they wanted it: her in their bed, all night, every night. Sam had moved in next door, with help from all of the guys, which of course, was the perfect reason to have another party.

Criminal charges were being brought up against Randa's ex, Simon. With the testimony of an upstanding member of the San Diego Police Department as an actual witness to the crime, and enough of the circumstantial evidence, the assistant DA was pretty confident the council member would be in county orange soon. Not to mention the charges of resisting arrest and assault to a police officer.

They wanted to get her away, to take her away from the house, away from dogs. Hell, with Sam just next door, he even volunteered to doggy sit. Romeo and the other two dogs were now their own pack of sorts. Uncle Sam would be totally outnumbered.

Randa had been told to pack a bag with swimwear, sundresses, and nothing else. They left it up to her whether or not to pack lingerie. Personally, they wished she would stop wearing it, as it just got in the way. They guessed it would create the need to answer questions at work, and they had already had to sign wavers there regarding sexual harassment.

All of them would be off the clock by two in the afternoon, so with a quick stop at home to walk the dogs and pack the Infinity, they could head to the location the men had picked out, but kept secret from Randa. They had contacted Kitty and asked her to make a special dessert and deliver it to the location.

Colton had also gotten involved. It turned out the head chef where they were going happened to be a good friend and mentor of Colt's. So, with a little planning, a special picnic would be made available to them, complete with an elegant basket and bottle of champagne.

Chase and Jack each carried parts of the surprise they would be giving to their lady the next day. It was something the two men had thought a lot about. They were nervous. What if she couldn't envision the life they would suggest? What if she wasn't ready? What if their last idea was something she wouldn't go for, at all?

***

At the house, the dogs outside working off a little excess energy, waiting for Uncle Sam to get home from work, Randa had her bag packed. She worried she didn't pack the right clothes, the right swimsuit. And shoes, she had just bought the cutest shoes, ones that would give her some height and yet be comfortable. Her men wouldn't give her a clue as to where they were taking her, but she couldn't care less. As long as she was with them, that was all that mattered to her.

Jack and Chase took less time to pack their bags. It was easier for men: jeans, casual pants, shorts. Unless the man was a metrosexual, packing for a mere two days was a piece of cake. When they sat on the edge of the custom bed and watched her fuss with her packing they were wise to hold back their smiles. With a groan she finally zippered her bag shut, looked at them and couldn't stop the shiver as they stared at her with such hot gazes.

"If you two want to get to where ever it is you're taking me, we'd better leave now, or we'll be ending up in that big bed of ours."

She boldly left her bags where they were and walked out of their room. She looked back at them over her shoulder and then laughed as they quickly got up, each grabbed two bags, and then followed her down the stairs and out to the car.

They drove for about an hour when Randa saw the sign for the Hotel del Coronado. She had never stayed in the hotel, but had been to the area many times. She had walked the beach and had even attended a reception. She might have been getting ahead of herself, though. She would have to just wait and see. She was remembering some girl gossip that the hotel was a common place for proposals and weddings and such.

***

Chase sat in the back seat, and Jack behind the wheel. Chase smiled at Randa's expression. He was sure she would get whiplash from her neck whipping back and forth. When they passed the sign for the hotel, he could have sworn she gasped. Still, neither man said a word. He just hoped everything they planned worked out.

He smiled to himself as she looked like a child pressed to the window of a candy store. The surprise he and Jack had come up with for her was packed in his bag and he was so tempted to just blurt it out there in the car. He looked up and saw Jack's face in the mirror frowning at him. He grinned when he realized Jack had seemed to read his expression and was warning him to keep it together. With a nod, he calmed himself, knowing waiting for the perfect moment was best.

The Infinity pulled up in front of the hotel and a uniformed employee came over to take out their luggage, as the valet was handed the keys. Randa was speechless and both men took a hand as they walked into the hotel. Since the suite was in Chase's name, Jack and Randa wandered around the lobby looking at the opulence surrounding them. Fresh, fragrant flowers and tons of crystals were everywhere. The openness and the wooden beams gave a bit of an old west saloon kind of feeling mixed with elegance.

The porter stood by with their bags and as soon as Chase was finished, took them to the elevators to the floor they would be staying on. Once there, the room wasn't far. Door unlocked and bags settled inside, the men took care of the porter, and then shut the door. They stood watching as Randa wandered the room, taking in the suite with awe plainly written on her face. She had walked to the doors to their balcony and after checking the curtains, had unlocked and swung them wide open, letting the slight ocean breeze and fading sunlight into the room.

He couldn't get over how she was framed by the light—all feminine beauty—calling out for pleasure. Her hair fell down her back in graceful waves. Her dress was light and flowing softly around her legs. She was truly a sight and he knew that image would be burned into both of their memories as the start of the best day of their lives.

***

Randa couldn't believe the view. From their fifth floor balcony, the ocean gleamed with the slowly setting sun. She hadn't stopped to see too much of the room, because the balcony called to her. When she realized how quiet the room was, she whirled and saw her men watching her with such love in their eyes, her own eyes welled with tears. How could she have gotten so lucky to have two wonderful men fall in love with her? Her. This was no insecure moment, it was more her being awestruck with two people and trying to figure out what she could have possibly done to deserve them.

"Surprise," they said softly to her.

She ran across the floor into their waiting arms, arms that immediately wrapped around her. She rained kisses on their faces and had them laughing and groaning at the same time. It seemed like forever since they had

328

been together, what with work, getting her car fixed, and all of the other every day stuff chiming in. She grabbed a hand from each of them and pulled them over to the very large bed, having them sit. She kissed one then the other deeply.

***

They had no reservations for dinner and no plans for the night, so they had the entire evening to do what they wanted. It was looking like room service would be in order, because Jack doubted they would be going anywhere.

When she came back to him to kiss him again, he pulled her down so she was lying in his lap and in Chase's. He couldn't be more thankful that the dress was a wraparound and it basically came off like a robe. With it untied, they pushed it off her shoulders and ultimately off her body.

As he continued to kiss her, Jack's hands went to her heavy breasts. Already, her nipples were hard, begging for his attentions. He couldn't help himself, he had to taste. Pulling away from her lips, he lifted her torso until he could swoop down and take one of those dusky rose nipples into his mouth, sucking, licking and lightly nipping through the material covering it. He said a silent prayer her bra was a front closure piece of fluff, so he snapped it open and pushed the sides off and away. Before him were two of the most perfect globes he had ever seen.

***

Chase had watched with envy as Jack took control of her upper body, kissing her and then untying her dress. The halves opened to reveal the body of the woman they loved. They knew every part of her, knew exactly where to touch. Chase knew behind her knees she was very sensitive, knew with her thighs spread, he could dive right to her sweetness. She needed that delicious torment of only the tips of his fingers softly running along her inner thighs. By the time he would reach her tempting sheath, she would be whimpering and tossing her head.

Chase decided the panties that matched her bra had to go. He needed to feel her heat against his fingers, needed to savor her and bring her to the point where she couldn't think. Or maybe so all she could think about was them, their mouths pleasing her, their cocks waiting to fill her. He pulled the silk down her legs and tossed them on the floor somewhere. Right about then was when he and Jack decided she needed to get a little more horizontal.

"Darlin', lie down and get comfortable," Chase's Texas drawl thickened in his arousal.

He waited as she eagerly scooted up on the bed and lay with her head on a pillow, trying to catch her breath. Jack joined her on one side. His head lowered to pick up the kissing they had started at the end of the bed. His hand found her breasts again, cupping and gently squeezing, working to her nipple where he pinched lightly and pulled. Then he would begin the

330

cupping and squeezing on the other breast. She was moaning softly against his lips.

Chase didn't waste any time. He eased her legs apart and for a mere moment just stared at her loveliness. The sight she presented to him was the same as every other time they'd been with her, but he knew he would never get used to how she glistened for them. She was more than ready, but Chase was never one to rush. He pulled his shirt over his head and tossed it somewhere in the direction of her panties. With his fingers, he opened her and he leaned down to run his tongue from one end of her slit to the top, nearing her clit. Her arousal hit his senses like ambrosia. With a flick of his tongue against that sensitive bundle of nerves, he could feel her legs begin to shake.

***

Jack lifted his head and looked down her body to where Chase was working on her. He groaned while Randa was keening and panting. He sat up and pulled his own shirt off, then stood beside the bed, unzipped, and kicked off his trousers. He was more than ready for her to pay some attention to his cock, but for the moment it was all about her. Back on the bed, he lowered his head to her mouth again, letting his tongue mimic the motion of Chase's on her sensitive labia.

Her hands came up to thread through his hair and pull him closer. His hands moved to cup and caress her breasts again. She filled his hand perfectly. He pushed them together and lifted his head to see those pretty

331

nipples just begging for his lips. His eyes turned to hers and the look he gave her could have melted steel. Head lowered, his tongue swirled around the hard tip. He could do that all night and never need anything else.

***

Chase looked up from what he was doing. His friend was again paying homage to their lady's breasts. Randa had her head thrown back and her fingers tightly intertwined in his hair. Not to be outdone, Chase held her labia open and flicked her clit quickly as he slowly inserted two fingers into her channel. He could feel her core weeping and he eagerly lapped her moisture, groaning against her. He held her still to continue his assault. Her body alternated between lifting for him and then for Jack. Never would he get enough of her. He could hear her moaning and crying out and took pleasure in it. The wetter she got for him the harder he got. He was already ready to lose it. He looked up her body and saw the almost death grip on Jack's head and knew she was close.

With his fingers filling her and his tongue flicking, he could feel her inner muscles grabbing hold. He brought his other hand up and dipped a finger in her juices until it was coated. His fingers continued to pump in her, and he took the newly glistening digit and brought it around to her backend. He used her natural lubricant to ease the way for his finger to push past the tight ring of muscle of her ass. With his mouth still working her clit, he growled into her as she cried out.

Both men continued to use their hands and mouths to edge her over again, but they also watched her face. She was a vision, worthy of the masters of canvas. Her head tilted back, lips slightly parted on a soundless cry, eyes clenched shut. Her back bowed, hips lifted in the air, and her chest was rising and falling from her exertions.

They both moved up the bed and lay on their sides. Each had a hand that softly caressed her body, needing to keep the contact high going, needing her to feel cherished. This was what they wanted for the weekend. A way for her to relax, recover from all the stress, to recharge and consider.

With his head propped on his hand, Chase looked down at her, love shining in his eyes. "Darlin', remember when we were talking a few weeks ago about how to work the three of us out? How we wanted the whole relationship deal and a family?"

"I do remember, love." She was still coming down from the massive climax, but paying attention. "We never really talked about it again, but you know I can't have any more kids."

"Baby, we know that. We've been doing some checking and would like to see about a surrogate," Jack said.

"I think that's a great idea. That way the baby is biologically one of yours."

"Well, here's the thing, hon. We want you to donate the eggs. We want you to be the momma in all but the birth. And...we were wondering how you would feel about two babies?"

***

That definitely brought her out of the climax stupor. Were they talking about at the same time? Two separate surrogates or one surrogate carrying both babies? Oh my god, she would have two babies to deal with? From past experience, she knew one baby was a handful. After a moment, she calmed down. If they decided on two babies at the same time, there were three of them, an endless supply of aunts and uncles, and a much older brother to help. With that thought, she suddenly accepted it. Hell, she was all for it.

"You're talking two eggs fertilized, by sperm donated from each of you, eggs donated by me, implanted in the same woman so they would be fraternal twins, right? Cause I want to make sure that we are all on the same page."

"Yeah, hon, that's exactly what we're talking about," Jack answered with a chuckle.

"So, what do you think? There would be plenty of help, if we needed it. Between the three of us, we could financially do it. And we've got plenty of room. Hell, we could even build on to the house if it came down to it. Pac would love the project." Chase looked at her expectantly.

"I say, let's find a surrogate and get this done. I can't wait to be a momma again. And you two will be awesome daddies."

She threw her arms around them and couldn't believe she just agreed to becoming a mother again, after so many years. True, it was by way of another woman, but Randa would be their momma. Then she looked at them. Here she was, buck ass naked, and they were still partially dressed. They were either going to get their clothes taken off or she would get dressed.

"So how do you want to celebrate our impending parenthood?" Randa lie back, holding herself up by her elbows.

"Your choice, baby. We can order in, spend the rest of the day in bed, or eat out and walk the beach."

***

Jack was hard and desperately needed to be inside her, and from the looks of Chase, he did too. But the offer had been put out there that it was her choice. If Jack had to hazard a guess he could almost predict her answer. The devilish twinkle in her eye was almost a dead giveaway. He looked at Chase and saw his friend's big grin. They all knew what she would say, but she had to confirm it.

"Hmmm, well the beach looked so lovely when I was out on the balcony..."

He inwardly groaned, but refused to vocalize it. Jack said not a word, knowing she was teasing them. But on the other hand, *if* she chose to go out, they would with no complaints. Any time they spend with her— naked or not—was worth it. But if she didn't make a decision soon, they would be tempted to try and convince her staying in would be the better choice.

"Okay, I vote stay in. But I want to eat a hot fudge sundae in this big bed—off your chests."

"Deal!" they both chimed quickly, their excitement bursting out of them.

Jack and Chase weren't going to give her the chance to change her mind. Jack would make sure he got extra towels brought up at some point, he had a feeling they would need them. It would not be fun to sleep in a beautiful and very luxurious bed that happened to be a sticky mess.

***

Randa stood at the door to the balcony watching as their dinner dishes were taken away and the sundae delivered shortly after. As Jack tipped the bell boy and closed the door, he toed off his shoes on the way back to the center of the room. Jack stopped where he was and looked at Chase. Seems her men both had the same idea as Chase had already removed the rest of his clothing. Randa started towards them, removing her dress as she walked. When she got to Chase, she pushed him to sit on the edge of the bed.

Randa took the tray with the sundae on it and placed it on the table near the bed. She dipped a finger in the extra chocolate syrup and knelt between his legs to paint the sauce on the head of Chase's erection. With a sly smile, she leaned forward and licked the tip free of the dark liquid. The taste of the sweet, mixed with his pre-cum, forced a low moan in the back of her throat. Chase leaned back on his hands to watch.

"That syrup is supposed to go on the ice cream, baby," Jack admonished.

"Oh, but it tastes so much better the way I'm enjoying it," she said impishly. "Would you like a demonstration?"

"Hmm, baby, you can do whatever you want to me as long as it includes that wet mouth and hot tongue." Jack slowly walked to the bed, stripped off his pants, and stood to the side.

She reached for the sauce again and with two fingers dripped the brown sweetness along Jack's length. Though warm, she knew the sauce would not hurt him. Instead, it made him suck in a breath. With one hand still wrapped around Chase, Randa lowered her head and licked all of the chocolate from Jack, making him groan low. She sat back on her heels, each hand now wrapped around a cock, looking from one very impressive length to the other.

***

Chase had wanted to enjoy more of the chocolate syrup treatment, but knew there was plenty of time. He pulled her by the arm until she straddled him. He wanted to be inside her, needed to feel her heat wrapped around him. He looked up at Jack and knew his friend was thinking and needing the same. He saw Jack looking as Randa sat on Chase's lap, her perfect ass just calling out to him. When Jack looked from the chocolate sauce to Randa, Chase could almost read his mind.

"Chase, lie down and have her lay on top of you."

Chase was more than happy to do as Jack instructed. He scooted back until his head was near the pillows, allowing Randa's body to cover his. He could feel her soft, satiny smooth skin all over him and willingly allowed his friend to do what he needed to do as long as Randa could stay just like this. Her breasts pressed against his chest, her thighs naturally separated to allow his between hers. He watched as Jack approached the bed with towels and the bowl.

Over her shoulder, Chase watched as Jack grabbed a couple of towels to catch any stray sauce then picked up the bowl. He dipped two fingers in the bowl and brought them to her mouth. She eagerly took both of Jack's fingers into her mouth and sucked them clean, imitating the motions she had used on them just minutes before. The sight of Jack's fingers in Randa's mouth, as she cleaned the sticky sauce off, made both men groan. Chase knew then what Jack was going to do. When he dipped them again and brought them to the crack of her ass and held them slightly above her, allowing the sauce to drip between her cheeks, both Chase and Randa groaned. Her head fell forward to rest on his chest. Chase didn't have a direct line of sight of what he was doing, but Randa lifted her head and looked into his eyes, her lips slightly parted. He lifted his head as she lowered hers and their lips pressed together while Jack still played with her ass. Jack's next words caused them to groan again. Chase needed more. He slowly, so as not to disturb Jack's movements, began to slide down her body, until her breasts were within reach.

338

"Relax, baby. Just breathe through it and let it happen."

***

Randa knew he was prepping her to take him. With him being bigger than Chase, the times Jack had actually entered her ass were not as often as Chase. They were afraid of hurting her. What they needed to realize was that a bit of pain mixed in was very enjoyable, and she planned on proving it to them tonight. With her concentration on Jack's fingers, she hadn't paid too much attention to Chase moving his body down hers, from under her, and was now at her breasts, her nipples sucked deep into his mouth.

The feel of his lips surrounding her flesh had her involuntarily moving her body over his. She needed more. But her body wasn't being too particular. It wanted more of Jack and more of Chase, more of anything they were giving her. She was getting impatient. She needed them so badly, but knew *this* couldn't be rushed.

***

Jack couldn't see her expression, but he'd learned to read her body very well. He also couldn't see Chase's, but knew between the both of them she was more than ready for the next step. His fingers were coated in chocolate and to see it smeared all over her skin made him want to lick it all off. The sounds she was making could make a monk masturbate in front of a nun. And he loved knowing he was part of the reason for those sounds. God, he wanted to shout it to the whole world that she was theirs. He would have to settle for working with his best buddy and show her.

"Jack, buddy, ease off, man. I got an idea. Hand me a couple of those towels and then you can play."

Jack grabbed a couple of towels and laid them on the bed then stepped back. Since they knew the ice cream wasn't going to be eaten in the traditional way, and the chocolate was definitely a good call for lube, he could see where Chase's mind was heading. Randa got up off of him and knelt to the side, watching him place the towels down. Then he lay back down and grabbed the bowl on the table. The vanilla ice cream had melted enough—though Jack assumed was still a little cool—for him to take the spoon and drizzle some of the sweet liquid on his very hot, hard cock. With a bit of mischief in his eyes, he even placed the cherry on the tip.

"My favorite way to eat a sundae." She laughed low and crawled her way between his legs.

Before she could get fully in place, Jack put a couple more towels down where she would be lying. Eagerly, she crawled up the bed until her head was just even with his belly. With a smile across her face, she held her body up on her hands and knees. Her head lowered and blew softly on the tip in front of her. Her lips parted, took the cherry into her mouth, and chewed slowly.

Jack watched as she ate the fruit off Chase's cock. He then walked around to the end of the bed. With the bowl of syrup in one hand, he used his other hand to lightly caress her bare bottom as it stuck in the air, practically screaming for attention. There was still syrup between the cheeks of her ass but he needed more for what he had planned. He could see Chase's face and could tell that with the bobbing of Randa's head she had brought him close, but then backed off. It was so hot to watch their woman please one and be about to please him. So. Fucking. Hot.

***

Randa hadn't taken Jack in her ass too often due to his larger size than Chase, but he was always careful to make sure there was proper lube so she didn't get hurt. She knew no matter what, they would always take care of her and she wanted to make sure they were taken care of too. It was a wonder she could even form coherent thoughts at all with everything she was feeling. Her body on fire and yet wanting so much more.

With all her attention focused on Chase, she lowered her head and slowly licked his length from tip to base and back up to tip. As her lips hovered above him, ready to take him in, she looked up his body and found he was watching with his eyes half closed. His tongue came out and licked his lips as though he were sending her a signal. She mimicked his movements with her own tongue, but didn't lick her lips. The head of his cock was what received the moist attention. She slowly lowered her head until the tip hit the back of her throat. Her tongue slid along the underside.

***

Chase had raised himself up onto his elbows and was watching as Randa lowered her head, inch by inch over him. The wet heat, her tongue, and the suction. All of it was enough to tighten the muscles in his legs, his toes ready to curl. He had to concentrate hard to hold back. He didn't want to lose it so soon. He focused on just the movements and not so much feeling what she was doing. He knew it would be the only way he could last.

Barely able to keep his concentration, Chase was vaguely aware Jack knelt behind Randa, chocolate syrup at the ready. Randa had stopped, but her mouth still held him tightly. He saw Jack dip two fingers into the syrup and move his hand to Randa's ass, assumedly to paint the tight ring of muscles of her ass. Chase felt relief. He knew it wouldn't be long. With short movements, Jack began to pump his fingers in and out of her. Chase could feel her hum her need against his flesh and her body rock to meet Jack's fingers. Then she stopped completely, again her mouth still wrapped around Chase and listened as Jack spoke to her.

"Baby, are you ready to take me? As nice as your ass feels around my fingers, I have a feeling you want more, yes?"

Since she couldn't talk with a mouth full of his cock, she managed to hum out her yes around him. Chase whole heartedly approved of her action. The bed dipped and he heard rustling, then Jack came back to the bed. Chase could see the bottle of lube he held in his hand. Jack popped the lid open and then started slicking it on himself.

Chase saw Jack was about to take her from behind and needed in on the action. With a gentle tap on the cheek, he had her release him. With a crook of his finger and a smile, he beckoned her to come up his body. Jack backed off and let her move. Randa straddled Chase's hips, her ass in the air. Chase pulled her down for a quick, deep kiss then sat her up.

"You know what we want, baby...Climb aboard."

***

With a Cheshire grin, Randa lifted up onto her knees. She didn't need any help guiding him into her heat, his aim was true and she was very ready for him. She eased down onto him and moved her hips side to side to just get the feel of him deep within. Chase groaned, put his arms around to her back, and pulled her back down to him until their lips met. As she braced herself above him, he thrust upward into her sheath, taking her lips the whole time. He drove into her, and she could feel herself start to head down the road to her happy place, her muscles starting to tighten around him. When she felt his hips slow until he was barely stroking in her, she whimpered.

"Oh please, Chase, please don't stop."

"Darlin', don't you want Jack in on our fun? Come lie on me, baby. Let him help take you too. You know we both need to feel you wrapped around us."

"Yes. Oh god, yes. Jack, come to me. I need you in me too."

***

Jack had watched as Randa had slowly lowered herself onto Chase's erection. He had never really thought too deeply about the voyeurism side of a threesome. To watch as his best friend and the woman they loved come together made the blood rush straight to his cock. When Chase lifted and lowered his hips, entering and exiting Randa, it took all of Jack's will power to hold back. However, it didn't stop him from stroking himself. He had been lubing himself up when Randa was sucking Chase, readying to take her from behind. The sounds their lady was making were enough to make him blow, but he again held back.

His eyes met Chase's. With a nod and a smile, it was almost like he was saying 'come get you some, pal'. His eyes were drawn back to Randa. Her body was made to be loved by them. He knew they would never tire of loving her. It just wasn't possible. Chase held her still as he was deep inside her. Almost as if he called to her, she looked over her shoulder and saw his hand moving up and down his length slowly, his thumb circling the tip, his eyes half mast while watching them. Her breath caught and she whispered his name.

"Jack? Honey, I need you. Come take me, please?"

Jack watched as Randa lie along Chase's body, Chase's cock buried deep inside her. He moved up close

344

to her back end and again applied lube to her and himself. With his one hand wrapped around his cock, he used his other hand to brace against her and slowly entered her. Gradually, taking all care to not rush, he pushed forward. That ring tightening at first until he could feel the tension ease out of her and could feel her start to push back toward him with the barest of moves. With a silent pop, the tip slid past and he had to force himself to hold still for her to get accustomed to the feel of the double penetration.

***

Chase could feel Jack's entry, the thin membrane the only thing separating them. He looked at Randa's face and saw her biting her lower lip. He knew no matter the lube or preparation, the initial penetration could still be a bit uncomfortable. He silently applauded Jack's control and stillness. They both knew the moment she was ready for more, though. It was like a switch flipped and she would make the barest of movements.

With both of their cocks inside her, the fit was tight. The need to rush down to the finish line towards their climax was strong, but drawing it out would make it all the more worth it. He ran his hands down her arms, then along her sides. Hell, he could have been holding her feet and he wouldn't care, he just needed to have his hands on her.

***

Randa loved the feeling of fullness they gave her when they were both deep inside her. All she needed to do was get past the first few seconds. She felt Jack's hands on her ass cheeks, rubbing softly, could feel his chest against her back as he had bent down closer to her and asked if she was okay. She couldn't answer; her breathing was too fast, so she just nodded her head. Seconds later, she needed more. Her hips began to push back against Jack and that was the signal they were looking for.

She certainly couldn't forget Chase. She felt his hands smoothing her skin. It was like every nerve in her body was connected to a live wire. Like their touch was a direct line to her clit. As if all they had to do was look at her or touch her with the tip of a finger and she would go off like a rocket. All she needed was them, any way she could get them.

***

Jack lifted up and grabbed her around her waist. He pulled almost all the way out until just the tip remained, then thrust forward. Within a few movements, Randa was gasping with each entry and whimpering with every exit. For every withdrawal, Chase thrust upward. Every time Jack pushed into her, Chase would retreat. They gave her no break from the sensations that they were giving her.

The room was silent with the exception of their labored breathing, the low moans coming from them all, and the sounds of flesh meeting flesh. The air was heavy with the scent of chocolate and sex. The end result was just within their reach, and it was rushing to the surface. Jack felt the need compelling him to move faster and to force Chase to do the same, their climaxes closer by the second.

If Jack didn't know any better, he'd swear that every drop of his blood had pooled in his cock. The feel of her tight muscles wrapped around him, taut and wet, and the sound of her nonsensical ramblings, were all enough to send him flying, but he grit his teeth and held on. Though he didn't know what she said, he knew what she wanted, what she needed. He knew what he wanted. Well, besides a release so powerful he'd not be able to do much more than pass out. No, he needed—*they*— needed her to have a bone melting climax, right then, no more waiting. Their hips were working against each other with the goal to get Randa to the point of no return, to please her and show her what a life with them would be like. They knew they could make her happy and knew no other could satisfy them. She was and always would be their one.

***

Within moments, Randa could feel herself about to go. Her muscles were throbbing around Chase's cock and she could feel that bit of an 'Oh my god' about to come crashing through her. It took all she had not to scream her pleasure from the rafters. Her body had a mind of its own. Never a screamer, but not as quiet as a mouse either, the loud sounds coming from her soon made her hoarse. But since she had never been a screamer, she just did what she always did and bit her lip. Her eyes closed and she concentrated on the two hard lengths as they moved in and out of her. She could feel every bit of them as her body was so sensitized to their every move.

She could feel the strength in both of their bodies. Chase's hard length under her, and Jack equally hard, pressed against her back. A part of her was still wondering why her, but the new and improved Randa bitch slapped herself and relished their desire. And right then she needed to get out of her head anyhow and concentrate on feeling.

***

Jack's instinct had taken over. His hips picked up their rhythm. He could feel that special euphoria starting to move from his lower back to his groin. He thought to their plans for the following day and the answer they hoped they would get. That thought alone threw him and made his hips stop their movement as he emptied into her tightness.

The sound of his climax echoed in the room, mixed in with the remaining pants and groans and growls. He'd wanted to finish with them, but she had felt so awesome around him he hadn't been able to help himself. She proved to be too much for him, this time. He tried to move, really he did, but he just couldn't pull himself away from her.

***

Randa felt Jack's warmth fill her and it spurred her on to her own release, making her cry out and fall forward onto Chase's chest. Her inner muscles were throbbing and she could feel Chase tighten his grip on her waist. She knew she would go again, it was just the way things were with them.

She felt Jack still deep inside her and she wished it could go on longer. Chase, she could feel was on the edge. She loved these two men and wanted this moment to last forever, even if it wouldn't. The emotions that ran through her made her tear up. She could feel the climax force itself to the surface and then explode. Her whole body shook from the intensity and power.

***

Chase heard Jack go, and Randa right behind him. As they climaxed together, Chase held onto her hips and began to pump up into her, trying like hell to get as deep as he could get. He would have crawled up into her if he could. He was dealing with the alternating throb and squeeze of her pussy, when with a final arch of his back and thrust up, he shouted out his release.

Chase felt the weight on him—basically both Jack and Randa—ease up as Jack extracted himself. The room quieted until the only sound was their heavy breathing and an occasional murmur from one or the other. His hand traced along her back, feeling the slight sheen of sweat covering her, as he assumed he and Jack were also covered in it. A lump formed in his throat as the feelings that arose hit him. He and Jack had been like brothers for so long and no other had really pierced his heart, until Randa. Now to have two people who he knew he could not live without in his life was awesome and terrifying at the same time.

***

Jack collapsed on his side of the bed and hooked his arm over Randa's waist. He smiled at Chase when he gently turned her so that she was on her side facing Jack, then Chase curled himself to her back. Jack couldn't have said what was going on in Chase's head, but it was probably something similar to his. All Jack could think of was how easily he could make himself look like a weak pussy by breaking down. The one thing that prevented this from happening was the thought of their plans for tomorrow.

He and Chase were confident Colton would come through for them and everything would go as planned. He wanted the whole experience to be one Randa would never forget. He knew he and Chase would be pouring a lot of themselves into the day and to what was going to happen. He twirled a lock of her hair then let it fall to land and curl around her breast. He leaned down to kiss her softly as her eyes closed and she began to drift off.

Jack was the first to wake the next day with the sun peeking through the floor to ceiling gossamer door coverings. Randa was still curled against Jack's side, but one arm was wrapped around one of Chase's that was draped over her hip. With a glance to the side, Jack saw it was after ten in the morning. They had slept through breakfast, but there was no need to rush. The next phase in the weekend wasn't due to happen for a couple of hours.

Though they still had time before they needed to get going, between showers and grabbing a bite, time would fly. Jack knew he should wake Chase and Randa, but chose to take stock of how Randa looked right then. He leaned down to caress her lips with his. His hand reached down to pluck her nipple then cup her breast. His mouth moved to her cheek, then down to her neck, and finally to her nape. He nuzzled and licked her, breathing in her scent. Taking in the scent of all three of them combined.

He whispered into her ear. "I love you, Miranda Michaels. There will never be anyone else to take the place you have in my heart."

***

Randa opened her eyes and luxuriated in Jack's kisses. The sheet had slipped to her waist and her breasts were pressed to his chest. She felt an arm slip up and under hers. Then there were two hands on her breasts, one from each of her men. When Chase's arm then pulled her onto her back so that they could say good morning to her in a more proper manner, she almost purred.

The combination of Chase's hand and Jack's mouth were enough to take her slow awakening into a full blown, wide awake state. When Jack spoke from his heart, her eyes filled with tears and threatened to fall. She wanted to respond, but the lump in her throat wouldn't let her. She smiled tremulously, raised her hand to each of them, and cupped the sides of both of their faces. Chase looked down at her and she saw the same emotion she saw in Jack, with a bit of mischief mixed in.

***

Chase had no problem letting Jack speak for him. He wanted to express himself too, but he was so much better at actions than words sometimes. When he saw Randa get emotional, he wanted to swoop in and kiss the tears away, but he knew they weren't sad tears. Instead, he moved between Randa's thighs and was softly playing with her silky skin, slowly working his shoulders between them so they were spread and he could see the glistening moisture waiting for him. He leaned down and ran his tongue along the opening of her slit and up to her little bundle of nerves that swelled with his touch. With a flick of his tongue, he tasted her essence and moaned against her. He heard Jack talking to her so he lifted himself up until he was lying next to her, his mouth near her other ear.

"Randa, you can't know how long I've waited for you. How long Jack and I waited. We had been talking about how we were skeptical it would ever happen and then you practically fell in our laps. Moving in next to you was the best thing we ever did. I love you, darlin'."

Randa turned her head from one to the other and her eyes welled up with tears. She reached up and kissed first Jack, then him.

"You two came into my life at the moment I needed you most. I never would have thought someone like me could ever have caught the interest of one again, let alone two very attractive, sweet men like you." She sounded so overcome with emotion. With tears in her eyes, she reached up to kiss both of them again.

Chapter Twenty-Three

Chase lifted himself up and stared down at her. He wanted to call her out on what she said, but didn't want to cast a shadow on their day. Today was too important for him to mess up by getting anyone riled. What would it take to convince her? He was hoping after their plans that afternoon came through, she would be thoroughly convinced. Hell, he hoped she liked what they were going to do, *and* reacted the way they hoped.

Deep down Chase wanted to say to hell with their plans and suggest they stay in bed all day, but they wanted to get her out of the room, needed her to know it wasn't all about sex. He got out of bed and walked to the closet to pull out his bag, grabbing a change of clothes.

"Babe, how about we take a walk on the beach before lunch? Then the surprise we have planned for you can be waiting and ready for us."

***

Jack could tell Randa's words affected Chase as much as him, but he had the feeling it was just a reflexive statement and she probably didn't mean it like it sounded. Hell, he knew if their friends weren't as honorable as they were, they would be panting after her like dogs. He had noticed the change in her in the time since they first met. He hoped their plans today would finally convince her she was worth every bit of their love, of their lust.

"I think that's a great idea, buddy. What do you say, Randa?"

He sat up and drew her back against his chest. His hand casually drifted to her breast so he could caress her. She looked up at him and her expression screamed she was thinking more of staying in bed, but now the idea of a walk was growing on him. It would do them good to get out of the room and maybe work up an appetite for each other, again.

She sounded a little confused but answered hesitantly, "A walk would be great. Is this surprise a casual thing or should I dress up a little?"

"How about a sundress, darlin'? You look beautiful no matter what you wear, but a sundress would be best, right Jack?"

"Baby, you'd look good in a potato sack, but yeah, I agree with Chase, a sundress would be great."

***

Randa was about to ask them for more details, but Chase excused himself to take a quick shower. Jack stepped out onto the balcony claiming he needed to quickly check on a patient. She could see him talking on the phone, but didn't want to interrupt, so she went to her bags and got out her clothes for the day. When Chase came out of the bathroom, she gave him a quick kiss and said she'd be out in a moment.

Before she stepped into the shower, she pinned her hair up off her neck. She thanked herself for the laser treatments that meant she didn't have to shave her legs. After a moment she stepped out of the shower, dried off and applied lotion. She was suspicious of what Chase and Jack were up to, but didn't want to over think anything. She left the bathroom with just the towel around her and stepped to where her clothes were hanging. With Jack watching through the glass door and Chase dressed, she looked at them impishly and dropped the towel. With the looks they were shooting her way, she didn't think— for once—about any extra curves or the stray stretch marks. She swore she could see herself through their eyes and she liked how it made her feel.

***

Chase stood there entranced as she came out of the bathroom, towel loosely wrapped around her curvy body. When she dropped the covering, his entire body heated and he could feel his cartoon howling wolf fighting to make its presence known. The sunlight only made what was already beautiful, worthy of a Michelangelo sculpture. He licked his lips and kept his eyes trained on her as she slipped into a filmy dress, thinking the whole time it was a crime to cover such delicious skin. *Temptation at its finest,* he thought.

***

356

Jack was standing on the balcony on the phone with Colton making sure he had arranged the whole picnic lunch, when he saw Randa come out barely covered by a towel. He barely paid attention when Colton reassured him all was good to go, even gave him the name of the head chef there at the hotel. The drop of the towel stopped all thought in Jack's head and he almost dropped the phone. His voice was a bit distant when he thanked Colton then disconnected the call. His hand unconsciously came up to his face to make sure his tongue wasn't hanging out.

His attention stayed focused on her until she finished getting dressed. He saw Chase walk to her and wrap his arm around her waist, then both of them joined Jack on the balcony. She stood looking out at the ocean, Jack standing behind her with his arms around her. The three of them were quite the sight. Randa's hair drifting back in the slight breeze, Jack with his head to the side of hers, and then one of Randa's arms wrapped around Chase's waist.

"I've heard there are some really good shops along Orange Ave here. Would you like to take a walk before we grab lunch?" Jack suggested in a strangled voice.

***

Randa still thought something was up between them, but couldn't figure out what it was. But being a typical woman, she was always up for some window shopping. She slipped into comfortable walking shoes, which still looked cute with her sundress, and waited as the men slipped into theirs.

After wandering around the tourist shops, they came to a store with paintings in the window. Chase and Jack stood back and watched Randa while she stared at a painting that caught her eye. She wasn't sure if it was water or oil paint, but the painting was a typical tourist beach scene. The tower of the Coronado was in the distance as the sun set.

Randa was looking at the painting and was really considering buying it, but it was a bit big to be lugging around. There was just something about the painting that called to her. In the forefront of the painting was a trio of birds. Their bodies were gracefully suspended in the air. The detail on their wings, right down to their feathers, was amazing. Sure the rest of the painting was very eye catching, but it was the three birds that kept her attention.

Chase stepped up behind her and wrapped an arm around her waist, Jack's hand clasped with a free one of hers. They looked at each other in the window of the shop. Their little trio looked really good together. She turned and tugged them away from the store. Smiling, she pulled an arm from each guy to her side. The smiles Chase and Jack exchanged could only be described as devious, but she wasn't sure if she really wanted to try and figure them out just then. They strolled around for about an hour or so, stopping at a couple of stores to get souvenirs for Randa's friends. Jack and Randa were in one shop looking at a bracelet that Randa had seen in the window. Chase stayed outside, saying he had to make a quick call. When she and Jack came out she started to question who Chase was on the phone with, but he gave her some story of checking on a patient. That was weird since Jack had said the same thing earlier.

"Are you ready for lunch? The next part of our surprise is waiting for us back at the hotel."

"I'm starved. But you two are acting weird. Want to tell me what's going on?"

Randa decided to just spit it out and get them to come out with it. Her past fears rushed to the surface and flooded her with doubt. Maybe they were doing this as a final goodbye. Her eyes welled with tears as the thought hit her heart first then made a bee line for her brain. *No*, she thought, *they would never do that to me*. Eyes dried up quickly, she still waited for one of them to explain what was going on.

"Baby, it's a good surprise, really." Jack stopped and turned her to face him. "Can you hang with us for a bit longer? We promise, not much longer...okay?"

She nodded her head, unable to speak. She was afraid if she did, her voice would be too hoarse to be understood. They looked at her, not with pity in their eyes, but with so much love she again choked up. *Damn, what's the matter with me?* They were wonderful men, always respectful of her and other women. They never acted like the players she had met, dated, and subsequently been dumped by.

***

Jack and Randa walked with their fingers entwined. Chase walked on the other side of her doing the same. Chase told them he would meet them back at the hotel, saying he had something he had to take care of. The other two walked away, Jack making sure Randa didn't turn to see Chase walk into the shop to purchase the painting she hadn't wanted to let on she really wanted. Jack knew after he made the purchase, it would be arranged to be delivered to the house. They would make sure it was hung before she got home as a surprise.

Back at the hotel, Jack and Randa went into the bar to have a quick drink. No sense in going back to the room when Chase would be along shortly. Jack sat with his arm around the back of Randa's chair. He was playing with her hair and running his fingers along the nape of her neck and the top of her shoulders. That was how Chase found them. Her eyes closed, lips parted, breathing erratic. Jack had moved to nuzzling, was nursing a hard-on, and had a hand ready to move under the skirt of her dress.

Jack wanted to behave, but he couldn't. After he had sat there touching and caressing her soft skin, he found he couldn't stop himself from tasting then touching her. He hadn't realized how far gone he was until Chase tapped him on the shoulder. They both turned at Chase's voice.

"I hate to interrupt, but our lunch is ready. I think you'll really like what we've got planned, Randa. I've even been recommended a spot that is shaded but has a great view of the beach. Can you two tear away from each other long enough?"

Randa turned bright red when Jack grinned at her and pulled his hand out from under the hem of her skirt. He shrugged apologetically, barely, and helped her down from the bar stool. He thought it was so cute she was flustered. She hadn't known it, but he'd been careful to make sure no one would have or could have seen their intimate display. They walked to the concierge desk and retrieved the basket and a light blanket.

The trio left the hotel and strolled in the direction Chase had been instructed. Pretty soon they were in a small copse of trees, though not enough to totally block out the sky and the view of the beach. Jack spread out the blanket and they all settled down to open the basket and see what the hotel chef had supplied them for their lunch.

Thinly sliced medium rare roast beef, bits of honey glazed ham, fresh mozzarella, cherry tomatoes, along with other tasty treats. Freshly cut fruits and a sliced loaf of crusty French bread. Two bottles of wine were also included. A Booths Tsarine Premium Brut to be enjoyed with the ham and a Ridge's 1999 Monte Bello to go with the roast beef. The dessert had been delivered by Kitty personally. She hadn't stayed for fear of giving away the surprise the two men had concocted. Of course the dessert and the Dom Perignon were in a separate section with separate champagne flutes and the surprise there too.

Jack was a bundle of nerves, tempted to just spit it out and tell her what was going on, but a warning look from Chase stopped him. Despite his angst he was confident she would be pleased and like what they were planning, but as is human nature, a slight moment of insecurity had rolled through him.

They enjoyed the ham and the Swiss paired with it, slices of the French bread, and bites of fruit in between sips of the Brut. Next they sampled the roast beef and the fresh mozzarella with the Monte Bello. Their conversation was kept light and casual, neither man directing, letting Randa take charge. They interjected when there was a lull. They did ask a young male employee, who happened to be walking by, to take a couple of pictures of their trio. As the young man turned to leave, Jack jumped up and asked him to return in about fifteen minutes or so and if he couldn't, to please send someone else.

When Randa looked at him with a questioning gaze, he merely smiled at her and asked if she would want dessert. She hesitantly agreed, but only wanted a little since they had already eaten so much. Chase pulled out the pine nut tart with rosemary cream, which made Randa narrow her eyes in suspicion.

***

Randa knew something was up now. She would recognize that tart anywhere. Kitty knew it was Randa's favorite dessert, ever. It was so rich and decadent Randa only allowed herself to have it on very special occasions. She also knew Kitty was aware of Randa's self-restriction to the dessert. When she looked at her men, they both had blank expressions plastered on their faces.

"Randa, darlin', could you get the fresh glasses out of the other compartment, please? With this last bottle, we don't want to mix the flavors."

She moved to the basket and at first she was confused. But when she looked up and saw the expectant looks on their faces, she gasped. There were three chains displayed in what she could only guess at their meaning. She knew she wouldn't have to take a huge leap to figure out what this was all about, but she didn't want to spoil the moment for her men. They went to all this trouble, so she wanted to let them continue.

No way was Randa going to be running around thinking she was a sex goddess, capable of luring any man into her bed. But right at that moment, the truth of the situation hit her. Jack and Chase loved her and desired her. She saw the truth of it in their eyes. But all of her past was still there to beat her down, to try and convince her she didn't deserve any of it.

She opened her mouth then closed it. Should she ask them or let them set their own pace? Should she just shout yes, to hell with everything else and go from there? No, she decided, they had gone to so much trouble to arrange this and she didn't want to belittle it or take control out of their hands. The looks on their faces were a mixture of confidence, love, and though she could hardly fathom why, a tiny bit of hesitance.

"Miranda Michaels, would you do us the honor of becoming our love; living with us, caring for us as we will care for you? Will you honor us with your love, with your happy times? To allow us to try and make your sad times easier? To protect you in any way necessary? To share in the financial burden of whatever the future will throw at us? If we are fortunate to have kids, would you be our babies' mother?"

Right then and there, she knew this was it. She had thought she found love twice before, but this moment had just proved she hadn't. With tears welled up and spilling down her cheeks, she nodded her head and replied.

"Chase Fargo, Jack Benning, I would be proud to be your love for as long as the time we are given together. I love you both so much my heart aches with it. I do promise all of me is yours. I trust you with my love, my heart—fully. Any sad times that are shuffled our way will be handled by the three of us. So, yes, I'll be yours, both of yours."

The chains were brought out to reveal all three were identical with the exception of the length. On each chain held three small rings, intertwined to represent their new life together. Chase lifted Randa's hair away from her neck, and Jack fastened the chain, letting the rings settle just above her breasts to be easily seen. Then Randa returned the favor for her men.

Right then, the male employee came back and he was again asked to take a picture, this time with their promise of happy years to come proudly being displayed. Randa sat sideways and her men each on a side. Wide, happy smiles were on all three faces as they all thought of how life couldn't get any more perfect.

Epilogue

"Chase, Jack, where are you two? We're supposed to meet with Vanessa in twenty minutes. The doctor is going to give us the news at the same time, and damn it, I don't want to be late."

She sensed Jack come up behind her before he wrapped his arms around her waist and buried his head in her hair at the nape of her neck. She would never get enough of this. It just would not happen. Not a day went by she wasn't thankful for having met him and Chase.

"Babe, calm down, it takes five minutes to get to the doctor's office. Chase is just powdering his nose."

"I fuckin' heard that, asshole," Chase said from the stairway.

She turned to see Chase approach them. The desire in his eyes was so hot she had to look down to make sure the clothes she wore weren't singed. If she weren't so nervous about this appointment she would make him follow through with that look. But this was baby related and the doctor had actually sounded like he was smiling when he had called. So their mutual need would have to wait until they got home.

"I know how long it takes, but I have such a good feeling. Even though we were told it might take more than one try, but I just think this is it. Am I crazy?"

"No, darlin', not crazy, just very eager to be a mama." Chase pulled her from Jack's arms and into his.

"And you're both sure you want to do this? A baby is a *huge* responsibility."

"Honey, we've had Max for a while and haven't lost him," Jack said with a laugh.

Randa turned and swatted him, laughing. "Not the same thing and you know it. Now, let's get gone. We're not going to keep anyone waiting."

***

Chase paced as Jack and Randa sat waiting for Vanessa. The door opened and in walked a beautiful young woman in her twenties. She looked around and, spotting the three of them, she blushed and headed their way. Randa fussed and got her a glass of water as Chase and Jack sat opposite of the young lady who was hopefully carrying their babies. After another five or ten minutes of catching up with Vanessa, they heard her name called. All four were brought back to a larger office than normal, since this was not a normal prospective parent situation.

He could see Randa was silently trying to read the doctor to get the results they all were hoping for. Damn, he would do well at the poker tables. Nothing. He chuckled, when with a sigh, she sat forward and waited, her hands shaking and twisting together. He looked at Vanessa, the young girl who would be carrying their babies. She had been recommended by their doctor because she was a patient of his already. She was twenty-four and in med school. She would only be carrying the babies, the eggs were Randa's since the doctor had checked her out and found her eggs very viable. So now all they had to do was hope for a positive. Another chuckle earned him a smack on the arm as Randa almost screamed when he began to shuffle papers.

"So, are we ready to have some babies?"

With a gasp and a cry, Randa turned to Vanessa and hugged her. Jack looked as stunned as Chase felt and he couldn't help the tears that welled up. Vanessa merely smiled and patted Randa's back. Then the room went silent as Randa turned back to the doctor.

"Are you sure both took? We're really going to have the twins we wanted?"

"Well, if you want to know for sure, even though we are fairly certain they did, we can do a transvaginal ultrasound to listen for the heartbeats, but all signs are pointing to both fertilized eggs sitting pretty in Miss Vanessa here."

"Please, doctor? Can we do that? I'd just like to be sure."

The doctor directed a nurse to take Vanessa to a room to get ready. Minutes later, the exam room was crowded with the five people it would take to bring in the two little ones that Vanessa would now be caring for and nurturing for the next nine months.

With the speakers turned up, the ultrasound transducer—looking very much like a wand—successfully picked up on two distinct heartbeats. Thank goodness Vanessa knew to come in with a bladder very full or one of the heartbeats could have been missed. They all listened as the one heartbeat would sound then the other would echo, then start over. Chase had never thought kids were in his future. He looked over and saw Randa openly crying and Jack trying to hide wiping his eyes. Then it hit Chase. *Holy shit,* he thought, *I'm going to be a dad.*

***

Jack didn't know for sure what the others were thinking, but he was floored. *Kids,* he thought, *oh my fucking god.* He looked at Chase and thought his friend looked a little green around the gills. They were both going to be daddies. Unless blood tests were done, no one would know who the biological daddy would be for which baby, but in their case, no one cared. Life with Randa was already a blessing, and in nine months their family would be complete. They looked at each other, then at Randa, who was pressing tissues to her eyes and sniffling. To them, she was and always would be the most beautiful woman in the world.

The End

Other Titles by Tanya Sands

The Chasers Series

Double Her Pleasure

Mobile Pleasure

Recipe for Pleasure

Constructed Pleasure

Captured Pleasure

Mechanical Pleasure

The Ink Chasers Trilogy

Wicked Education

Wicked Triplicity

Wicked Following (coming soon)

Standalones

There's No Tomorrow

About the Author

Tanya Sands is the pseudonym of a stay-at-home mom who, having written but not published short stories for years, finally took the leap in 2014 and published her passion. When she's not writing she's raising her 2 young boys and 4 furbabies in the Dallas, TX area while her husband supports them all by driving all over the country as a long-haul truck driver. She is the youngest of 6 and a proud veteran of the US Air Force.

You can connect with Tanya through her email (tanya.sands@yahoo.com) or through her Facebook page: https://www.facebook.com/TanyaChasers.

Made in the USA
Monee, IL
03 July 2023